I DON'T LOOK LIKE

WHAT I'VE BEEN

THROUGH

D1275794

Angela Marie Holmes

Dedicated to the one love I lost...

TABLE OF CONTENTS

CHAPTER ONE

I do...

S o where was I? Oh, I remember Brian and I were off to get our marriage license. Nothing was going to stop us this day, not even the thunder storm. We had gone out to Brian's mother's house to see the white dress she had picked out for me to wear. Once we arrived it was laid out on the couch all ready for me to try on.

Brian's mom was deaf but she was able to sound some words slightly. Some you could understand and some you couldn't. Ironically, Brian had a little girl who was also deaf. I thought that was special. Something only God could have orchestrated, a bond between her grandchild that no one else could share. Brian was the only one in the family who learned sign language. The rest of the family just moved their lips slowly and yelled as if she would hear what they were saying. She tried to teach me basic words in sign language. Words like, "how are you, thank you, hello and good bye and especially I love you." She made sure I knew that one.

"Turn around." She directed.

She tucked, pinned and hemmed where she saw fit. I held my arms up and followed her instruction.

We were supposed to be at the church by six o'clock. My father met us there. The church was just up the road from Brian's mother's house. It was actually their family's church. Brian sang in the choir and taught youth bible study. I was real impressed and proud of him.

We all got into the car and headed to the church. My father pulled up right on time. It was just the four of us. Nadia had stayed with Michele. I had previously met the minister that was to perform our intimate ceremony. I felt comfortable talking with him. He was a great Christian man, full of humor and wisdom when it came to relationships. He had engaged with me and Brian on several occasions after church and over dinner. Everyone thought we made a good couple and was happy he was settling down.

As we stepped to the alter we prepared to take our vows, it all became so real to me. There was no wedding party, no audience of friends and family members, and that is how a marriage is after the wedding is over just the two of you until death do you part, full of sunny skies, lingerie and Marvin Gaye, unless somebody lied. I was ready to get it on!

I looked into Brian's eyes and recited my vows. Never stopping to think, this was really serious business. I had no time to be nervous. *Just go with the flow, you know this man and you feel you love him enough to marry him, I voiced in my head as the vows exited my mouth. You'll be fine, I convinced myself.*

Brian starred into my eyes with the biggest grin trying to keep his calm on. I couldn't tell if he was actually nervous or not.

Whatever he was feeling he made me at ease as he looked into my eyes. I was good.

"I do..." I confessed.

"You may now kiss your bride." The preacher announced.

We didn't put too much on it with my father present. They were both overjoyed. We were husband and wife! The lightning struck once more and the lights in the church flickered. I didn't think anything of it.

"Let's get out of here." My father stated.

We drove back and got into another car other than our own.

"Whose car is this? Where are we going?"

"This is my homeboys ride and he got us a room over in Albany as a wedding present, since we can't exactly go on a honeymoon right now."

"Oh, okay that was nice."

We were on the road with the rain and the lightning. Guess this was a typical rainy night in Georgia and I was married now. I had fallen asleep during the 45-minute ride.

"Baby, wake up we're here." He whispered

"Oh wow, I fell asleep that fast?"

"Now you know you were sleep before we made it a good distance down the highway."

Brian ran around the car to open my door. It was still raining. We made it up the stairs to the Motel room.

"Watch your step baby, be careful." He warned as he held my hand and guided me up the staircase.

When he opened the door, he threw the bag in and swept me off my feet to carry me over the threshold. I giggled at his ploy to carry out all the after-wedding rituals. As he held me in his arms we looked into each other's eyes while the light from the lamp post was glaring into the doorway. The moon was nowhere in sight in this weather. That kiss sent that sensation through my body. We both realized it was just the two of us from here on out.

Our kiss became more passionate. He let me down gently from his arms and held me close around my waist. I rubbed his head gently in our embrace. He unzipped my dress then unhooked my bra. All within seconds they dropped to the floor and I stepped out of my heels. He guided me onto the bed face down as he held my breast in one hand, pulling off my sheer stockings with the other. While kissing my ass, he slid off my white string thongs with the Rhinestone butterfly positioned like a tramp stamp. Positioning me in the air licking me as his tongue then guided between my ass cheeks into the next hole. Tasting every inch of my body gave him undeniable pleasure.

He stood and quickly undressed himself as I played with my clit waiting for his grand entrance. He slowly entered inside me from behind, going deep with one stroke, the pain caused me pleasure. He liked to tease me with long stokes. I invited the pain as his thrust got stronger and stronger. Unable to penetrate my walls any deeper as he grabbed my shoulders to keep me in his grasps.

His position teasingly massaged my clit and we both reached an uncontrollable climax as he groaned out catching his breath, my cry was that of an unheard tune. That never stopped him. It only made him want more. He positioned me on my back as he taunted the last breath of my cry out of my mouth with his tongue. Our kisses were the connection to our souls.

We didn't sleep at all that night. We even agreed that our wedding fingers felt different. Could it be that our rings were cutting off the circulation in our minds of the thought of no longer being single, that now we both belonged to one another after vowing 'til death do us part. That the addiction of our sex would not be the only thing to tie us and hold us together, without that we were still bound to this relationship now called a marriage.

We woke up the next morning, still filled with the anxiety of being newlyweds. Check out time was approaching as we showered together. I had no desire for any more samplers, appetizers or main course of his sex he wanted to dish out. I wanted to head right over to IHOP for my real breakfast sampler!

CHAPTER TWO

W e returned back to work that Monday. My coworkers had placed gifts on my desk. Everyone was curious as to how our wedding ceremony and night went during the storm. I shared the ceremony details. We laughed and they joked once more in regards to the weather, that the thunder storm was a bad sign.

Everyday Brian and I went to lunch together. My shift ended up changing from 8am-5pm to 11am-7pm. So, I slept in and Brian took Nadia to school, he would pick up Nadia when he got off. Brian would have dinner ready and Nadia's homework done once he picked me up from work. The next few months were smooth. We always went to his moms for dinner on Friday nights or went visiting on Saturday. His family always spent time together and they loved to eat, and of course church on Sunday and dinner once again. They loved Nadia and she went to youth bible study with Brian on Wednesdays and my dad would pick me from work.

She would spend the night on a few occasions. Nadia's

classmates lived on the corner and they were more than happy to have her over.

"Well babe what shall we do tonight? Would you like to go to   dinner?" I asked.

"Sure, I could use me a good steak from Shoney's."

"Cool we can go there."

After dinner, we were ready to enjoy each other for dessert. Brain ran the water for us to shower together and once we went into the bedroom. I lay on the bed and Brian went into our walk-in closet.

"Want to try something new tonight?" Holding up a pair of handcuffs.

"Oh my, where did you get those from?"

"Don't worry about all that." He said with a smile.

I put my hands to the headboard anticipating what would be next. I hated when he would pin me down as he sucked the very last orgasm I had in me. Now that was torture. *What would he do? I've never done any crazy shit like this before.* I was hooked up. It wasn't too comfortable but I soon forgot once he started to taste my thighs and all that was waiting for him in between. He had my thighs and hips up in the air at his total disposal of his tongue as I released one orgasm after the other. I was cumming over and over again. My body was weak with ecstasy.

"Okay okay! I can't take it. Let my arms down. I think my hands are numb."

"Okay baby." Brian kissed between my thighs.

He went into the closet to get the key.

"What are you doing? Hurry up!"

Now I feel crazy lying here butt ass naked waiting to be unhandcuffed.

"Baby I can't find the key..."

"What did you say?"

"I can't find the key. It was in this bag I swear!"

"Quit playing games!"

"I'm not playing."

"Oh crap! Are you for real? So how am I supposed to get out of these damn things?"

"Yo' daddy got a key?"

"Man, I know you crazy. I wish I would call my dad."

"Well we gone have to call somebody. Baby I'm going to have to call the police."

"The police?"

"Baby, that's the only people we can call to get them handcuffs off." He replied.

"Okay, whatever. So how am I supposed to put clothes on?"

"Here put your shorts on and then I'll cover you up."

"What if it falls down? I don't even have a bra on!"

"I'm sorry baby." Brian teased as he called 911.

The doorbell rang. It was the police. Luckily it was just one officer. And the first thing he says as he walks in the bedroom...

"No need to be embarrassed ma'am. You wouldn't believe how many calls we get for this same situation. You'll be free in a jiffy." He reassured.

In a Jiffy I was. The officer left right back out and wished us a good night. Brian walked him to the front door. I got up and put on all my clothes.

Brian walked back in the room and he just laughed his ass off.

"It wouldn't be so funny if it was you." I said as I smacked him in the chest.

CHAPTER THREE

I had an admirer at work. I was all for being polite but it seems as though this man was a bit forward. I seemed to always end up on the elevator with him. I mentioned it to Brian thinking nothing of it. He knew exactly who I was talking about. The guy got on the elevator right before Brian. Brian grabbed the guy by his throat and choked him threatening,

"If I catch you near my wife I'm going to kill you! If I even hear you spoke to her you'll have me to deal with."

The doors of the elevator opened and Brian got off. The guy remained inside and reported the incident to his supervisor. They immediately located Brian and called him into the office. He explained the incident and both of them were terminated.

"It's your fault, you set me up!"

"Set you up? How did I set you up? I didn't tell you to go and choke the man out. I was just telling you he was being extra friendly."

"Well what the hell did you expect me to do if you come tell me some shit about another man being extra friendly?"

"I didn't expect you to go and put your hands on him, hell you can't go around putting your hands-on folks!"

I was ironing my work clothes and Brian slapped the ironing board right from under me. I was standing there literally holding the iron in my hand. My clothes went flying with the ironing board. Oh shit, he was mad now for real. I didn't know what to do or say. I unplugged the iron and took it and placed it in the kitchen and sat on the couch. Brian walked through the living room and out the front door. My heart was pounding.

"Lord, what is he going to do next?"

Brian blamed me for what happened. It was an entire month that went by before he found another job. This time he worked at night. Good. That way I wouldn't have to look at his ass when I got home from work. By this time my shift rotated once more, I was up for the 7a-3 pm shift. My dad picked up Nadia for school and Brian would catch a ride because his shift was 3p-11p.

We were constantly at each other's throats. I couldn't say one word without starting an argument or him catching an attitude. Things just weren't the same after that incident.

May was almost over. It was my birthday and I decided to call out and stay home and relax. Brian wondered why I wasn't getting ready for work.

"Baby, you not getting up, you're going to be late for work."

"No, I'm staying home today for my birthday."

"Why didn't you tell me now I have to call out!"

"Why do you have to call out, what does that have to do with you going to work?"

"I'm not going in if you're staying home, I'm skipping out too!"

I wondered why he always felt he had to be up under me all the damn time. I couldn't even go to Walmart without him always wanting to go for me. If I wanted to take the car to go to my dad's, he had a problem with that. Wanting to drop me off and go chill with his homeboys. *Umm hello, why can't your homeboys come visit you or pick you up? This is my car in the first place, damn! I thought to myself.*

I was getting real sick of him. He had to be in control of everything. I told him to take the car so I could spend some time with my friend.

"Hey friend, you mind if I wash a load of clothes over your house? We could go walk the road while they're in the washer."

"Yeah, that's fine come on."

Lynn was the first person to do my hair when I got to town. She was known for her clean cuts. Brian used to drop me off at her shop as well. At least he didn't wait around until my appointment was over.

Lynn arrived shortly after Brian left and put a load of clothes in the washer. We left to go walking. When we returned, Brian had made it back home. My stomach turned at the thought of seeing my own car in our parking space. We walked in and he was sitting on the couch.

"Where you been?"

"Oh, we went walking."

"You didn't ask me if you could go walking."

"I didn't ask you? Who the fuck is you? And why would I need to ask you to do a damn thing, I'm grown!"

"I'm your husband and I need to know where you are in case of an emergency!"

"Please what type of an emergency?"

We argued the rest of the night. Lynn took her clothes out of the washer and took them down the street to the wash house to dry in the big dryers. Nadia was over Michele's who had moved to town so she wouldn't be alone in Atlanta while her husband was on the road driving trucks.

That weekend Brian wanted to go and look for houses. I thought it would be cool and we could finally have a good day and go out to eat. We drove all the way out of town to go look at trailers. *Are you serious? Who is about to buy a trailer?* You should have heard him talking all this big talk to the guy knowing we ain't had no money or any thought of buying nothing. I caught a straight attitude and turned my nose up at all those stupid trailers.

On our way home I sat in the back seat with Nadia. I didn't want to hear anything he had to say nor did I want to argue in front of my daughter. That didn't stop him from running his mouth.

"Why you always have to catch an attitude about everything?"

"I don't have and attitude it's more along the lines of fed up!"

"Fed up, you want to know who is fed up? Me! You and your   picky ass ways!"

"I don't give a damn what you are fed up with! Your fake ass, pretending to be more than you are acting like you so damn Holy in church, teaching youth bible study, singing in the choir and you the devil."

I had gotten so heated from arguing with him before I knew it I snatched his Bible and threw it out the window! It was over at that point.

CHAPTER FOUR

M y next decision was to leave Brian. We could not get along and I couldn't stand him. He had gotten a little too controlling and had gotten used to always dropping me off and taking my car. I couldn't even drop off Nadia to basketball practice. He would always drive us and say, wait her babe, I'll walk her in. At first I thought that was sweet, then I saw he was just once again being controlling, always wanting to show off.

I had become friends with one of my coworkers. Heather, she was a cool white girl. We had started having lunch together most days. I confided in her of my plan to leave Brian. She was all for it she could not stand him either.

"There is an apartment available in my complex and it's by the same property management."

It was the same layout as my current place just slightly older. I went to my property manager and let her know I was filing for divorce and asked if I could move into the vacant apartment at the other complex, and sure enough she said it was available and it was fifty dollars cheaper.

"I'll take it!"

"Sorry to hear about your marriage, didn't you two just get married on Valentine's Day?"

"Yes, ma'am we did."

"Well you never know someone until you live with them in your case until it's too late..."

"When will you be moving?"

"Tomorrow, I'm friends with one of the tenants in Bldg. 3."

"Okay, come by tomorrow to get the keys and I will draw up a   new lease for you to sign."

"Okay thank you."

I left and put my plan in motion.

"I'll get my boyfriend to get his truck and we can haul all your stuff in one trip while Brian is at work." Heather plotted.

The next day I got the keys after work and her boyfriend backed up his truck to my apartment and we moved everything out. I had the lights and the phone transferred to my new apartment. They were scheduled to turn off in this apartment by midnight. I didn't care what happened to Brian at this point. I usually would drop him off when his shift changed to later and he would always catch a ride home. This particular night he decides to take my car to work.

"Okay fine." I thought to myself. "I will just go and get my car when it gets late."

I took the living room set and the washer and dryer we financed together. Once everything was in place I had them to drive me up to Brian's job to get my car back.

"Look he has your car parked in front of another car so you can't get it. That old bastard knew he had no business taking your car to work. I would call the police." Heather griped I got out of the truck and asked the security guard if he could have the car parked behind my car moved. He went inside the building and returned with Brian.

"I need my car can you tell whose ever car this is to move?"

"I sure cannot."

"What do you mean you sure cannot, I need my car?"

"For what, you're supposed to be in the bed."

"It don't matter what I might need it for, you know you can't leave me home with Nadia without a car. That makes no sense! You ain't been driving my car to work during this shift."

"Well I ain't asking my homeboy to move his car."

"Call the police, they'll make him give you the car."

Heather yelled from the truck.

We called the police and they came out to his job.

"What seems to be the trouble folks?"

"I came to get my car and it's blocked in on purpose."

"Is that true sir?" The officer asked Brian.

"Yes, it is. This is my wife and she trying to take my car."

"Your car? This is my car. I drove this car from California asshole!"

"Well technically ma'am if you two are married it is half his property."

"Well I always drop him off because I have a child at home, and I need my car in case of an emergency."

"That sounds like a valid reason, is there a certain reason why you would leave you wife at home alone with a child while you're working?"

"No sir can't think of any."

"Go have the owner of this vehicle come out and move it

so this lady can get back home." The policeman instructed the security guard.

"Thank you! And I need the key because I can't find mine."

I got my car and went to pick up Nadia from Michele's. She had agreed to watch her while we moved.

"You got everything out of the apartment?"

"Yep, he had the nerve to take my car to work, knowing I always drop him off."

"Oh, no he didn't, see that's that controlling spirit. He knows good and damn well he shouldn't leave you and that baby home alone without a car and it's your car too!"

"Yeah, I had to call the police because he had my car blocked so I couldn't get it without him knowing. And I made him give me his set of keys."

"Wow! He is too much. Well love ya, call me tomorrow."

"Ok I will. Love you too, thank you."

There would be no way he would ask anyone to ride around trying to find me or my parked car. I felt relieved to be in a different apartment all by myself. I slept like a baby.

CHAPTER FIVE

W eeks went by and I hadn't heard any talk about what I had done. No calls or pop up visits from Brian on my job. I confided in one of Brian's friend Cary who worked in receiving at the hospital. Brian introduced me to him when we first started working there.

"I ain't seen Brian around nowhere. I ain't never had a chance to ask him why he got fired."

"He choked that maintenance man out in the elevator when I told him he always speaks to me."

"What! That nigga crazy man, you can't be puttin' yo hands on folk's man!"

"You alright? You needed anything?"

"Oh, I'm fine. I moved in the apartments down the street. The ones next to the cleaners."

"No shit, right down the street. Ok, ok I'll be checking on you and little Nadia. She still playing ball for the Rec?"

"Yes, she is. I'll catch up with you later then. I just wanted to fill you in."

Brian's sister told me that he caught a bus to San Diego

to stay with one of his Marine buddies. So, I was free for the summer. My dad's side of the family had a reunion scheduled in the month of July in Atlanta. So, that was our next family outing. I saw my cousin's I hadn't seen since I was eight years old. Everyone knew I had recently married and asked about my husband and how come I didn't bring him.

"Oh, he's out of town right now, I guess you would say..."

I was too embarrassed to say I made a horrible mistake in marrying him. I started to feel empty and alone. Once I returned to the room me and Michele shared I sat out on the balcony and began to wonder what Brian was doing. I almost wished he was here with me. The moonlight was so romantic I hated to have a night like that wasted alone. Now isn't that something. I actually missed him, his touch, and his smell. He had always been so charismatic. I did love that part about him and how we kissed. He always knew how to caress me. I felt my heart beating between my legs. Oh damn! You better not even start that shit! I was trying to do those Kegel exercises. I was actually missing my husband's sex. *Oh, now he's your husband I told myself*...this was crazy! This was not a good combination. He hadn't even called, I hadn't changed my number. Did I expect him to know that, not really because at the time I didn't care if he jumped off a bridge, but now my heart began to speak something different?

The next day I spent the morning with my dad. He had the motorhome towed to the shop. Something had gone wrong with it and needed to be fixed. That was fun. We followed the tow truck to some shop. It was a gang of Negros up there. I almost felt embarrassed to be looking so cute in front of my dad with them peaking and not speaking. I remained friendly though. We ate at a Bar BQ joint next door while we waited. I was really liking Atlanta if you know what I mean. When we walked in they had the jams blasting. Then wouldn't you know Maxwell, "'til the cops come knocking" came on...just rub it in why don't you! The motorhome was going to need to be delivered later that evening. Seems the work would take longer than we anticipated.

We headed back to the hotel just in time to hang out with my cousins. They were planning on going site seeing, shopping and out to eat. My dad was all for it as well. We all walked over to the CNN building and took a tour. He was good at orchestrating tours. We walked through downtown and ended up at the Underground back in a circle to Macy's and Hard Rock Café to eat. I loved my family. I think that's when I'm the happiest.

The banquet dinner was at six. We had to get back to get dressed for that. Everything was wonderful. My dad did his usual speech about how he grew up. The motorhome got delivered and we would be leaving that next day by check out time.

When we returned home my feelings didn't seem to get any better. I went to church with my dad. During the sermon, my heart was heavy and I began to cry. My dad put his arm around me and said, "He'll be back you'll see, just give it some time."

I became friends with my fine neighbor upstairs. He was really cool and protective. His name was James. He lifted weights and boy was he fine. I confided in him about my marriage and he helped me along the way emotionally with advice from a man's perspective. Making sure I knew my worth.

CHAPTER SIX

My dad was right that next month in August Brian's money and luck had run out. I received a call from him alright. He was trying to figure out where my head was. I played along, not giving up too much information. He had no place to go and couldn't stay out there on the other side of the world too much longer.

We started talking every night for the next two weeks. I made the decision to let him move back home. I purchased his bus ticket. It would take almost a week for him to return that next Sunday morning. I had to admit I was rather excited for him to come home. All I could think about was his sex and how he licked between my legs, how he felt inside me and gave me multiple orgasms.

It was Sunday morning, the phone rang.

"Hello."

"Hello?"

"Are you here?"

"Who was that that just answered the phone?"

"What are you talking about, I answered the phone."

My voice was a bit deep in the morning. It wasn't the sweetest first thing in the morning. It had to warm up.

"You got some nigga over there?"

"Brian shut the hell up with all that, why would I have some other nigga answer my phone and I know you come home today?"

"I don't know it sounded like someone else answered the phone."

"Are you here?"

"Yeah can you come and pick me up?"

The bus station was not too far from my apartment. I jumped up and washed my face and brushed my teeth. I grabbed a piece of chewing gum. Put some lotion on my face and Vaseline on my lips. I wanted a kiss as soon as I saw his face.

When I pulled up I got out of the car and opened the trunk so he could put his bags in the back. When I looked up Brian had put one hand around my waist and the other hand behind my neck to bring my lips to his. I embraced his touch and my heart melted at the warmth and passion of his kiss. I missed my husband.

Brian put his bags down at the door, took me into his arms and kissed me as if he never wanted to be apart from me another day. He undressed me as we stepped in the living room. I began to unzip his pants to feel his erection. My boxers fell to the floor as he lifted my t-shirt over my head. As he kicked off his jeans and I lifted his shirt over his head, kissing him all over his chest. Brian picked me up as we still kissed and lay me on the couch. He went straight to the wet center where my love lies, softly licking me to the point of no control. I screamed out in ecstasy as my body released that indescribable climax. Clinching Brian's head pulling him in for more, it felt so good I thought my body was going to explode over and over.

"Fuck me, Fuck me now. Put it in baby!"

"You know I haven't had sex since I left. I don't want to come   too quick baby."

Brian's was as hard as a brick and he was about to burst.

"I don't care baby fuck me! Oh, yes baby harder, harder."

He came into my wetness. He pushed harder and harder filling every inch of me. He grabbed my thighs and his thrusts became harder and harder, faster and faster. He groaned and grunted louder and louder. I could feel him so deep I couldn't catch my breath. He stood up positioning one leg on the other side of the couch placing my legs on his shoulders with the thrust continuing deeper and deeper. He pulled me up on top of him directing my body up and down, up and down faster and faster. He was in full control. I didn't care about the pain it hurt too good. He was beating into my stomach. I didn't have to move a muscle. His upper body strength led my body in whatever direction he desired. As he exploded he held me tight with his head between my breasts, our hearts beating out of our chests as if they were one. Sweat dripping down my stomach from between my breast. I fell back off of Brian onto the couch lying there lifeless.

We talked for hours about our marriage and what we now desired from one another. Brian didn't have a job and I assured him I would take care of everything until he found one. I accompanied him on most of his interviews. It wasn't long before he landed a job at a Youth Detention Center. I actually accompanied Brian on that interview. They seemed as if they were recruiting me as well. It was rather odd for his second interview to be on a Saturday. It was definitely different environment for those young boys. It was as if they were already in prison by the treatment I observed.

Everything was going great, over the next three months Brian had two jobs. My dad had been working to get him on at the jail so that position fell right into place as well for the day shift as a jailor. He worked the Detention Center at night. It was a ways to travel and he wouldn't arrive home until after midnight.

As for finances Brian gave me his whole check from his night job and kept his check from the jail to support his personal needs. He bought a car and openly began smoking. He just couldn't smoke around me or in the apartment. He kept gum and mouthwash on hand. He was succeeding on both jobs and began to attract more attention from his staff and coworkers. I was proud of him until his attitude began to change. He walked around as if he was better than everybody, always bragging about his accomplishments and job performance. I began to tell myself, here we go it's only a matter of time before this turns ugly.

Our sex life began to dwindle dead and when he would normally be home like clockwork shortly after midnight, he began coming in past two sometimes even three in the morning claiming he was doing over time.

"I would prefer for you to call and let me know, I get worried with you traveling on that two-lane highway alone."

"I'm sorry baby we never know until our shift is almost over and I don't want to break your sleep."

"Well I'd rather you do, you know I can't sleep long without you in the bed."

I couldn't rest until I saw the headlights shine through our bedroom window waiting up most nights to make love to my husband for him only to be too tired to even touch me. I would always raise my head past his pillow to see the time... 3:26am Bastard!

We began to have several disagreements. It seemed as if Brian had his own agenda coming in and leaving the house whenever he got ready with no regards to my schedule. With Brian working all hours over time on weekends without consulting me, I started spending most of my time with Michele. He got up and got dressed for work on a Saturday.

"You're going to work over time again?"

"Yeah baby, can you make sure you take my mom's grocery shopping. I promised her I would bring her into town but I have to work."

He said that all in one breath like it was a direct order. I just stared at him looking all smug as he tucked in his shirt with those damn clamps he used around his legs to keep his shirt flat against his waist without wrinkling as he fastened his pants. He was too much for himself.

I called out to his mothers to see when she wanted to be picked up and his sister answered the phone.

"Hey Trudy, how you doing?"

"Fine and yourself?"

"Oh, I'm fine. I was calling to check and see what time your mom wanted to go to the grocery store. Your brother is working over time again today and he promised your mom he would take her."

"Oh, child don't worry about that, she don't need nothing and if she come up with something I can take her."

"Are you sure, I don't mind."

"Yeah child I can run to the store if she needs something."

"Okay, well I'm sure we'll see you tomorrow after church."

"Okay baby, see you then."

I called Michele to see what they were up to for the day.

"We're thinking about going to Florida to the mall in Tallahassee."

"Ooh I want to go."

"Come on, where's your hubby?"

"He's working overtime today."

"Oh, okay well ya'll come on, my husband went to fill up the truck."

"Ok we're on our way."

Me and Nadia were already dressed and made it over to Michele's. He was just pulling up and they were loading in the truck.

"Hey sis, how ya'll doing? You ready to ride?"

"Yep!"

I backed my car in and we hopped in the truck. We spent all day at the mall and even picked up a Matinee. We didn't get home until 1 o'clock in the morning. We were so sleepy. We were walking directly to the car.

"Nadia can stay over and you can just come get her tomorrow."

"Okay cool, see you tomorrow."

There was a note on the windshield, it read, "It is imperative that you get in touch with me as soon as you get this, Brian."

My heart dropped. He was looking for me, but why? He left for work without consulting me. As I rode home my heart was pounding. I didn't know if he was upset, if something had happened. What was he going to say? I pulled into the complex and his car was not in his space. I felt relieved. I hurried up and ran in the house, got out of my clothes and got in the bed. I stood on the bed and unscrewed the light bulb. Every time he came home he had a habit of flicking the light on to wake me up. I thought that was so rude. He wasn't home and he wouldn't know what time I got home. I tried to hurry up and fall asleep or at least calm down and act like it. Within minutes' headlights shined through our bedroom window. He was home. My heart stated to race. I held my breath trying to slow my heartbeat down so he wouldn't feel I was scared. I had closed the bedroom door so that if I had fallen asleep I would hear him come through the door. I turned toward the wall with my back facing the door.

As Brian walked in the front door I could tell by the slam of the door he was upset. The window in the bedroom shook. He busted through our bedroom door. He flicked the light switch. (told you, asshole!) I didn't want him to see me flinching trying to pretend I was asleep. I didn't know what was coming next.

"What the fuck is up with the light?" He asked himself. I could tell by his movements that he was doing his normal routine. He takes off his necklace, his watch, and then his wedding ring. He puts his wallet on the dresser, then takes his pants off and throws them on the floor in front of the chest. He went to the bathroom then when he returned he closed the bedroom door. He plopped in the bed trying to wake me up. I didn't move or make a sound. My heart was pounding so hard I just knew he could hear it.

"Danielle!"

I laid there stiff as a board.

"Danielle!"

"Hmm?"

"Where have you been?"

I didn't know how to answer the question.

"We went to the mall with Michele." I moaned again as if I was coming out of a dead sleep.

"Did you take my mom to the grocery store?"

"No, she said she didn't want to go and Trudy was there and said if she changed her mind she would take her." I replied still moaning from out of my sleep.

"What mall did you go to cause I looked for you for hours and I never saw your car at the mall."

"We went to the mall in Tallahassee."

"Tallahassee! In Tallahassee?"

Brian pounced on top of me in an instant. Grabbing both my wrist yelling,

"Tallahassee, Tallahassee! You went to Tallahassee?"

"I know we are not going to do this again? Get off me." I pleaded calmly.

"You went to Tallahassee without asking me and you didn't even take my mother to the grocery store?"

"I told you she didn't want to go. Your sister was there and said if she needed anything she would take her. Now get off of me!"

"My mother said you never called or came to take her."

"I told you Trudy answered the phone. Why would I lie about that? Call your sister and ask her."

"I don't have to call anyone! I told you to take her and you felt going to the mall was more important than doing something for my mother after everything she has done for us."

"What the hell are you talking about? Get off of me!"

I was not waiting for him to pull any military tactics and pin holds. I began to buck my body and kick and fight to get loose. He was straddled across my waist holding both my arms by my wrists pinned down by my shoulders. As long as he didn't put his knees on my shoulders like before I had a chance to get loose.

"Let me go, get off me! Oh, my God why are you doing this again!"

I was able to knock him off balance and get my leg free. I kicked him off me and he grabbed my legs. When he did that I punched him in the face. He grabbed me around my neck and choked me while he hopped right back on top of me. My mind flashed back to when Juelz choked me unconscious. Was I really going through this again? Did I really deserve to be abused by all the men I had thought loved me? Why is this happening to me? I couldn't yell he was choking the life out of me. I began to panic, I thought this time he was going to kill me. I had told my neighbor that whenever Brian came home late to listen out in case he started an argument or started a fight with me so he could call 911 or come to the door to see if I was calling for help.

There was no way he could hear anything. I went for Brian's eyes. I figured if I poked them or scratched his face he would let me go. He would not stop choking me. I couldn't breathe and this time I thought he was going to kill me. I didn't know if my eyes were opened or closed. Everything was black. I couldn't even hear at this point. My hand motioned across his face out of desperation. He finally let go. I grasped for air and only saw stars spinning around the room. We wrestled to the floor as I tried to break free onto the side of the bed. This time I knew to kick and scream for my life. I was not going to let him pin me in the corner. He pulled me by my feet and dragged me across the floor. I kicked him to get lose to try and stand up. I ended up on my stomach and he grabbed me again from behind and put me in a headlock with both my arms behind my head. I tried to kick off the wall to get some type of leverage to get free. I thought if I kicked out the window someone would hear the glass shatter. All it did was land outside the window onto the pile of pine needles below.

No one heard a thing. He tried to slam me face down on the bed. I remember him doing that last time so I resisted with all I had and we landed on the floor by his dumbbells on the side of the dresser. I miss hitting my head by just an inch as I looked to my left and saw the weight by my eye. Brian had gotten tired. He got up and walked in circles in the middle of the bedroom by the closet.

I got my balance and used the wall to get up off the floor and ran into the bathroom. I locked the door and turned the light on to look in the mirror. My t-shirt was ripped and full of blood from scratches and my nose was bleeding, my hair was all over my head, and my eye had broken blood vessels. I immediately began to cry. I couldn't believe this happened again. Brian knocked on the door.

"Danielle? Danielle open the door!"

"Leave me alone. I thought you said we weren't going to do this again?"

"I know. I'm sorry, open the door."

"No, leave me alone!"

"I promise I won't touch you again, open the door so we can talk about this, Danielle please open the door, and I'll leave you alone. I'll be in the room if you want to talk."

Brian went back into the bedroom. I just stood there looking in the mirror trying to stop my tears. I came out the bathroom and went into Nadia's room and lay down on her bed facing the wall.

Brian stood at the door.

"Can we talk?"

"I have nothing to say to you, leave me alone."

"Please Danielle, I'm sorry."

"I don't want to hear that shit. You know what to do next."

"You talking about move out?"

"Hell yeah, and I'm not going to discuss it with you, get your shit and get out!"

"I will. I remember the agreement."

Brian walked over to the bed and kneeled down behind me.

"Can you just look at me? I love you and I'm sorry. I had no right to put my hands on you again. I just got so upset, and I couldn't control myself. Can you please turn over and talk to me?"

"I have nothing to say to you, leave me alone!"

Brian touched my arm.

"I love you."

I snatched my arm away, and screamed out in pain. It was if my hand had to catch up with my arm.

"Damn!"

"What's wrong?"

"My arm is soar. Leave me alone and get out of my face!"

I sat up to position my arm continuing to face the wall. He touched my back.

"I'm sorry Danielle."

"Don't touch me!"

Brian stood up, "I'll move out in the morning."

"Good!"

I lay there for a while, making sure I didn't hear any noises coming from our bedroom. Had he fallen asleep? My arm was still soar. I went to get off the bed and damn it hurt so bad again. What was that?

I tipped toed to the door to listen for any movement coming from the other room. My heart was pounding. If he was awake, he could probably hear it beating out of my chest. I tried to catch my breath. He probably heard that too. I tipped to the ledge in the kitchen and felt for my car keys.

I went to grab them with my right hand and pain shot up my arm and I dropped the keys. What the fuck! I picked up the keys with my left hand and tipped toed quickly to the front door. I thought I would faint right there on the spot if I heard the bedroom door open. I slowly unlocked the deadbolt, it clicked. Damn! Why does everything seem ten times louder when you're trying to be quiet? Next I had to open the door. When I tried to open it slowly it squeaked. I just open it quickly in one motion and closed it behind me. I ran and jumped in the car and locked the door. I started the car and left the headlights off. I put the car in reverse and backed out praying Brian wasn't running out of the apartment behind me. I sped out the parking lot so fast I didn't even turn the headlights on until I was a ways down the street. It was 4 o'clock in the morning and I was the only car on the streets. I went to the phone booth at the Flash Foods station on the corner down the street from Michele's. There was always some change in the ashtray. Since I didn't smoke it stayed full. My brother in law answered the phone.

"This is Danielle, can you open the door? I'm at Flash Foods. Brian jumped on me and I ran out the house."

"Yeah come on!"

I could hear him telling my sister...that was Danielle, Brian jumped on her...

I jumped back in the car. I didn't have any shoes on, just my ripped bloody t-shirt and my boxers. I ran up the stairs to my sisters. My brother in law opened the door, let me get Michele. I followed him down the hall and he turned on the spare bedroom light on and motioned me to go in there. I went in and sat on the bed. My arm was in so much pain, I was holding it up with my left hand like a sling. Michele peeked through the door and slowly came into the room. I looked up at her and she began to cry,

"What happened?"

"He jumped on me when I told him I went with you guys to the mall."

"What's wrong with your arm?"

"I don't know, it just hurts really bad."

Michele touched it and tried to see what happened to it and I flinched.

"Ouch that hurts!"

"Dan your arm is broken. You have to go to the

emergency room."

"No. I can't go to the ER then they'll know what happened."

"You're going to have to, you can't keep your arm like that, and your shirt is full of blood."

"I know look at my hair can you put it in a ponytail for me in the morning?"

"Yeah."

"I'll go in the morning. I just have to think up a lie to tell."

"Let me get you some clothes to change into."

"Okay thank you."

CHAPTER SEVEN

That morning Michele put my hair in a ponytail. I didn't want Nadia to see my arm so I went on into the emergency room before they woke up.

I tried to make sure I looked to my right so that no one was able to see my busted blood vessels. I was taken to the back and sat on a gurney waiting for the Doctor after my X-ray. He bought the X-ray into the room and hung it in front of the lighted box to read.

"You have what they call a boxer fracture." He stated

He showed me where the fracture was. The bone on the outside of my hand under my pinky finger was shattered which connects my wrist to my arm. No wonder why my arm was in pain and I had to support my hand and wrist. When he asked me if anyone had done this to me my mind flashed back to me punching Brian in the face.

"No, one of my dad's weight's fell on top of my hand while we were cleaning his shed." I lied.

I didn't want my coworkers looking up my ER visit. They took me off of work for one week. They put a blue cast up to my elbow. I was right handed and didn't know how I was going to function. I was surely going to have Michele come with me to the house to make sure all Brian's things were gone. I needed to get my affairs in order. I wanted to go see my family. This year has not been that great at all. I called Evelyn to let her know what had happened.

"For real girl, are you serious?" She asked in amazement.

"Yes, my arm is in a cast all the way up to my elbow and it's my hand that is broke."

"I want to come up there for Thanksgiving, but I don't have any money to buy two tickets for me and Nadia."

"I know right and you know short notice they are going to be a grip."

We caught up some more and then I was tired of holding the phone with my left hand. It seemed so awkward.

"I'll talk to you later. Wish I was coming there for Thanksgiving."

"I know girl, Bye"

"Bye."

CHAPTER EIGHT

“**W**hat's up girl? What you doing? You talk to my girl?”

“Wow, she just called and said she wanted to come down too, but she didn't have enough money for both of them.”

“For Thanksgiving? Tell her I'll pay for her and the baby to come if she need me to get their tickets.” Juelz replied.

“Let her know I got her when she gets here.”

“Okay I'll let her know she can come. Let me call her back.”

They were working with some dude that had credit card numbers and would purchase the tickets. Evelyn called back that night and said my flight would be leaving that next morning at 6:30, and I could pick up my tickets at the gate. It was already 11 o'clock at night and I had to wash and pack with one hand. Oh shit!

I was running around the apartment like a chicken with my head cut off. I had to fill up my gas tank before I got on the highway. I didn't leave until 4o'clock in the morning. I was scared I would miss my flight. I was flying down 75 like a bat out of hell. We made it to Atlanta airport in an hour and thirty minutes. I was going 90 mph. I was basically the only car on the road that time of morning, thank God. We struggled with our luggage, but we made it to check in. I was nervous, I didn't know how this credit card thing was going to work. It was all worked out. I picked up me and Nadia's boarding passes and made it just in time through the gates, down the escalator, onto the train, up the escalator, down the moving sidewalk, to the gate. The line to board the plane was already in motion.

Once we were settled in our seats I took a deep breath and looked over at Nadia.

"We made it!"

It had been a whole year since we left and I was ready to see my family. I was not a size 9 any longer, more like a size 13. Evelyn warned Juelz not to say anything when he saw me.

"What you mean is she pregnant?"

"Hell, no nigga, her arm broke."

"How did that happen?"

"Her and her husband got in a fight and he broke her arm."

"Not the preacher and the preacher's wife." He laughed.

"Shut up nigga!"

"I ain't gone say nothing, just call me when she get here."

"I need some gas money I have to go get her from San Francisco."

"I got you mama, don't trip."

CHAPTER NINE

We landed safe and sound. California airports were so much less hectic than the Atlanta airport. Through the gates, down the escalator, straight to the baggage claim and out the door. Evelyn was coming in just as we were coming out.

"Hey Nadia!" Evelyn said smiling as she hugged her.

"Mom I can put my arms around her waist two times, she can hula hoop in a Cheerio!" Nadia laughed.

Nadia really like telling that joke. Evelyn was like a size zero. We had an hour and forty-five-minute ride. I told Evelyn a whole years' worth of stories in that hour and forty-five minutes. We never talked on the phone anymore since Brian was always the hot topic.

I was able to see all my family. Thanksgiving for my family was always like a family reunion. We usually had all our gatherings at Aunt Chellie's. She had the biggest house space now. I remember growing up all the family functions were held at my house because we had the biggest space, and a huge backyard with a pool.

Everyone was happy to see me, and they also asked why I didn't bring my new husband. My grandfather immediately pulled me to the side after observing my handi-cap.

"I'm going to ask you a question and I want you to tell me the truth. Have you been fighting?"

"No, Daddy." I lied

I hated to lie, but I didn't feel like confessing and opening up my feelings to anyone about what I had been going through. Everybody painted this picture of me being a bad ass and so far, I hadn't given them anything different to go on.

Juelz showed up at my aunt's house, of course he was sitting outside in the car. He had followed Aaron. The family loved Aaron, but they didn't have anything good to say about Juelz. Especially since I went to jail behind him. He didn't care, *fuck your family he would say.*
I walked outside.

"I would come in but..." He yelled as he walked up the driveway.
I cut him off in mid-sentence...

"Yeah sure you would. You're a big chicken."

"Naw, I don't want nobody trippin' on a nigga. I know they don't care for ya boy. So, what's up withcha' baby? "How you break your arm?"

"Fighting with my husband."

"Not the preacher?"
"Shut up!" I laughed

"You thought I was crazy and you run off and marry some nigga you don't even know."

"Be quiet, you're right. You're right. It's alright I'm getting an annulment."

Juelz looked at me with those sparkling eyes as if he missed me being home.

"Why you had to leave me man?"

"You know why I left. You didn't want me, you wanted Justice. All those years and everything we been through and you still chose her over me."

"She was holding my dope."

"That wasn't all she was holding; your ass wouldn't come home. So, it was evident who was more important."

"Did you have to take my money too nigga shit?"

"Hell yeah, how else was I supposed to eat? You didn't even get me a car when I got out of jail. You didn't buy me any clothes, you didn't do anything for me! Four years later you still fucking with those same hoes. Look I don't even want to talk about it anymore. It's over and done with now. You still giving me some money?" I laughed

"Yeah nigga shit. How long you staying all week?"

"Yep, they have me off all week because of my arm."

He reached in his pocket and gave me two one hundred dollar bills.

"Here you go mama."

"Thank you."

We continued to catch up and talk about other things. I knew I had truly out grown him and was very happy with my decision I made to leave him.

"So, we gone kick it tomorrow? Where you staying at Evelyn's spot?"

"Yeah."

"Tell that nigga Aaron to call me. I'll let you get back to your folks. Call me tomorrow, Evelyn got my number."

"Okay, I will."

I hugged him and he stole a kiss from my lips. You know you still my nigga man." He said as he gazed into my eyes.

"No, I am not!"

"Nigga you gone always be my nigga!"

"Okay Juelz, thank you!"

"Fo' sho' anytime mama. I'll see you tomorrow. Call me!"

CHAPTER TEN

I went to Tavia to get my hair done. We were all going to the BET comedy show. They actually came to Sacramento. I gave Darwin's sister who was also working at their new spot the money for my ticket to the show. She was having them Fed Ex'd in that evening and we were all meeting up.

"So, I heard yo' boo flew you in from Atlanta?"

"Yep!" I said with a smile.

"You know that man loves you. You a cold piece! You must got some powerful snapper down between them legs, shit! And you got married too?"

"I'm getting a divorce already, he was crazy!"

"Awe damn Gina!" She laughed.

Candy's old fling KT *"The King of Cali"* we call him came through the door of the shop as I was leaving. He saw my cast,

"Who you been down there whooping on in Georgia?" He joked.

I just laughed with no reply. If he only knew I stepped out of the fire into the frying pan.

CHAPTER ELEVEN

I returned home and pressed charges against Brian for assault and battery. I went to my dad's office to talk to him about it.

"Are you sure he did this to you? You're not just making it up to get back at him, are you?" He suggested.

Are you kidding? I thought to myself. That shouldn't even be an issue, this was the second time he had lost his temper and used physical abuse towards me. Certainly, I didn't want him to become a police officer or some other protective authority figure to lose his temper in any other type of situation. I didn't care anything about his record, he did it and I was pressing charges.

After the charges were filed Brian was terminated from the jail and later lost his job at the Detention Center due to using excessive force on a minor.

Cary saw me at work, he asked me how I broke my arm. I was embarrassed so I stuck to my story about helping my dad in the shed. He knew I was lying. He was looking at me like that doesn't make sense. He also saw the broken blood vessel in my eye.

"That nigga did that to your arm?"

"No!"

"Okay, let me find out you lying to me and that nigga den put his hands on you. I'm going to have a talk with Brian. I don't believe in no man putting his hands on no woman period. I know you lying to me, I don't know why you trying to protect that nigga."

I couldn't do anything but walk off.

I was able to get Nadia a new bunk bed set from Walmart for Christmas. It was the metal framed style. It came in red, white or blue. I got Nadia the red set. Brian had asked for Nadia's bike back that he had bought her the Christmas before. I made sure that bike was at my father's during the winter season. Cary actually put the whole set together. It didn't take him no time. I see he knew exactly what he was doing and I was relieved. He had gotten the truth out of me the more we talked. He had started coming over a few times to check on me and Nadia. Either of us hadn't heard or seen Brian anywhere.

Spoke too soon. It was Valentine's Day and the thought of it made me sick. I returned my wedding ring to the Jewelry store and exchanged it for a necklace, a bangle, a watch, a tennis bracelet and some diamond hoops. I was happy to be free! When I got off work and walked to my car there was a red rose on my windshield. I picked it up, looked around to see if I saw any sign of someone unfamiliar and threw it in the street. I got in my car and went to pick up Nadia from school. I always gave her a pair of pajamas, and stuffed animal and balloons on Valentine's Day!

I was on my own now in the apartment. I was still collecting my AFDC from California and my food stamps. Shelise had warned me about welfare fraud and how they will catch up with you. I had been using Vanessa's address and she had gone months without picking up the food stamps while I was trying to stack a few more checks that were being deposited on my card. They started sending them certified, but she was never home to sign for them. So, I decided to call and report that I moved to Georgia and that I would no longer need the assistance. Boy, did I hate to see that money go, but it was the right thing to do since I had seemed to have gotten away with it for a year. I called my worker and he actually thanked me for calling.

"The world needs more honest people like you. Thank you for calling to inform the office that you have moved."

"Well thank you." I stated with guilt.

"Good luck to you in Georgia."

"Okay thank you."

There had been a subdivision of duplexes that I ran across behind the school where my nephew attended a Head Start Program. I had put in an application.

"There's a waiting list a mile long."

"Okay, well here is my application to keep on file."

"Okay we keep the applications on file for up to one year, but always check back and update any contact information," she advised.

It was a quiet Sunday morning and I was cleaning up my room. Nadia was over Michele's as always. She and my nephew were only two peas in that same pod. Six months apart. As I sat on my bed a voice told me to call and check on my application on the duplex.

"On a Sunday?" I asked myself out loud.

"Yes, call and check on your application..."

"Okay." I spoke back to myself.

The manager lived on site so maybe she would answer.

"Pertilla Place." A voice sounded on the other end of the

phone.

"Good afternoon, I hate to bother you but I had put in an application in last month and I was told to check on my application periodically since there was a waiting list."

"What was your name sweetheart? I'm the new manager to the property." She asked.

"Danielle Manning,"

"Let me take a look, that name sounds familiar."
I thought to myself, *it does?*

"I'm looking through this stack of applications. Here it is!"

"Okay so you're looking for a two or three bedroom. All we have available is a three bedroom, but they are only twenty-five dollars more.

"Okay."

I'll tell you what, I am going to put you at the top of this stack. We may be having a unit coming available. I'm not certain, but I will make sure I contact you first. Don't get your hopes up it may be a few months." She warned.

"Oh, that's fine with me whatever you have, whenever, I can wait."

"How much are you paying now?"

"Five Fifty for a two bedroom."

"Oh, yes dear our units are three-sixty and you would gain an extra bedroom and bathroom."

"Really!"

"Yes ma'am! Just check back with me."

"Okay thank you so much!"
I figured I could pay a few more months in hopes she would call.

It was Thursday and I had walked in from work. The phone was ringing.

"Hello."

"Hello Danielle, this is Anita from Pertilla Place. I have good news. We have a unit coming up. It's a three bedroom, two baths. It should be ready by the middle of next month. You could move in and we could prorate your rent on April first."

"Really! Oh, my God! Something told me to call and I thought it was weird to call on a Sunday, but I listened to that voice!"

"That was the Holy Spirit sweetheart. Everything happens for a reason. You can come take a look at it once it's empty, but it will have new carpet and paint when you move in."

"Okay I will put in my 30-day notice. *This will work out perfect!*"

I couldn't wait to move. Brian wouldn't know where I lived and if he did it was because he followed me. He wouldn't know where I was going or what I was doing.

CHAPTER TWELVE

I was still paranoid so I moved room by room at night while it was dark. Then I asked Cary to move the beds with his truck. I had let the sofa and the bedroom set go back that Brian had talked me into getting, that he never paid for not to mention the washer and dryer. I hated to give that up, but the complex had a nice big clean laundry room I could use. It was perfect. I had my new place, new paint and new carpet. I took another look around I went into the kitchen. Hey! Where is the dishwasher? I just knew there was a dishwasher in here. Ah man no dishwasher. Crap!

I pulled up to my duplex and a girl was walking out of her unit from the set of duplexes next to mine.

"You Jackson's wife?"

My heart dropped. Oh Lord, what was she about to say?

"No."

"Isn't that his car?" She hesitated.

"No, this is my car."

"Oh, because I know I seen him driving that same car to work."

"Oh, you work at the Detention Center?"

"Yeah, I'm C-Money girlfriend."

C-Money was Brian main ace, partner in crime homeboy.

"Please don't tell him I live next door to you. I am trying to stay clear of him." I confessed.

"I promise you I won't. Them mothafucka's ain't no good and both of them get on my got damn nerves."

"I don't give a fuck as long as he stays away from me. He's a stalker!"

Just as I spoke those words there was a burgundy Mustang driving down the main road.

"There he goes right there!"

"He must have followed me."

"That's a damn shame."

"Does he know you live here?"

"Yeah, they've been over here before."

"Damn! And I never met you. I'll just say I was coming to see you. He doesn't know when I could have met you."

"It really ain't none of his fuckin' business!"

"Well let me go in the house before he drives back by. He'll just think I'm at someone's house."

She and I became good friends. Her name was Shannon. We were literally staying up until one or two in the morning every night talking about all the dirt these two negros were doing.

I was in the house watching television and my phone rang.

"Hello."

"Hey baby, you know that crazy ass nigga sitting in his car down here by Shirley's place." Cary stated.

Brian pulled into the parking lot. He backed in to get a clear view of my car. I guess to see when I would come out of one of the duplexes.

"For real?"

"Yeah! I'm watching his ass out the window. I'll be down there to check on you when I leave here."

"Okay."

I knew Cary liked me but I couldn't actually see myself with him. He was a nice person, he seemed to be crazy about me because anything I asked for he made sure I had it. Money for a bill, gas, even toilet paper if I ever ran out and he wasn't cheap. I had kissed him a few times. It was nice in those awkward moments. He had soft juicy lips. He seemed real passionate, I had to admit I was a bit curious...

Cary called to let me know he was on his way down and Brian had left a while ago. I had just gotten out of the shower and put on my burgundy velvet panties and bra set. I had candles lit in the living room. When I opened the door, Cary looked around in confusion. He could see my silhouette, and I saw he had a big grin on his face wondering what was in store. He sat on the couch and I straddled myself across his lap. I instantly felt a budge in his pants.

"What you doing girl?" His country accent sounded in my ear.

"What does it look like?"

I began to kiss him ever so gently. He squeezed my back, his hands unhooking my bra. He began to fondle my breast as we kissed passionately. I never thought a kiss from him would make me feel this way. I was soaking wet as he sucked my pretty brown nipples. Licking one then the other as I kissed the top of his bald head. I wanted him inside me now, as I unbuttoned his pants and he unzipped them and pulled them off past his knees. As I pulled my thong to the side Cary directed himself in that warm wet spot.

Damn this shit feels good. I thought to myself as he grabbed my ass and directed my body so he could go deeper and deeper. *Damn this feels good. Where she get this pussy from. That nigga crazy to let this get away.* Cary thought to himself.

I did that famous froggy position with that twist as I held on to the back of the couch.

What the fuck is she doing? Got damn! I ain't never felt no shit like this and I know I'm the number one Stunna'! This pussy about to make me forget my damn name. Look at her sexy ass, them titties floppin' up and down, I can't even keep them in my mouth. Damn! This girl fine. Oh, shit I'm about to skeet all in this pussy.

"I'm about to come baby" Cary whispered as if he couldn't catch his breath.

He pushed me off just in time. I enjoyed the show with a smile as he held his head back. I climbed back on top of him for some more, but he couldn't take it.

"No baby, hell no, you trying to kill me."

I laughed and sat beside him as he got himself together. When he left, he walked out shaking his head. You a mothafucka' boy! After he left I walked down the hall to the bathroom to jump in the shower with a smile on my face...

You are a mess... I said to myself.

That next day I went down the walk way to visit Ms. Shirley. Ms. Shirley was an old friend of Cary's. I met her that school year when Nadia started walking with her twin boys to school. Ms. Shirley became a mediator and counselor between me and Cary. She would always give me advice about men and slip in hints about Cary. What she meant by that I did not know. She knew Cary better than I did, but she saw he was extremely fond of me and whenever I needed him he was there for me.

"When it comes to these men you have to make sure you respect yourself and your children first. They can only do what you allow them to. It's up to you to set the standard for yourself." She stated.

"I respect myself. I don't have anyone around my daughter. My company only comes at night after she is asleep. If they want to fuck with me they gonna have to give me some money first, cause I ain't fuckin' for free. I'm picky about who I talk too."

Ms. Shirley gave me the worse look of disappointment ever while shaking her head.

"Why do you have such a nasty mouth baby? You are too pretty to have such a filthy mouth. That just doesn't look good and that's not a way to think. Men don't owe you anything. It's up to you to set an example for your daughter. You are such a pretty girl then when you open your mouth it just makes you look so ugly."

My mouth dropped open. I couldn't believe she said that to me. I was so ashamed of what I had just said. That I even thought of myself like that. Did I sound that bad? In that instant I thought of the girls I saw in public cursing at their kids and calling them out their names even at two and three years old. I used to be that girl. I didn't think twice about stopping that. If I could help it, I told myself I was not going to curse anymore. And I didn't, don't get me wrong I didn't say I forgot how to curse. So, watch it! I just started watching how I spoke and voiced my opinion. I believe that was my first lesson in the change of ME. No man is obligated to pay my bills, if they choose to date me. I am responsible for me and my own child. It's more attractive when you're not so needy, but it doesn't hurt to have help from someone you're dating. If they offer...what? It's a process.

CHAPTER THIRTEEN

I pulled up to Michele's with Nadia. When we went to walk up the stairs my nephew was coming down.

"We out in the back Aunty, Ms. Kim is barbecuing."

It was getting dark and they were just about to wrap things up. I came from the breeze way and everyone was sitting around in chairs making plates before they started clearing out the food. Hey Danielle, how are you? A sweet voice sounded from the crowd. That was Kim. She and her fiancé lived directly under Michele. She was very pretty with a very sweet spirit to match.

"Hello, how is everybody?" I asked into the crowd.

"Hey sis." Michele yelled.

"Let me introduce you to my parents."

"This is my mom Ms. Pam and this is my daddy Mr. Charles."

"...Nice to meet you both."

"Nice to meet you too, pull up a chair."

Kim had two boys. Nadia ran off with the rest of the kids. She seemed to be surrounded by boys. She was the only girl. A guy came from the breeze way. He was packing up pans and trash asking Ms. Pam what else needed to go where. He seemed to be real helpful. I didn't pay him much attention. He went back into the breeze way.

"Which one of you ladies does my son like?"

"It must be Dan." Kim stated as her and Michele laughed.

"I'm married." Michele added.

"Me? Why you say that? Who's your son?"

"Oh, that explains it! He must like you because he's running around like he's crazy knowing you can't get that boy to take out the trash let alone help clean up." Ms. Pam stated. They all laughed together as he returned.

"What's so funny?" ...

I ran into him a few days later when I pulled up at Michele's. He and another guy were standing at the bottom of the stairs as I walked up. We were never formally introduced.

"How you been?" He yelled

"Fine"

"I see that! What's your name again?"

"Danielle and what was yours?"

"Charles."

"That's right Kim's brother right."

"Yeah."

"Okay, nice to see you."

I know he's watching me walk up these stairs. As I looked back...Yep! I knew it.

I knocked on the door and slowly turned to look back down the stairs. There he was watching my every move as the door opened.

"What's up? How you doing?"

"Fine! Girl look whose outside."

"Who?"

"Kim's brother." As Michele peeked out the blinds...

"He's coming up the stairs Dan." Michele said with that giggle.

"Oh Lord. Guess we have a stalker."

There was a knock at the door.

"Answer it, it's for you." Michele gestured.

"Yes sir?" I asked as I opened the door.

"Can I talk to you for a minute?"

"Sure." I stepped outside.

"So how you doing?"

"You asked me that already remember."

"Oh yeah." He laughed. So, Michele is your sister?"

"Yes."

"How come I never saw you before?"

"I don't know? My daughter is over here all the time."

"Little Nadia? Oh, that's your little girl? She cute just like her mama. How old is she?"

"Nine. She'll be ten in October."

"Where you work at?"

"The Hospital."

"Oh, for real? I can't believe I've never seen you before. My mom is a nurse at the hospital. What floor you work on?"

"I work in registration."

"So, are you dating anybody?"

"No."

"You?"

"No, no not the kid."

"What is that supposed to mean? So, you a playa, then right?"

"No, I really don't have time to date, but you can make time for what you really want." He said with a glare in his eyes.

I knew what that meant. He was going to ask me out. I was just wondering how long it was going to take him to spit it out. He was cute enough. Here it comes...

"What you doing this weekend?"

"Nothing."

"Let me get your number and we can discuss where you want   me to take you over the phone."

I reached in my pocket and pulled out my number.

"I already knew it was coming, here you go." I stated as I handed him the piece of paper.

"Oh, is that right?"

"Yes, that's right since you starred me all the way up these stairs like you were taking my clothes off."

We both laughed. Charles's friend came to the bottom of the stairs suggesting he was about to take off.

"Let me go we have a couple of runs to make. I'm going to call you."

"Okay."

He ran down the stairs and this time I watched his every move before I went inside.

CHAPTER FOURTEEN

C harles called me that same night. We were both so excited we stayed on the phone for hours. He called me a little before eleven. We talked about our families and what I had been doing since I had been in Tifton. I never mentioned being married. I basically wished that never happened, so as far as I'm concerned it didn't.

It was almost the month of May. Once again, another year had passed. I talked to Charles on the phone every night that first month. Then I invited him over for dinner. I made a broiled T-bone, baked potato and a broccoli medley. He seemed to be impressed.

As he ate he was looking around at my place.

Her house is so clean, I mean spotless. She can cook and she fine. Ain't nobody hitting that and I'm the lucky one to get a home cooked meal. Her phone hasn't rung one time. Yeah, I can see myself over here with her. Her daughter is the same age as my nephews. She's the same age as my sister. Everyone should get along fine. I'll tell her about my baby mama another time.

After dinner, we sat on the couch. I turned off the lights and let the glow of the candles light the room. We talked more and agreed that a month had gone by and we had talked every day. We definitely had chemistry. The next thing to happen was the first kiss. That told it all. A kiss told if there was a connection, if you were passionate, even if you had love making skills. *Like roller skating, yeah that tells a lot about a brotha'.* The connection was there alright. *I was going to enjoy this one.* Charles had full soft lips and a thick tongue. Unlike Brian, he had thin lips and a long skinny tongue. His tongue was good but we hadn't kissed all that much. He was too busy licking between my legs all the time. Damn!

As we kissed Charles's hands moved right to my breast. What did he do that for? I was already wet from those soft juicy lips. The next thing I knew he had pulled me on top of him. We might as well been making love with our clothes on. Oh, I hope he had a big dick. I would hate for all this passion to go to waste. His body was so strong and thick. He was holding me so tight as we grinded against one another. I couldn't take it I wanted to feel him inside me. I stopped kissing him and stood up. I pulled him off the couch and directed him to follow me to my bedroom. He kissed me as he laid me on the bed. *Damn! What happened to my 90-day rule?* His kisses were perfect. The way he held me and squeezed my breast felt so good! He squirmed out of his pants and our bodies were soon skin to skin, wrist to wrist and cheek to cheek. As he found my warm wet spot he paused.

"You're not on your period, are you?"

"Why would you ask me a question like that at a time like this?"

"Why your pussy so wet?" He asked.

"It's always that wet. That's how my body is." I whispered.

I never felt this feeling before. Damn her pussy is warm and wet and she huggin' my dick. Damn! She didn't ask me to use a condom. I hope she don't do this to every dude she meet.

I can't believe how his body fits with mine. This is so good, shit! I hope he wants this pussy every night. If he wants this he ain't gonna leave.

Charles was there every night for the next month. He got off work and every day at the same time I would see him coming down the street pulling up in my complex. Daddy's home! My heart would just flutter. I made sure dinner was in the oven or on the stove.

"Hey baby, how was your day? What we eating for dinner?" Looking in the pots on the stove giving me a big kiss on the lips.

I thought that was so special. Once he moved in. He picked up the light bill and transferred his phone line to my address. We started a lot of double dating with his sister and the kids. They were due to get married in August.

So, you're the one who has gotten my brother out of my house. He must really like you, we hardly ever see him now. I smiled nervously. I was always shy until I got to know you. We started meeting over there regularly. They were always doing something or going somewhere. I could get used to this. Charles had two sisters. The other lived in Atlanta. I hadn't met her yet. He told me we would get along well, that we had similar personalities. I looked forward to meeting her she was actually Shannon's best friend.

CHAPTER FIFTEEN

"**G**irl, you know your brother is messing with my neighbor."

"Who?"

"Her name is Danielle. She real cute, but girl they are so loud!"

"Loud they arguing already?" His sister joked.

"No, girl fucking. They do it every night for hours. You know our rooms are right next to each other and girl, me and my boyfriend laying in the bed sleep and here they go. It was funny at first, but now girl I be wanting to bang on the wall and tell them to take they ass to sleep or go in another room."

"Oh, my goodness, you crazy girl, too much information" She laughed.

"I'm sorry girl."

"Kim told me he had a new girlfriend. I can't believe he has gotten rid of that other baby mama? I'll believe it when I see it."

"Well, he be over there every night." Shannon added.

"I'm sure I'll be meeting her then."

The next few months seem like a fairytale. It was as if I had known Charles forever. Everything was perfect. We had gone on a weekend get away with his sister and her fiancé and the kids of course, to a waterpark in Florida. We met for dinner Friday night, then Saturday morning spent all day at the park, had dinner and stayed overnight in a Hotel. It was so fun to be away from home with a love interest. Nadia had a great time with his nephews. I never had to worry about money whenever we went anywhere. We met for breakfast the next morning before getting back on the road.

I was meeting Charles over his sister's. When I pulled up I saw he was already there. I was always so excited to see him. I knocked on the door and entered. They were all sitting in the living room talking.

"Baby, you feel like riding out of town for dinner?"

"That's fine." I replied.

"I have a taste for a steak and a margarita." Kim added.

"Do you drink?"

"No, I don't. I've tasted Daiquiri's before."

"Ok, we'll get you one of those." She laughed.

Charles drank socially. As I recall he brought some Crown Royal and it was in the cabinet above the refrigerator.

We arrived at the restaurant. Charles ordered my drink and my meal. While we ate, I sipped on my daiquiri. I felt a buzz half way through my drink. Somehow, we got on the subject of different couples in Tifton.

"Do you know Lynn Denton?" Kim asked.

"Yes, she's my best friend, well one of my closest friends here. I met her when I first moved to Tifton. I had a short T-Boz cut and I would let her do my hair and we have been close ever since."

"I can't picture you with a short cut. I bet it was cute.

You have a pretty face. Your hair is beautiful too!"

"Thank you, you're so sweet."

"Hey didn't she marry that faggot Rich?" Charles interjected.

"He is not a faggot. Rich is nice. That's a mean thing to say."

"I say that nigga a pussy bitch, and I don't like him!"

"Well I think he's sweet."

Charles looked at me like I spit in his face. I picked up on that quick. I thought I was tripping for a minute off my drink. Did I say something wrong? The table was totally silent. I started to sweat and got light headed. Charles didn't speak to me the rest of the night. If I made a comment, or try to speak he cut me off.

This was our first argument or disagreement. What was he going to say next? Was he going to break up with me behind our disagreement? I didn't understand what I said wrong. I lost my appetite. I tried to finish my drink but I really had a stomach ache now. I never liked confrontation.

Kim remembered she and her fiancé had an appointment to take pre-wedding pictures with a friend of theirs that was a photographer. Luckily that ended dinner and we left the restaurant. We followed them to the photographer's house. It was total silence in the car. It was actually raining. I didn't know what city we were in. I tried to talk to Charles to find out why he was mad or what did I say that was so wrong, but that didn't work. He still was not speaking to me. We looked as they posed for their pictures. That kind of lightened the mood. They even encouraged us to take pictures. We took a few. This made me nervous. When we finished, we headed home. The whole ride was still in silence. Once we made it home I didn't know what to do. I undressed and got in the shower. He didn't join me as he usually did. He sat there on his side of the bed waiting for me to return. I turned the light off and climbed in the bed leaving him sitting in the dark. I didn't know what else to do. He wasn't speaking to me after all my attempts.

"Dan." His voice sounded in the dark.
I didn't know if I should reply. Was I mad now or just confused? I didn't know why he was mad and shut me down.

"Dan?" His voice sounded again.
"What!"
"Why did you embarrass me?"
"When? What do you mean embarrass you?"
"You talked against me when we were talking about Lynn and Rich. If I say that nigga a faggot you're not supposed to say anything. Like you siding with the nigga over me."
"What? Choosing him over you? All I said was he was cool."
"And I said he was a punk. Why you defending him? He like you or something?"
"What in the hell? That's my friend's husband. I was just voicing my opinion. So, because you don't like him, I shouldn't like him? That's crazy, but I get it. I think that's retarded, but fine whatever you say."
"It is whatever I say, that nigga don't pay no bills over here. What you defending him for?"
"Okay, okay I heard you, I'm sorry."
I had nothing else to say. The silence became sleep.

"Dan? You okay?" Charles asked.
"Yeah."
"Come here, you know that was our first argument?" He pulled my body against his by placing his hand around my waste.

Oh, now he wants some.

"Yes."

"You just made me so mad."

"I'm sorry." I apologized.

"No, I'm sorry." He said as he kissed the side of my face.

Putting my hand on his penis so I could feel how hard he was. He rolled over on top of me, spreading my legs as he guided himself inside me. *I forgot what we were even arguing about, hell he probably didn't know his damn self. Maybe it was that drink he had.*

Since our first argument was out the way. I guess we both figured it was time to fess up to our other secrets, me and being married and he about his baby mama situation. She was still under the impression that he still lived with Kim until someone had mentioned to her they saw his car parked every night at my house.

My situation was easy. All I had to do was file for an annulment.

"So, you mean that you are married and you didn't think that was important to tell me before now." Charles asked.

"I did but I blocked him out so much it hadn't even dawned on me to take the appropriate steps." I replied.

"Well you know technically this man could come up in here and I would be in the wrong because you're his wife."

"I wish he would. He doesn't even know I live here. I haven't seen or heard of him since I left."

"Well how much does an annulment cost?"

"I don't know. I guess I could ask my dad to find out."

"Or go down to the Courthouse and find out. I'll pay for it. Hell I might want you to be my wife."

I looked at him with that smile of relief. Glad that was over. One down and two more to go, I never mention about going to jail for murder or being shot. The appropriate time will present itself I'm sure. When it came to the baby mama, I don't think I had any control over that situation. He was too worried about paying child support if she found out he was with someone else. These men and this child support. I can understand if the father is not supportive and has the money to help, but I don't get these chicks who are irresponsible and have a baby daddy that buys the child everything they need while they don't do shit, worried about getting their hair and nails did while the child looking a hot ass mess. *Oh, sorry I said I wasn't going to curse*, but man it makes no sense to me. The scandalous females always get the good ones and the decent independent females always gets the knuckle heads. They have too much power over their heads with that word "Child Support". It's almost frightening at the thought of the extent they will go not to pay it. In his case, he is letting it control his future for happiness. Point blank!

Charles pulled up to drop off his daughter some shoes and an outfit that Kim had picked out. She lived with her mama.

"Here go some shoes and an outfit for my baby."

"When are you getting her dress for the wedding?" She asked.

"I don't know you'll have to talk to Kim about that." He replied.

"Where you been hiding? I've been over to Kim's and she says she hasn't seen you. Who you staying with now? And you ain't returned any of my calls?"

"I'm not staying with anybody. They changed my schedule at work. I don't get off until the morning sometimes. Why? What you needed something?"

"Don't think you slick? My cousin Quetta already told me you be in that complex with those duplexes where her baby daddy aunty stay. She say your car be parked over there every night."

"Well tell Quetta she need to mind her fuckin' business and don't worry about my damn car, and don't be calling me about no he said she said bullshit." He said as he got in his car and drove off.

"Yeah, let me find out you lying. I will take you to court!" She yelled.

Now it seems that what Charles thought was comfortable and no one knew everyone was talking about our relationship. He didn't like people in his business and it seemed his baby mama knew more than he thought. Now he would have to pacify both situations.

He had actually had his own apartment. I guess he and his baby mama lived together, then he put her out. His cousin Candice was living there. Since he was always at my place she moved in. That's why he transferred the phone. I had wondered why he had a phone at his sister's. I had never been over there until one day she invited me over and told me the whole story.

CHAPTER SIXTEEN

The wedding was soon approaching. Kim had asked me to do her makeup. Charles was in the wedding. I was finally able to meet his other sister that lived in Atlanta. She had come down a few times to help with the wedding planning. She stayed next door at Shannon's and we all stayed up late talking. Charles was right we hit it off just fine and we were the same age. This would be my first time meeting his whole entire family. I had picked out the perfect short dress that had a skinny scarf like wrap with the same pattern. It was cute and sexy for summer, but sophisticated enough for a wedding with some Metallic strappy heels. I loved my Steve Madden sandals.

As I arrived to the church I was so nervous. Charles was in the wedding so he was already at the chapel. I never confirmed with his sister if I was still to do her makeup, so I figured they had it together. I was so nervous. Not to mention his baby mama would be here somewhere since their daughter was in the wedding. I knew most of his family but this would be everybody from out of town. I walked through the door of the chapel. It was beautifully decorated in white with flowers and crystals. This was nice. I imagined if I too would one day marry Charles and we would be here next. I found a seat with a friend I knew, that made me feel more comfortable. I hated going places by myself. I guess that's why I was never too much of a club person. I would seem to have a panic attack if I had to do something alone. Hopefully it was something I would grow out of. I also had the pleasure of seeing the baby mama. That was uncomfortable for me especially since I knew Charles lived with me and she didn't.

As I sat and waited with the rest of the guest, Charles peeked out to make sure I was there. Once he spotted me he winked and bit his bottom lip. I knew what that meant. He looked so handsome in his tuxedo. He was so sexy too me. Bells started ringing. The bride is coming! The bride is coming! The little flower girls ran down the aisle screaming as they dropped their petals. Everyone turned to the door as the groom and his party stepped out behind the curtain and took their places at the Altar.

The ceremony was beautiful. As I walked out of the chapel wouldn't you know the first person I ran directly into, *no literally*, Charles's baby mama? Oh, brother I thought. It was as if we knew exactly who each other were. I waited off to the side to be noticed as the wedding party grouped to take their pictures. I wondered if Charles would acknowledge me and he did.

"Damn! You look good baby. He kissed me on the cheek. We're about to take pictures."

"Okay, I'll be here." I replied.

I was relieved that one of his cousins greeted me with a hug. I guess that confirmed it. The baby mama left and I was able to relax. They were really sweet to me. I admired their poses. Once they finished I was able to give Kim a hug.

"You look so pretty."

"Where were you? You were supposed to do my make up?"

"Oh, I'm sorry I wasn't for sure if you had changed your mind. I didn't want to impose on your most important day."

"You weren't imposing, you're like family now. I wanted you to do it. I did my best with what I had."

"You did good. I apologize."

"It's okay. We ready to take off. We are meeting at the reception hall in an hour."

"Okay."

"We going to get changed over to Danielle's."

That was Charles' cousin and his sister from Atlanta.

"Okay."

"Can I ride with you, I'll get dressed at Shannon's?"

"Sure." I happily replied.

"Baby I'll be right behind ya'll, let me make sure everything gets locked up at the chapel." Charles instructed.

We all arrived at my house. Charles was coming down the road as we were getting out of the car. His sister went to Shannon's and his other cousins pulled up and came into my place.

They all were getting changed as Charles and I went into the bedroom. He was tired and it was hot.

"You want to take a nap?"

"Baby you tired?" I asked.

"Hell, yeah and I want to rub on you for a while."

"We about to go next door to Shannon's" a voice sounded from the other side of the door.

"Cool! We're about to take a nap. Wake us up in an hour." Charles yelled.

We lay there first talking about the wedding, and the fact that I literally ran into his baby mama.

"Yeah, she's going to be a problem."

"For who?" I asked.

"I don't know, she full of shit. She going to try to take out child support now."

"Don't you buy everything already?"

"That's my point she lazy, and don't want to work. So, I don't give her my money I buy my daughter whatever she need. After seeing how fine you was looking today, I know she mad." He laughed.

"You're so crazy!" I laughed.

"This ought to be an incentive enough to get her shit together, hell."

He started feeling under my t-shirt. He rolled on top of me and lifted my shirt to get full access of my breast, sucking one then the other.

"You know I was a tittie baby, don't you?"

"I see." I replied.

We made love quietly and the next thing we knew we were knocked out. There was a knock at the door.

"It's time to go, y'all still sleep."

"Awe damn what time is it? We coming." He said looking at the clock.

"We'll meet ya'll there!"

We pulled up to the reception. Everything was under way as we walked in.

"What were you two up too, you're late."

"Man, we fell asleep."

Kim gave me that sly grin. She was too funny. I loved her already. I sat with their parents. They always made me feel so welcome. The food was so good. The music was good. It was time for the bouquet toss. My co-worker was one of the servers. We sat next to each other at work. She was single too and you didn't have to tell her twice.

Everyone was lined up, go on Danielle, you single. Get up there girl you might get lucky and catch it. I laughed and ran up at the last minute.

As soon as she tossed it, and it landed right in my hands and my co-worker snatched it before I could get a grip on it. *Story of my life.* They all knew it landed with me and looked at Charles teasing him that he was next.

CHAPTER SEVENTEEN

I was terminated from my job. I had work in registration and was chosen to be the registration clerk in the new Oncology center because I processed the most registrations. After being pulled back and forth between departments I had decided to apply to permanently be placed in Oncology. Next thing I know they stated they had a hiring freeze and shortly after I was terminated due to a conflict of interest. Really?

I was too embarrassed to tell Charles. I figured he would still be supportive.

"Who gets fired from their job?"

"What do you mean?"

"I mean you got fired for no reason?"

"Well that is what they told me, that going back and forth between departments was causing a conflict of interests. How could that be when they chose me to go? I tried to transfer and then this is what I get." I replied.

"Well it is what it is. What are you going to do now? Are

you going to apply for unemployment?"

"I guess so."

"In the meantime, you should start looking for another job."

"Yeah, but where?"

"Go to McDonald's they are always hiring." He replied.
No, he did not just tell me to apply at McDonald's. What in the hell? Is he for real?

I started to see another side of him after this. Cary would stop by to check on me to see if I needed anything. We were standing outside talking when Charles came home. I introduced them and he went on in the house.

"Who's that nigga?"

"My boyfriend."

"He stay with you?"

"Yeah!"

"What the fuck you got that nigga staying with you for?"

"What do you mean? We've been dating since March."

"So, cause y'all dating, the nigga got to live with you?"

"No, but he does. Why you trippin'?"

"You know why the fuck I'm tripping but I'm gone let that go."
Charles called me to come in from the house.

"Let me go see what he wants. I'll call you later."

"Yeah you do that." Cary replied
I went back in the house to see what Charles wanted.

"Who's dude?"

"Oh, that's Cary. He works at the hospital."

"He like you?"

"No, why you ask that?"

"I'm just asking, you know I come home and see some other nigga talking to my woman."

"He's just my friend. He cool."

"Well I don't want you talking to no other dudes."

"What do you mean?"

"I don't see any reason for you to have any male friends. You don't see any other chicks calling my phone. I even had my home phone transferred to your house. That should speak volumes."

He had a point, but I don't believe that means we should cut our friends off. But then again, most relationships between a male and female had to start with some physical attraction that resulted in sex. It's rarely a case that the relationship is strictly platonic. One just may decide to cut those sexual strings in hopes to agree to continue the friendship. In other cases, if the other party is over looked they may have feelings that they never felt should be shared in risk of losing the friendship that they have established, and in the end, are noticed as a piece of the puzzle that now cannot be replaced. So, cliché.

I agreed to disagree with Charles to keep the peace. He wanted me to actually tell Cary he couldn't come by any longer, and like he asked I told him not to call the house. That was all I told him.

I was home during the day now and I finally got a chance to run into my neighbors that shared my porch. It seemed to be a lady and her daughters. Looks like two girls and one had a little girl. She was really cute. I guess the one with the baby was older. She was always driving their van and seem to have the little girl all the time.

I was coming from the laundry room and one of the girls was coming in. She looked familiar.

"Hey don't you work at the hospital? I remember you when I came for my ultrasound."

"Yes, I did. Heaven, right?"

"Yep, don't tell my mama. I haven't told anyone yet. You stay next door to us."

"I do and oh, I won't. I leave so early I've never gotten a chance to meet you or speak. I see your mom through the window running out after I get home from work."

"Yep, she work at the Marriott from 3-11."

"Oh, okay and the other girl with the baby I see driving the van is your sister too?"

"Yeah, that's Sunny, she's my baby sister. I'm the middle girl and that's our oldest sister's Neveah's baby."

"Oh, okay so it's three of y'all, and your mom? Cool. Well I'm glad I finally got to meet one of you. Yeah, we see you too

leaving out in the morning. That's your boyfriend that lives with you?" She asked.

"Yes, he has been living with me for a few months now. Like since June." I replied laughing.

"Oh okay."

We hit it off and I soon met the whole crew. They were really cool. They started coming over and we started hanging outside talking about everything. They had been friends with Shannon too. We cooked breakfast and dinners together. I told them all my war stories the closer we became.

They became like family to me. Sisters I never had the pleasure of hanging out with. They were so shocked to hear all about what I had been through. They stayed glued to the couch as I told one story after the other. Sunny would ask a zillion questions.

"Girl naw shut the fuck up! You is a real live gangsta!" She would say.

I would just laugh because I can remember everything like it was yesterday without the emotions. Sunny was another feisty one. Nice shape with an average height of 5'7. She got in the most fights. She talk hella shit but she backed it up too. She was classy and trendy in her appearance, always on point and she kept you on your toes for sure. Her hair and nails stayed fly with all the accessories to match every outfit from the earrings to the toe ring. She had a number one sponsor on deck. He gave her anything she asked for.

Heaven on the other hand was quiet and very personal. She too had pretty thick hair and pretty brown eyes. We all had hair on our lip. They were actually hairier than I was in a good way. Me and Heaven took pride in our eyelashes being long and Sunny always pulled hers out from her nervous condition. Don't even ask. It was just something she did. Heaven didn't want anyone knowing her business. She didn't have many friend girls unlike Sunny. Sunny was always the life of the party, always shinning. Heaven was short, cute and petite with a nice shape. Always so sweet, never out of character. She wouldn't even dream of cursing you out. When she heard my story it dang near brought her to tears and she would always say,

"Thank you, Jesus! That wasn't nothin' but the Lord."

I never got to know Neveah, she was more street and was always gone somewhere getting crunk from one house to the next. She didn't live with them, they only kept the baby to ensure her safety. That sister there was off the chain.

The summer was over and I thought things could only get better between me and Charles. My father stopped asking me to go to church but everybody was talking about the revival at Friendship Baptist Church. The Pastor's son came every year. They say he's a prophet.

I got dressed and me and Nadia headed out the door to church. When I arrived, I noticed my father and step mother were sitting in the front pews on the left side of the church. Michele motioned me to join them. A friend of mine noticed me as I sat down in my seat. She made her way over to give me a hug and say hello. It was Sabrina. Ever since she met me she took a liking to me as if she had known me for years. She was always so excited to see me and would just love on me like I was her best friend in the world.

We began to talk about the revival, the prophet and the things that God had been blessing her with. Speaking of that I asked her about the Holy Spirit.

"What is it when people shout and jump around screaming talking in tongues?" I asked.

"Girl it's just the spirit of the Lord. When it comes on you it's just something you have no control over and you really can't explain when it happens."

"I've never had it before, I want that to happen to me."

"It will sweetie, you just have to ask God to touch you. It will happen just pray for a closer relationship with Him and you'll be in there."

We both laughed and gave each other another big hug and took our seats.

During the service, I really paid attention to the preaching. I never liked to go to my dad's church because I hated the routine of the service. Four offerings, six hymns, two more worship prayers then the choir would sing. That took up most of the service, then by the time the preacher started preaching I was sleepy, wishing I would have just stayed home.

They asked if everybody would stand and worship the Lord. Close your eyes and just think of all the things God has brought you through. Have you just really told God thank you from the bottom of your heart. From the depth of your soul have you just stopped and told the Lord thank you?

I never thought of it that way. I did have a whole lot of shit *oops...* stuff to be thankful for. I could have still been in jail, I could have been cocked eyed or dead from getting shot in the head or the accident alone could have killed me. Not to mention the abuse I suffered from Juelz and Brian. I really didn't hold a grudge against Nadia's dad. I never loved him, but man when you look at all that stuff I went through I am thankful, so very thankful that I'm still alive. I could have never awakened when I went unconscious. God did that, He saved me. He saved my life, He is the reason I am here today.

"Thank you, Lord, thank you, thank you, thank you!"

The more I cried out to the Lord tears started rolling down my face, my eyes were closed and I was screaming thank you to the Lord. I started jumping up and down, shouting waving my hands crying out thank you to the Lord for saving me.

"Move back just let her go, the spirit is on her." My father instructed everyone in the pew. Michele picked up her son so he wouldn't get hit.

I fell in my seat not knowing what had happened. All I knew was I was exhausted and dizzy. At the end of the service the prophet asked who ever wanted to come up for prayer to come to the Alter. If you felt you needed answers or a word from God to come up and let him pray for you. I found myself in a long line waiting for prayer. I didn't know what exactly I wanted prayer for. I just wanted to hear anything the Lord had to tell me.

When I made it to him the first thing he did as soon as he looked at me was begin to cry, his face was frowned up and he spoke in a weeping voice,

"Everything is going to be okay, don't worry everything will be alright. I see your heart and you are crying inside, but don't worry everything is going to be alright."

I could not get the image of his face out of my mind. Was

my heart really sad, was I just going through the motions of life? What did he see?

That night I wanted to tell Charles what happened. When he came home I was excited. He was raised Jehovah's Witness although we never talked about religion. I never thought he would have an opinion about what I experienced. I didn't really know how to start the conversation.

"You know how those people in church be shouting and jumping around when the spirit is on them?"

"Yeah, that stuff ain't real." He replied.

"Yes, it is!"

"No, it's not."

"It happened to me tonight at the revival."

I explained to him everything that happened that night. He didn't have much of a response. We never considered the fact that we were from different religions. If we had gotten married would I convert to Jehovah's Witness? A family that prays together stays together, but that was one thing I don't believe I would consider doing and that may cause a problem. I couldn't see bringing him to church since he seemed so heartless when I told him about what happened at the revival. It was never even discussed again.

I had the opportunity to tell him those last two secrets I had been holding on too. I told him to get the full understanding of why I was so thankful and grateful. I wanted him to know that my crime was not intentional and that being shot in the head was nothing but a miracle. People get shot all the time and die. Just drop dead, and God allowed me to live. He saved my mind and my body through all my circumstances, and I don't look like what I been through because you would have never thought looking at the beautiful smile I keep on my face.

"Why did you tell me that?"

"What do you mean? You asked me if I had any secrets and I felt that sooner or later I would have to tell you."

"Well how did you know I would be able to handle a secret like that?"

"I never thought of it being too much to handle. It's not like I did anything on purpose, and it was ten years ago. Do I look like I would be the type of person that could casually commit a crime of any sort?"

"No, baby I'm not saying that it's just that that type of information took me of guard, and no you don't look like any of that could have ever happen to you. I know you didn't mean to kill anyone. I'm just not used to even having to process that type of information from someone I'm actually in a relationship with. I mean that's the type of stuff you hear on television not up close in your home."

"I see what you're saying. I'm sorry I didn't mean to spring that on you, but I guess there never would be a good time to tell anyone something like that."

"It's okay baby. I can't even imagine you going through that."

He pulled me close to give me a hug. It felt weird. I didn't know what was going on in his head now?

CHAPTER EIGHTEEN

C harles shift actually changed. He was getting off at eleven now and for some reason started parking his work truck in the back. He had surprised me when I went to his sister's in Atlanta for the weekend. He called up there to see what we were up to.

"What y'all doing? He asked.
"I'm doing your girlfriends hair. What's up?"
"Let me speak to her."
"My brothers on the phone for you."
"Hey what's going on?"
"Nothing too much I got a surprise for you?"
"For me? What is it?"
"I got us a truck!"
"A truck?"
"He got a new truck? What kind did he get?" His sister interjected.
"What kind of truck did you get us?"
"99 Ford Expedition, it's clean too Dan. I think you're

going to like it!"

"Oh! Those are nice. I've only seen this year's model. Is it any difference from 98 to 99? He got a 99 Ford Expedition" I whispered.

"Just little added features with a few more bells and whistles, you know."

"What time you all think you're going to make it in tomorrow?"

"I don't know we should be leaving around four. We're going to the mall when she gets done with my hair."

"Okay then, enjoy your day. I'll see you when you get home. Love you."

"Okay, love you too."

"My brother said he love you?" His sister asked.

"Yeah, he's been telling me he loved me a few months after he moved in."

"Well if my brother telling you that you better run."

"What you mean by that?

"I'm just saying. I'm not saying he don't I just know my brother. My whole family loves you now, so I'm happy to see he is finally trying to settle down." She added.

"Okay." I hesitated.

One thing you have to remember don't nobody know a man like his sister, so always listen closely and very carefully.

Charles honked the horn. His baby mama came out of her mother's house and got in his new Expedition. Charles had decided to take her on the gambling boat with Kim and her husband.

"This is nice of you. Where's your girlfriend?"

"She's not my girlfriend, but if you're referring to the chick at Kim's wedding she's out of town." He replied.

"So, when you get this." She asked as she looked around the truck taking in the new car smell.

"I got it yesterday."

"Oh, so am I the first female to ride in your truck huh?"

"If you want to believe that, I'll let you have that."

When Charles met up with Kim she had a strange look on her face, as if to say what the hell are you doing with her? And he returned the look as if to say, don't even ask.

They spent the day on the Gambling Casino Boat and went to dinner. After dinner, they checked into a Hotel for the evening. Charles had no reservations. *Why should I? Dan is with my sister in Atlanta. I'll be back by the time she gets home.*

We came back from the mall and I tried calling Charles. It had gone straight to voicemail. I didn't bother leaving him a message since we already talked for the day. He ended up calling back letting me know he would be on call for work if he didn't answer. So, that usually meant it was no telling when he got off work at the plant. He was an engineer and he was the fix it guy.

The next day his sister cooked a big breakfast. I helped clean up the house. We cleaned out her closet and swapped a few outfits. Before we knew it, it was time to hit the road. I called Charles as soon as I made it home. *Still no answer so he must've got called in again.*

I unpacked my clothes. The house was clean so I sorted some clothes to wash. He used the spare bedroom closet so I went in there to check to see if he had any dirty clothes. He took most of his clothes to the cleaners and I washed the rest. When I opened the closet, there were some clothes from the cleaners hanging up still in the plastic. His duffle bag was on the floor. He would usually put his dirty drawls and shirts from work in there. I went to look in it and there were some dirty shirts and socks along with a Hotel receipt. My heart started to pound out of my chest. Surely this was old. It had his baby mama name on it as the guest. I searched for the date. It was from yesterday. I looked for the address. It was some hotel in Florida. Son of a bitch! So, that bastard wasn't at work, he took her out of town, in the new truck he claim he got for us! Niggas ain't shit.

I called his phone once more. No answer. I didn't want to keep calling then he may have thought something was wrong. I went over to Shannon's to see if she was home. She was and I filled her in on what had happened. I asked her if she had seen him at all the weekend. She said she saw him earlier in some big truck and that he didn't stay long and left.

"That dirty mothafucka!"

"Yeah, I can't think straight. Oh, but I got something for him."

"What are you going to do girl?" She asked.

"You'll see. You have any tools, like a screw driver. Yeah I'm sure my boyfriend has some?"

"Can I borrow them?"

I switched my front door lock with my back door lock and broke the key off in the key hole. He never had a key to the back door. I packed up all his clothes in his duffle bag and the rest in the laundry basket neatly folded and placed them on the grass in front of my walk way.

It was a few hours before Charles returned. I patiently waited for him to pull up. I closed all the blinds and camped out in Nadia's room with all the lights off and slightly tilted the blinds so I could see out. He arrived just before dusk. I placed his Hotel receipt right on top of his neatly folded dirty clothes. He attempted to open the door, and then he tried using his key. He rang the doorbell like a maniac, he went around to the back door, then he banged on my bedroom window and I just sat in the window watching as he returned to the basket as he read his Hotel receipt. He threw his bag and the laundry basket in the back of his truck, he jumped in and drove off.

I began to cry. I went back into my bedroom and lay across my bed screaming. How could he have done this to me? He said he loved me. We got along so well. I even loved his mama. You bastard I yelled as I continued to cry. I never moved from that spot. When I woke up it was almost two in the morning. I hadn't taken the phone off the hook, but it hadn't rung either. He already knew there was nothing to be said.

I knew that my relationship wasn't going to be the one I wanted with Charles. He had let his new truck go to his head. He made a few drive-bys to my apartment when things cooled down. He never gave an apology or attempted to ask me to take him back. He was just popping up trying to see who was at my house. I figured that out right away and every time things where just as quiet as when he moved in. He never offered me a ride in his truck until he got his windows tinted. What the hell? He asked me to lunch at Ruby Tuesdays. He played Jagged Edge during the ride home. I loved that song and I was still in love with him. He could have cared less. I thought that would be an attempt at us getting back together. Not so much he dropped me off and never even asked to come in let alone stay the night.

I ran into Brian as he drove through my complex. I'm sure that was not a coincidence. He asked me if we could go for a ride and talk. I agreed and hopped in the car with him. It was dark when we decided to go to the picnic tables on the Campus of the College. I already knew what that meant. We've been there several times. It's dark and quiet and no one rarely goes there. It seems as if you're all alone under the stars in the sky. I would always wear some type of skirt with no panties. He desired the taste of me. I sat on top of the table and he sat in front of me with his head on my chest. He would begin to rub my legs under my skirt and confirm that I wasn't wearing anything underneath. I leaned down holding his face to kiss him gently on the lips. The more we kissed the further my skirt was raised up my legs. He pulled my hips off the table as he positioned me to lean back. He placed his mouth between my legs and my mind went back to how he used to please me with his tongue. It felt so good to feel that instant gratification. He knew my body so well and I was over whelmed with the sensations. I didn't want to lose total control outside under the stars, but I was close to it. I had to stop him after the second orgasm or else he would hold me until I had no more strength left in me. We ended on a good note. He dropped me off at home and I was hesitant to invite him in so I thanked him for the ride and went into the house.

"Can I call you?" He asked.

"You staying at your moms?"

"Yeah."

"I'll call you."

I went inside and took a shower and got in the bed, as I lay there alone I began to think about what just took place. I would never tell anyone that story or that I wanted him to come back. My body wasn't satisfied...

That morning I heard that loud work truck pulling up, it was nearly seven o'clock in the morning. You have got to be kidding. I looked over at Brian, he was dead asleep. I got out of my bed to tip toe and look out Nadia's window. It was Charles. Oh shoot! Just as I went back to climb back into bed he started knocking on my bedroom window. Are you serious right now? Brian jumped up.

"Just be still. Don't even ask." I stated.

"Who's that at your window?

"Nobody, I'm not even going to answer the door."

He continued to knock on my window calling my name. I just laid there as Brian placed his gun on the night stand.

"What the hell do you have a gun for?"

"I keep me some protection."

"Oh, my gosh! You are so retarded."

Right then I remembered why I couldn't stand him and wished he was not even in my damn bed, and now I ruined the only chance I might have had to get back with Charles. He might have been coming over for some make up sex! So much for that! Charles ended up leaving and Brian got up and left shortly after that. I was stuck feeling stupid so I went for some comfort next door with the girls. It was time for breakfast anyway. They always made me feel better when we got together and cooked. They saw the whole thing.

"Who you had in your bed girl? Charles was bammin on the door, we saw him go around the back." Heaven stated.

"Yeah, he was knocking on my window."

They fell out laughing.

"What you be doing to these negro's honey. Your pussy must be some damn dope or something, hell! That's what he gets. He needs to see two can play that game." Sunny laughed.

"Yes, but I didn't want him to see that. I don't want him knowing nothing about what I'm doing, especially that!" I added.

A few weeks later I kept noticing Brian's car in the next parking lot of our complex. I didn't think anything of it until I started leaving in the morning and his car was covered in morning dew. He was staying with some chick. It was late and me and Sunny was walking around the complex.

"Ain't that that boy car parked over there?"

"Yes, I wonder who he messing with? I've been seeing his car over there a few weeks now and I know he staying somewhere because his car is parked in the same spot when I leave in the mornings."

"We should egg his car!" Sunny suggested.

"Are you serious?"

"Yes, he is a clown! How is he going to mess with some chick in your same complex? It doesn't matter if y'all together or not. Just raggedy!"

We ran in the house.

"Wait who eggs we gonna use? I need my eggs hell?"

"We just need a few girl, I'll buy you some more eggs!"

We hopped in the car. It was almost ten o'clock at night. Sunny sat in the back seat and rolled the window down and threw the eggs from one side of the car to the other. It was actually funny. Just a little harmless humor, I wonder what the eggs did to his paint job on that Cutlass?

CHAPTER NINETEEN

T hinking back from the revival I decided I wanted to know more about God and what I needed to do to get it. I turned on the television in the morning. School had started back for Nadia and I was waiting to wake her up. It was 6 am. A black man out of Atlanta I had never seen or heard of before named Creflo Dollar. What kind of name was that? Was that his real name? Was that his real name or did he give his self that name when he started preaching?

I listened to him and I liked the sound of his voice. It had such authority and he spoke so clearly. He was really speaking truth. My heart felt different this time listening to the Word. I felt the Lord was then speaking to me.

"You could have still been in jail, but it was God that brought you out of that situation, that car wreck could have killed you, but it was God that lifted you up and saved you, that gunshot could have took you out, but by God's grace you are still here!"

Did he just say gunshot, Oh my God! He *is* talking to *me*. "Thank you, Jesus, thank you Lord!" I cried as tears rolled down my face.

I want to pray for you, those of you who are watching from home I want us to touch and agree that the grace of the Lord is upon you. I want you to touch the screen. Put your hands on my hands. He placed his hands to the screen and I placed my hands on top of his. We are going to touch and agree that you received that prayer and as he declared it is so I felt something through my body. It actually felt like a surge shot through me from my fingertips. I could not believe it! Did this really just happen to me? God spoke to me! He really spoke to me! That word was for me. I sat and reflected back on those incidents. I believed that if it really wasn't for the Lord I could have still been in jail or dead from the accident or the gun shot. The Lord saved me. He really saved me...

I couldn't wait to tell my dad. He did not believe me and was not the least bit excited?

"It was probably radio waves through the television you know..."

"So, you don't think it was real? You can't question the power of the Lord when He wants to speak to you? The Lord works in ways we can never even imagine. He always seems to get our attention one way or another. We just have to be willing to listen."

CHAPTER TWENTY

It was basketball season. Nadia played with the Recreation Department the previous year. I had never gotten out the car when she had been dropped off to practice. Brian had always taken her inside. So, they had try outs to sign up for teams.

I walked Nadia inside the gym and sat on the bleachers. Nadia warmed up on the court. My child was good! She made every basket. There was a guy instructing the kids on the court. When I saw him, my heart stopped? He was gorgeous! By the end of try outs I asked Nadia who he was. He's our basketball coach. I walked on the court to introduce myself.

"Hello, how are you. I'm Nadia's mother. Are you the coach?"

"Yes, I'm Preston Scott." He replied.

"So, will you pick teams today or give a schedule?"

"I will post the teams next week and also a schedule of the games."

"Okay. Are you working tomorrow?"

"Yeah, I should be here."

"Can I take you to lunch?"

"Sure." He replied in surprise.

I could tell there was strong chemistry between us by the visual there seemed to be fireworks! I liked what I saw. He was tall, every bit of 6'4, chocolate brown skin, broad shoulders and a chest out of this world. The natural kind not the kind from lifting weights. He was all man and very athletic.

We never met for lunch. He said he had a meeting and asked if he could make it up to me by buying me dinner. I agreed. We began to talk everyday over the phone. That was when I learned he was married. We had actually both gotten married at the same time in the same year. We realized if I had gotten out of the car that previous season we could have been married. Our conversations were so engaging, we had the same views about life and relationships. We began to see each other privately. I would park my car in an empty parking lot and get in the car with him. The chemistry between the two of us was so strong we could not resist the temptation of one another. Just to ride and be in each other's company was satisfying to Preston.

"I've never met a woman like you. You are so sweet and passionate."

"I try to be, you bring that out of me." I replied.

I got so caught up in Preston I blocked out the fact that he was married. The more time we talked the more we thought we should have been together. Charles still had a tiny piece of my heart. He just got so big headed over that truck that it was just ridiculous.

CHAPTER TWENTY-ONE

I had worked at Bo 'Jangles. I couldn't take working there any longer. They had denied my unemployment. Charles had wanted me to work anywhere as long as I was working. *And now we weren't even together.* This job might as well been McDonald's. I had to work on the weekends, so Nadia would chill with the girls or down to Ms. Shirley's with her boys.

Charles had discussed our situation with his mom.

"How are you going to tell that girl to get a job at McDonald's? If you lost your job would you go work at McDonald's? You were living there you need to help her, now that's just not right."

Charles tried to argue his views. Then he brought up the fact of my past.

"You cannot blame her or judge her for something she did in her past. Everybody makes mistakes. I think she's a very sweet girl, and you are wrong to treat her that way."

He failed to mention he had taken his baby mama out of

town overnight and I found out about it. I was close to his family and we all got along so well. He had to go and mess it up.

I put a Christmas tree in Nadia's room. I asked her to make a list of everything she wanted for Christmas. When I read the list, it was all boy toys. A train set, remote control car, a table top pool table, a basketball, the list went on. It was an easy list, but why was she such a tomboy. I purchased everything on her list and placed her gifts under her tree.

The next trip Charles' sister made to Tifton she stayed at my house instead of Shannon's. She and her mom had come over to visit.

"Yeah, girl come stay with me in Atlanta until you can get on your feet. I can't see how you can stay in this stupid behind town to begin with."

"The town is not stupid. It just might not be the place for everybody to live." Her mother interjected.

I did like Atlanta. Every time I went I hated to come back. I started looking for another job that I could transfer to. I could work somewhere for six months and then transfer. I'll go back to school and finish up my prerequisites for Radiology, and then start a program in Atlanta.

I quit that chicken box to start the next semester of classes. I drove thirty-five minutes away from town to take classes. Michele was also taking classes at the same school, only this time we were not speaking to each other. She had told Kim that I had an abortion.

When the conversation began, Kim played along with the story as if she had no clue. When in the back of her mind she was like *wow she is really jealous of her sister's relationship with my brother.* I was the type of woman that catered to my man in the kitchen, in the bedroom, and most definitely his ego.

Charles would always make a joke that he knew Michele's husband would had to have thought, *Damn! I married the wrong sister.* He never came home to a cooked meal. Instead it was baskets of clean clothes, basket of dirty clothes, sink full of dishes, and a dishwasher full of clean ones. Instead of leaving them there he would fold the clothes, wash the clothes, put the dishes up, wash the dishes, then order pizza if my sister didn't get up and cook.

Kim knew the situation between me and Charles, but she felt no need to correct or confirm the allegations being told. Charles and I had decided during our relationship that I would use an IUD device as a method of birth control since I was allergic to latex. The more we had used the condoms they made me itch. I had gone to my OB and had it inserted in his office.

"So, is it in place?" Charles asked.

"Yes, the doctor put it in during my appointment."

"What did it feel like? Did it hurt?"

"Heck yeah, it felt like a long pinch, but you couldn't control the pain. You just had to wait for it to stop."

"Will I be able to feel it?"

"No, you shouldn't. It's a string that hangs down, but you're not supposed to feel it." I added.

"Let me see."

All he had to do was touch me between my legs and his dick got hard. He put it inside me as we began to kiss. Over the course of our love making he could feel the string.

"Baby, that string or whatever it is you keep talking about keeps poking the top of my dick."

We kept trying with different positions as long as we could, but it was really uncomfortable. It gave me cramps, and I was constantly spotting. We couldn't last two weeks. He took me to the emergency room one night to have it removed. We were in and out no problem. What a relief, that thing was too aggravating. I guess I just had to keep the pills going.

We told Kim about what happened and how we went to the emergency room late at night because we had got stopped by the police. They are always bothering black folks. That's why I always say you have no business out in the streets after midnight. He explained he was taking me to the emergency room and the officer let us continue.

"They are so stupid. There was no reason to pull us over." I complained.

After Kim's conversation with Michele, she mentioned it to me and Charles when we had stopped over there. I couldn't believe she said that to her. Kim and I were close but at the same time she is still a stranger over blood. I hadn't even talked to Michele since me and Charles started dating. We were so wrapped up with our relationship I was enjoying our outings with his family. I never mentioned to Michele what Kim told me she had said but I was pissed. Months had gone by. It got so bad my father noticed the change in our relationship. Before I started going to school I would pick up my three-year-old nephew from daycare for my sister. I kept him until she got out of school. He would stay until like seven. I always made sure he ate dinner. Michele never asked me to keep him, my father asked one day if I mind picking him up from school and I said I didn't. That turned into an everyday thing for the full semester. She never said thank you and when she came to pick him up she never got out of the car she would just honk the horn and I would have Nadia walk him out to the car.

I had no problem not speaking to her, my feelings were extremely hurt. I still couldn't figure out how my sister even came up with the thought that I was even pregnant. It was just ridiculous for her to betray me like that and with a stranger.

While I was in school I started working at Applebee's as a hostess. My neighbor had mentioned they were hiring. I finally got a chance to meet the girl's mom. Ms. Marie was her name, Sunny and Heaven's mom. She worked there as a waitress. Once the semester was over I also went over to the Winn Dixie and applied for cashier. I was trying to work anyplace I could so I could transfer to Atlanta. I worked in the morning as a cashier from seven to eleven then I went over to Applebee's from eleven-thirty to four. Since Charles and I had broken up I was determined to move to Atlanta.

It was New Year's Eve. Shannon and I were going to the club to bring in the New Year. I was usually the homebody who let the girls come over my house after the club because they couldn't dare come in after midnight at their house. They would be so pumped up telling me all the stories of what happened. I would have them bring me a bacon cheeseburger and fries with a strawberry shake from Steak N Shake. It was the only place open after midnight. This time I was going with them. Preston mentioned he would be stepping out and I wanted him to see how cute I was even if we couldn't talk in public. That made it all more exciting.

The night was kind of boring in the beginning. I had spoken to Preston about my plans to be at the party that night so he knew I would be there. I kept watching the door for my dream man to walk through. As the night grew old the crowd got thicker. I spotted him walking through the crowd. He made his way over to the bar, where he hung out most of the night. Me and Shannon were sitting at a table next to the bar. I wasn't much of a drinker so I was still sort of uptight with the crowd. I had a few sips then we went to the dance floor once we loosened up. Once I caught Preston's eye I felt better. He nodded and winked his eye. I didn't know he wasn't going to say anything to me at all that night, but I was cool with that. I wanted to rub up against him, sneak a kiss in the dark or something. His eyes told all he couldn't say as he watched me dance. *Damn, this woman is fine! What in the hell am I going to do with her? I ain't felt this way over no woman in years. Look at her, just so damn sexy...*

I stayed on the dance floor for the rest of the night with some random dude wishing he was Preston. As long as I knew I had him for an audience that was all I needed. Just as I turned around from my dance partner laughing I looked up and there was Charles standing at the edge of the dance floor watching me. He walked up to me and yelled in my ear over the music,

"I'm ready to go home, are you coming?"

I looked at him and couldn't help but smile. I shook my head yes since he wasn't able to hear me my voice. I could have leaped through the roof. I signaled to the dude I was leaving as Charles took my hand and lead me through the crowd. I didn't care what happened after that. I just wanted to go home with him. *Oh, shit what about Preston? I'm sure I can just sneak out, he'll never know.* I ducked through the crowd. I waited for Charles at the door. As he approached me some girl was trying to get his attention. When he stopped to look back I immediately grabbed the arm of his black leather jacket and said, "You told me you were ready to go home, so let's go!"

As we walked to his truck I thought *yeah, the one I never got to ride in until the windows were tinted, same one he called and told me was for us, my how things change. He really let this funky truck go to his head. Preston has the same truck.*

I went to get in the front seat of the truck. Baby hop in the back I'm about to drop my homeboy off at his old lady house. What the hell? I know I'm tipsy but he's trippin'. Did this nigga just put me in the back seat like I was some trick?

He dropped his homeboy off and I stayed in the back seat. When we got to his apartment Charles didn't even open the door for me. Hey! I yelled. The automatic door locked and I couldn't get out. I banged on the window to get his attention. Brother! I know this is all to satisfy his ego. It took the thrill out of what I knew was about to take place.

I had never been to his apartment with him living in it. As I walked in he didn't turn on any lights. I could still tell my place was much nicer. He directed me straight to his bedroom. He had a nice bedroom suite. Solid wood, sturdy post on a king size bed. Now that was nice. I didn't know what to do so I sat on the edge of his bed. I guess by now I was nervous for being treated so ugly. Do I take off my clothes because I know exactly what I'm here for? Or do I just wait for him to climb on top of me. Or do I just make myself comfortable and wait for the invite into his bed? I sat there on the edge of his bed, not even comfortable enough to take off my coat.

Charles came out of the bathroom. Why are you still sitting on the edge of the bed? You're supposed to be butt naked in my bed. I should have known to follow my first mind, and to expect no more than what I got.

It was just like I remembered, his thick penis fitting perfectly into my vagina. How our bodies felt against each other. His wet kisses which expressed how much our bodies longed for each other. My dark chocolate nipples melted in his mouth. The feeling of his hands caressing both of my breasts as he squeezed each one in his hands felt so good.

I was so overwhelmed with emotion all I could do was cry. I missed him so much, I loved him and he couldn't see that his actions really hurt me.

"Are you crying?" He asked as his body froze.

I could see his silhouette as he rolled off me and flicked on the light. I was ashamed of my tears over this asshole.

"You're really crying? What are you crying for?"

I had a frog in my throat. I couldn't bring the words to tell him I loved him and that I missed him so much since it seemed as if he never loved me at all or spoke those three words to me.

"What's the matter Dan?" He asked as he pulled me close to him. I propped my head on his chest.

"Why were you crying?"

"You don't miss me at all?"

"Of course, I miss you. You're here with me, now aren't you? I don't bring females to my apartment."

"But you don't even call me. I haven't seen you in almost two months."

"I'm sorry Dan, but you hurt me when you put me out. That just did something to our relationship."

"What do you mean? You got a lot of nerve!" I sat up to see what was exactly about to come out of his mouth.

"You through my stuff out on the lawn and changed the locks."

"You lied and said you were working when you knew you took your baby mama out of town. And you took her with Kim and her husband. That was messed up. How do you think I felt when I found that receipt? It slapped me in my face. I always go in your bag to get your dirty clothes to wash."

"That was sort of foul, huh? But we didn't sleep together and I mean that."

"You said that already and I still don't believe you. So, at this point it doesn't matter. Then you had the nerve to start acting funny when you got your truck, and you were the one that called me telling me you got something for us."

"I was just trippin off my baby mama because she kept

threatening me with child support, and I felt like why should I give her money when she stay with her mama and don't want to work."

"Well you can't be scared to have a relationship and move on based on that."
We could have gone on all night with the same argument. No need to kill dead roses.

"Let me take you home."

"Take me home? So, you take me from the club so you can get some ass and I can't even stay the night? I haven't even been here two hours. The club is still jumping and you want to take me home!"

I put the key in the lock in disbelief. *No, this nigga didn't pull this shit!* Charles walked in behind me. I loved him, but I had to keep it moving. I hated putting him out but I just refuse to be lied to and cheated on. Then to deliberately sneak around behind my back like I'm some fool. I don't think so!

"Can I get something to drink?" He asked as he helped his self to my refrigerator. His bottle of Crown Royal was still sitting on top of it. Man, I left this here I didn't know where it was. I knew I couldn't have drunk the whole bottle. I thought one of my homeboys stole it out of my truck. All right I'll call you. He said as he walked out the door.

I stood there in shock. I know this didn't just happen. I looked at the door and turned off the lights. As I turned to walk down the hallway, I could see the clock on the microwave... 12:48 am. Damn!

CHAPTER TWENTY-TWO

"Hello, what happened to you last night?" I heard in my ear as I answered the phone. "Oh nothing, I went home."

"I see. I looked on the dance floor and you were gone."

"Yeah, I didn't know I wasn't going to be able to speak to you so it was pointless to be there."

"I'm sorry dear. You know I don't want anybody in our business."

"I know, I know. I just thought being at a club would be different."

"Well I'm sorry sweetheart. Are you going to let me make it up to you?"

"Of course, when?" I asked with excitement.

"You tell me"

"Whatever I want?"

"Whatever you want?"

"Okay, I'll think of something, you coming to see me today?"

"No, not today, I'm just staying around the house, but if I can get away I'll be over tonight okay?"

"Okay, I'll talk to you later."

I made up in my mind I never wanted to even see Charles' face. My feelings turned off in an instant at the thought of what happened last night. Ugh!

This year would be solely set on getting out of this town and getting to Atlanta by any means necessary, and while I did it I would get over Charles by spending time with Preston.

We had such chemistry I could never resist touching his chest and those shoulders. It seemed he was always wanting to talk while I was always trying to screw him every chance I got. When we rode in the car I always rubbed on his body or over his jeans between his legs to his penis to keep us company along the ride. He actually enjoyed being taken advantage of for a change. He said he had never met anyone like me, and that I didn't have any idea what affect I had on him.

Over the next few months the connection between Preston and I grew stronger. We were together every time opportunity that arose. I finally invited him to my place for dinner. This time I made spaghetti with French bread and salad. Yes, he ate my spaghetti. He was a grown man and thought nothing of the foolishness everyone associated with that dish. He trusted me and knew it would never get that serious. That was just nasty and desperate! He adored me. He loved the way I looked, my smile, the way my skinned smelled every time he hugged me. He could still smell my scent in his mind. I was all he thought about.

We had several private outings. Meeting different places to have sex, we did it anywhere. A back road in back of his truck, late night on the picnic tables in the park. I couldn't get enough, and he said he loved my spontaneity.

"What are you doing tomorrow dear?"

"Nothing." I replied to his deep soothing voice in my ear.

"I'm going to need you to drive my car for me from Lake Park."

That was a first for me, we could never be seen in public and not to mention in the day time.

"Do you think that is safe?"

"Yes, it will be fine. No one knows the car you're going to drive back. I just bought a Honda with tinted windows and I'm getting it serviced so I need to go pick it up."

"Oh, okay sure. I'll be happy to." I said with a smile as big as Texas

"I'll come pick you up in the morning."

I enjoyed having Preston all to myself. After we picked up the car we stopped along the way to grab a bite at Popeye's. I couldn't believe it.

"Are you okay?"

"Yes, dear I feel fine."

"Why are you starting to be seen with me in public?"

"I don't know, I guess I just don't care anymore. Maybe I want to get caught so I will have a reason to leave home."

We gazed into each other's eyes over our two piece with beans and rice.

"I still have some time to be out of pocket if you want to head back to your house to rape me."

"Sounds good to me!" I replied.

Preston felt good to me. Now this was chemistry I never felt before for a man. Not Brian, Cary not even Charles. This was different, and I couldn't explain it. It was all I ever thought about in his presence. He enjoyed every minute of it. I always climbed on top of him, I wouldn't have it any other way. His strong arms would pull me up and down his thick long penis. He would move me faster than I could catch his rhythm so I would just let him take over as he watched my breast bounce up and down.

Preston wasn't much of a kisser. I didn't like that part, but I would stick my tongue in his mouth anyway and tease him as I traced his lips with my mine. One thing about our encounters I never knew when he was about to nut. I was wondering because he never pulled out. Did he want me to have his baby? Was he insane?

Basketball season was almost over. The girl's team was on a winning streak. They started their tournaments in other cities and who do you think was going away for the weekend? Preston asked me to join him out of town while the teams competed for the championship.

"Yes, I'll go. I'll have to see if Nadia can stay with my sister for the weekend."

Nadia's team was done for the season. This was the big girls turn. That Friday we dropped Nadia off at Michele's and headed down the highway. I made sure I packed my pretty panty and bra sets that Cary bought me and made sure I had my scented candles. We were supposed to meet up at the restaurant after checking into the motel. The room wasn't anything to write home about so the candles would come in handy. I unpacked and placed the candles on the dresser and my soaps and bubble bath in the shower.

"I never met a woman like you. You brought candles and bubble bath, then to top it off matching panties and bras. I always wonder what color you're going to have on next." He stated.

"You're so funny. You have to have matching sets. Your wife doesn't wear matching panties and bras?"

"No."

"Oh wow. Okay…"

After dinner, we headed back to the Motel. I noticed that some of Nadia's friends were there with the other team. One was my friend's daughter. We used to work together at Bo 'Jangles. We became close friends and she was always hanging out with Nadia.

"Nadia could have come with us. Those are some of her friends in the room next to ours."

"Oh really, she would have enjoyed herself then. She would have fit right in."

"Yep, she could have just slept over there." I said laughing.

The night was like no other, to be able to wake up next to this man. The anticipation of our bodies against one another, the warmth of our skin touching. This time Preston was in total control. He was on top wanting to satisfy me and taste my soft breasts.

Her skin smells so good. This woman drives me crazy. The warmth between her legs makes me want to explode inside of her. I think I'm in love with this woman.

I wrapped my legs around his neck. I wanted to give him all the pleasure I had. Let me do it baby, I whispered as my hip swiveled around his penis in a rhythm up and down. I had him hooked. The rhythm was foreign to him, he couldn't control the surge. He came. *Damn! Already are you serious? I was just getting started.* I thought there was about to be some serious love making going on up in here tonight. He lay on top of me and went right to sleep. No! What the hell, my pussy is still hot and wet! I had to pry myself from underneath him. I went to the bathroom and washed up, but not before I got some oil and

110

began to give myself some satisfaction. It was built up, I don't believe I had cum in our last encounters. I was too worried about pleasing him. That release sent me in a head spin that made me dizzy. I was exhausted now. I returned to the bed and squeezed my way between his arms. He immediately received me kissing the top of my forehead wrapping his arms around me completely.

We woke up the next morning. I ran his shower and placed his tooth brush on the counter with toothpaste.

"Thank you dear, you are just amazing!" He smiled.

He also put his clothes in the cleaners so I laid our outfits on the bed. The day was full of basketball games. I was bored out of my mind but I tried to act excited for the girls. We met up at the restaurant for dinner. The girls won two games and lost the third so we would be going home tomorrow. I asked Preston if we could go somewhere else for the day before going home.

"Where would you like to go? I know there's a big mall in the next city. We can go there and stop somewhere for lunch."

"Oh, that would be perfect!"

That night was much different from the first. When we made it back to the room, I ran his shower and joined him after I lit the candles.

"You are so perfect for me." He said as I washed his back.

I was not trying to get my hair wet this trip so I made sure I got him out so I could finish my shower alone. When I stepped into the room the sheets were pulled back and he was laying on top of the bed taking in the candle light flickering of the walls in the room.

"You always been this romantic? You just drive me wild just watching how you are."

"Yes, I'm a Taurus remember, romantic and loyal in

love."

We were only two days apart. I climbed on top of him, as we talked I teased him with little kisses all over his face. Biting his bottom lip, he rolled over on top of me gazing into my eyes as we kissed.

"I love you dear."

"You do?"

"I do. You just make me feel so good. You're easy to talk to. You're all I think about."

"I feel I could love you too, but you belong to someone else."

"I know, I know. That sucks. Why couldn't you have just gotten out of the car?"

"Don't remind me, geesh. I wish I would have. My life would be so much different if I had met you first."

"We would definitely be married right now."

"That makes me so sad that I can't have you." I replied.

"Well we don't know what the future holds."

My mind couldn't comprehend that at the moment. The thought was a lovely feeling of possibilities. I held on to that and enjoyed his body next to mine for the night. We made love in so many positions. He must have been too excited the night before. His face dripping with sweat. I wiped his face as we continued to kiss as he penetrated deep inside me. This man felt so good to me, I couldn't resist the touch of his shoulder against my lips. He loved how they caressed his neck and the back of his ear. We ended our night in each other's arms as I lay on his chest, his arm around my shoulder and the other around my waist.

We checked out and headed to breakfast with the rest of the teams. A few hours later we found the mall. We strolled from store to store holding hands, window shopping.

"See anything you like?" He asked with a smile.

"Not yet why?"

"Cause if you see something you like I got you."

"Really?"

"Really."

"How about some tennis shoes, I don't own a pair of those." As we approached Lady Foot Locker.

"You don't own a pair of tennis? Oh, I forgot you're such a lady. You always dress so nice when I see you."

I looked at most of the shoes and went back to my favorites. A pair of orange and white K-Swiss with a matching shirt and I had to get the socks too.

"I should have known you were going to want the matching socks too. Just like your panties and bras."

"Well, I can't help it that's the way..."

"I'm not complaining, believe me I love that about you. I told you I've never met a woman like you. My wife doesn't even do half of the things you do."

I looked at him with a smile as I handed him my bags to carry.

CHAPTER TWENTY-THREE

While working at Applebee's a regular customer had noticed my smile and professionalism. His name was Dave. Average white man, so I thought, in his mid-thirties early forties. He came in everyday at the same time for lunch and ordered the same sweet tea to drink. I picked up on his ritual and I made sure as soon as I seated him I got his sweet tea myself.

He called me over to his table.

"I want you to come work for me."

"Where?"

"The Hampton Inn, I'm the General Manager. Come talk to me tomorrow morning before your shift to discuss the shift and job description."

"Okay, thank you."

I went over there and met with him that next morning, but he needed a hostess from 5am to 11am. No-way Jose'. I would not be getting up at 5am. I let him know that I was a cashier at Winn Dixie in the mornings and came over to the restaurant until 4.

"Well thank you for your honesty, if your schedule changes I will make a spot for you on my team."

"Thank you, I will do that."

Later that week Mr. Dave came in for lunch as usual and this time another gentleman was with him. He motioned for me to come to the table once he got my attention.

"Danielle this is Mr. Scott. He's the General Manager of the Courtyard by Marriott here in back of the restaurant."

"Hello, nice to meet you." I said as I extended my hand to shake his.

"I was mentioning to Mr. Scott how impressed I was with you, not to mention that gorgeous smile of yours."

"Well thank you Mr. Dave," I replied trying not to blush.

"I have a 3-11 position for front desk clerk if you're interested.

"Really? That would be perfect!"

"Well come over sometime today or tomorrow and fill out an application."

"Okay I will come over as soon as I get off. Thank you so much and thank you too Mr. Dave"

"You're very welcome, glad I could help."

I started that next Monday at the Front Desk. I couldn't wait to tell Ms. Marie. We both worked at Applebee's and now we both worked at the Courtyard. My relationship grew stronger and stronger with her and her daughters. I worked three jobs. I didn't know the area I would live in Atlanta. When it came time to talk to Charles' sister she already had house guests and would not be able to let me stay. She never came out and said it she would just insinuate it was too many people at her house and how tired she was letting people stay with her. So, to me that's what that meant.

"Have you put in any of your transfers?" She asked.

"No not yet. I don't know what area to put in for because I don't know where I will be staying. I'm going to see what area the hotels are in, I really don't want to work two jobs if I don't have   to."

"Oh, okay well let me know."

"Okay, I will."

Let you know for what you were the one who told me to move in the first place.

Ms. Marie helped me research different properties in Atlanta from the catalog. All I knew about Atlanta was College Park. She had spoken to her best friend, about my situation which happened to be my aunt on my dad's side. She was married to one of his cousins. She had a daughter named was Raquel. We had taken a computer class together and became acquainted. She had another sister I never met that lived in Atlanta.

"That would be good for them to be roommates. They could help each other with the kids and save money by splitting the bills. Give me her number and I'm going to call her and my daughter and try to get this thing together."

"Hello."

"Hello Danielle this is your aunt Cathy."

"Oh! Hey Aunt Cathy."

"Marie was telling me about you wanting to move to Atlanta and I thought it would be a great idea for you and Robyn to get together and help each other out."

"That would be fine with me, I've never met her." I replied.

"Well you will love her. She's my oldest. She lives in Alpharetta. It's about a forty-five-minute drive from where I work and that's at the top of 285. I work for Verizon in the Perimeter Dunwoody area, so it would be nothing for you to jump on 285 and go to Alpharetta."

"Sounds good to me."

"She has a two bedroom two and a half bath upstairs townhouse. She pays six-hundred and fifty dollars a month for rent. You guys could split that and the bills."

"I am willing to do that. I will see what Marriott property are around there, Perimeter you say?"

"Yes."

"I've already talked to my daughter and she would be glad to have you. I tell you Danielle I'm so excited when young woman can come together to save some money and help each other. So let me know what you find out. I'm going to give you my number and if you need anything just let me know. I'm willing to help you guys get on your feet and settled."

"Well thank you, I will. I have to be into work at three so I'll look in the book for properties."

I found a Courtyard right in Dunwoody. I actually called and inquired if any positions were available for transfer. I was in luck. They had a front desk position in the morning from 7-3 and some nights 3-11.

I faxed my resume to their General Manager. It was the month of March. I figured by the time I did get a transfer it would be by the time Nadia was out of school in May.

I was asked to interview that same week. Oh, my Goodness this has got to be God! I asked if there was a grocery store near the property in walking distance. They informed me there was a Publix around the corner. I called and explained to the manager that I was currently a cashier at Winn Dixie and asked if they had any positions available.

"Sure, we are always in need of cashiers. When you come

up come see me and put in an application."

"Okay, I sure will."

Charles had come into Applebee's while I was working, cursing me out about his phone bill in front of my customer waiting to be seated. I walked in the foyer for some privacy.

"Why you didn't tell me you didn't pay the phone bill? When I went to have it switched they said the last bill was never paid."

"I'm sorry, I forgot all about it."

"When can you give me my money for the phone bill?"

I looked at him like he was crazy. Was he really up at my job sweating me over a phone bill? I was so embarrassed when he finally left. I told him I would give him the money when I got paid, knowing I would not have any money to give especially for a bill, might want to chop that one up playa'!

Once I interviewed at the Courtyard I was offered the 7-3 position to start the following month! I accepted the position and went down the street on the corner to Publix. I asked to speak to the manager and introduced myself. I put in an application. She interviewed me on the spot. I let her know I was just offered a 7-3 shift at the Marriott down the street and she offered me 3-11 shift. I explained to her that some days I might need to work a 3-11 shift at the hotel, and she said that would not be a problem to let them know my schedule at the Hotel and if I had to work an evening shift they would schedule me off the next day at the store. If that ain't favor I don't know what is. By the time I move to Atlanta I'll have two jobs.

I told my father about my new job offers in Atlanta and let him know they wanted me to start sooner than I expected. My start date would actually be in three weeks. I asked if they could keep Nadia until school was out while I worked in Atlanta.

When I accepted the position, I didn't realize I would have to leave so soon. I was hoping to be able to prepare to move after Nadia had gotten out of school. I would need someone to keep Nadia until school was out. It would only be like a month and a half.

I asked my father if Nadia would be able to stay with them. He said he didn't know and that I would have to ask my stepmom. I hated when he left it up to her to make a major decision concerning me because the answer was always no. That was a selfish lady when it came to me and Nadia. One time we ran out of toilet paper and while we were visiting I asked if I could have a couple of rolls. She said no and my dad sat there and acted like he had nothing to say. Michele gave me five dollars so I could just go buy some. I agreed to ask me stepmom if Nadia could stay when I stopped by after work that evening.

We all sat in the living room as usual. That was always our meeting place when everyone got off work. Michele's kids always stayed over there after school until she got off work. Nadia was able to walk home from school until I got there. She was a latch key kid. I hardly ever had time to visit anymore working all the time.

"I have to start work in Atlanta in three weeks but Nadia won't be out of school by then, can she stay with y'all until school is out?"

I watched my step moms face expression, but I didn't expect the response I got.

"No, Nadia has a bad attitude."

My mouth was lying on the floor from complete shock.

"Bad attitude?" I replied.

"Yes, I just don't think it's a good idea."

I watched as my father sat in the chair acting as if he

heard none of the conversation taking place. Was he really going to sit there and let his wife deny my child, his grandchild? Just two years ago, they let Michele's son live with them for his whole third grade school year when she and her husband were having marital issues.

Wow, are you really going to look me in the eye and tell me my daughter can't stay here because you think she has a bad attitude. Mind you my daughter is as quiet as a mouse. She has so much going on in that little head of hers from all my shit you never know what she's thinking.

Nadia was the sweetest and respectful child you could ever know. It was always evident to her if she was being treated unfairly. I got to the point where I would feel uncomfortable leaving her over Michele's if my brother in law was not there. He was the fair one and made sure the kids were straight. My sister favored the baby at times over the two, in some cases it was understandable since he was the baby. Nadia said her and my nephew had to eat noodles while my sister ordered a pizza.

"Okay." I replied to my stepmom.

"Well let me go, Nadia walked home from school so she should be waiting for me at the house." I voiced.

"Okay baby doll, you taking off?"

"Yes" I replied as I rolled my eyes. I walked toward the recliner to give my father a kiss on the top of his head.

I couldn't believe what just happened. What was I going to do?

"Hello." A sweet voiced sounded over the phone.

"Mom." I blurted.

Remember I told you I got the job in Atlanta?"

"Yes."

"Well they want me to start as soon as possible so I turned in my two week notice at the hotel. I asked my dad could

Nadia stay with them until school is out while I work in Atlanta."

"Well what did he say?"

"It wasn't a he, it was a she. My dad told me to ask Carol."

"What did she say?"

"She said no!"

"No!"

"Yeah, she said Nadia had a bad attitude."

"Give me a break! That's a bunch of bullshit. Didn't Michele's son live with them when he was in the third grade or something when his mother was living in Atlanta?"

"Yep!" I replied.

"I ought to call you father and tell him a thing or two, but I not even going there. You don't even want to get me started on that!" She griped.

Me and mother continued to give them a tongue lashing. They were also a part of the reason why I was leaving. When it came to my daughter I never had their support. I always had to seek outside friends to help me with Nadia.

She and my nephew were both playing sports for the Recreation Department. It was always such a big deal to be on time for his games, and when it was time for Nadia's games no one ever showed up. It was just me cheering her on from the bleachers by myself, and it was the same for basketball. She couldn't play football but she was always rooting for her favorite cousin.

There was a knock at my door. It was Heaven.

"Hey, girl."

"Hey, what's going on?" She asked.

"Nothing, what's going on with you?"

"Oh, just waiting for my mama to get home. Girl, my granddaddy died. My mama been over to his house every night this week."

"Oh, I'm sorry to hear that. Was he sick?

"Yeah, he had been sick for a while. We knew it would be just a matter of time. Now we are going to have to move in my granddaddy's house because mama won't be able pay rent and a Mortgage."

"Move? How soon?"

"Girl, as soon as possible from what mama say?"

"Well I got the job in Atlanta and they want me there in three weeks. What if I ask if you all stay in my duplex and I pay all the rent while you transition to your granddaddy's and keep Nadia for me until she gets out of school?"

"Sound cool to me shoot, we just have to ask mama."

"I know, huh?"

"What your daddy and them say? They won't keep your baby until school is out?"

"Girl, no! He told me to ask my stepmom and she said no."

"Oh, uh uh. She be having your sister's kids all the time don't she. That's a shame, that's not your daddy's daughter, but that's her mama?"

"Yep, but I'll ask your mom."

"Yeah honey I would, Mama will probably say yes."

CHAPTER TWENTY-FOUR

Everything was settled. Ms. Marie and the girls would move into my place so she would be out of their duplex before the first of May and move out by June first. They would keep Nadia and I would come home on the weekends until she was out of school. I would pay the rent and the utilities as if I was staying there in exchange for them looking after my baby.

I was so ready to go. All my notices were in at the hotel and Winn Dixie. I remember the one time I needed my dad to keep Nadia I had to count down my drawer and didn't get to his house until 11:30. He got on to me and just fussed saying I was supposed to pick her up at eleven. I explained to him how I had to count my drawer and couldn't leave exactly at eleven. I don't know what he thought, but Michele worked at night as well but she had a key to their house and her kids spent the night most nights when her husband wasn't in town.

I quit Applebee's to catch a break before my three to eleven shift at the Marriott. I spent more time with Preston. He stayed over a few nights a week and had gotten so comfortable in my bed he over slept his curfew.

"Babe, its 4:30. You over slept."

"Damn!"

I laughed as he jumped up and grabbed his clothes. He couldn't put them on fast enough.

"Lock the door behind you." I instructed.

I smiled at the thought of him not making it home. He is slippin' for real.

Sunny had called me earlier in the day to ask me if she could have a get together at my place. I told her that was fine as long as my dream man would be there. He was actually homeboys with most of the younger cats. Not too much younger though. I got off work at seven and headed straight to the house.

Once I arrived, I walked in to a crowd of people. Dudes were everywhere. They were playing Dominos and some were hanging out in the kitchen eating. They had made a crab boil. I was allergic to Sea food so the smell of the crab made me sick. My eyes started burning from the steam in the kitchen.

"Hey honey, how was your day?"

"Hey girl, fine! It's crackin' up in here. Where all these dudes come from? You don't know any females damn!"

"You know we don't do females." Sunny replied.

I laughed and looked around and shook my head. Make sure you tell me when my man get's here, I'm going to my room to take a quick shower that took longer than I thought, I was anxious to see Preston so I wanted to make sure I was fresh and wash all the day's work away. As I got out of the shower to dry off there was a knock at my door.

"Who is it?" I yelled hoping to scare whoever was on the

other side of the door away. It was Preston.

"What are you doing dear?"

My heart started to pound, he made it. I opened the door in my towel and a big smile. I pulled Preston into my room and locked the door. I let my towel drop to the floor and wrapped my hands around his neck and planted a big juicy kiss on his lips.

As he squeezed my naked body our tongues melted in each other's mouths. I traced his lips with mine and sucked on his bottom lip. He slipped his fingers between my legs. His thrust so hard and strong, I wanted to climb on top of his hand. I motioned him to go deeper with my hips.

"We can't do this with everybody in your house."

"Yes, we can, come on Preston!"

I pulled Preston to the edge of the bed on top of me. Whenever he was on top he would get a rhythm going with his hands where he would make my ass jump. I never understood that, that's why I preferred to be on top. This time I just want some hard dick fucking me right now.

When we finished, we joined the rest of the house. I watched as Preston sat in on the Domino game.

"You tell him you about to move to Atlanta yet?"

"No, not yet." I replied.

"What are you waiting for, him to see you packing your stuff?"

"I'm going to tell him, maybe tomorrow." I griped as I gave Sunny that look.

CHAPTER TWENTY-FIVE

It was time for me to start packing, but first I had to have a talk with Preston to let him know my plans. I never considered telling him since he was married, it's not like we could make any future plans together.

I spent the morning moving what I could to storage. Preston was over bright and early with his truck. We didn't discuss the fact that I would be leaving. He didn't say a word, he just helped and stayed supportive of my decision.

We spent the day together and attempted to say a short goodbye that lasted all night. We had fallen asleep on the floor, when we woke up it was the next day. I slept in his arms all night.

This woman is really leaving. She lets nothing get in her way. She looks so beautiful and peaceful in my arms. I really do love her. What am I going to do without her here? She is all I think about. I wonder when our next trip will be to Atlanta. I believe she might be the love of my life. The love of my life is moving to Atlanta and there was nothing I can say about it...

"Preston, its seven-thirty get up!"

Wow! He finally stayed all night.

"I'm not leaving yet." He replied.

This time he wasn't worried about staying out all night. My duplex was almost empty. Ms. Marie and the girls would be moving in and seeing after Nadia. I had to get on the road. I would be meeting my cousin for the first time. Preston held me in his arms looking into my eyes.

"I'm going to miss you dear. I still can't believe you're leaving me." He expressed.

"I'll be back on the weekends until Nadia gets out of school."

"I know, but then my heart will just break each time you have to go back."

"You'll be fine babe. You'll be the first person I call once I'm at the exit!" I replied kissing his lips.

"Once I make it to that Enmark off the highway, I'll call you to get directions."

"Okay drive safe cousin, can't wait to meet you."

"Okay see you in a few hours."

Robyn was small framed and light skinned. She was even much shorter than me. She was just as skinny as Evelyn. I thought to myself. Then I thought about that joke Nadia always told when someone was skinny about the hula hoop and the Cheerio. She had a little boy around two or three.

When we arrived at her house it was a small complex of townhomes. They were really nice on the inside. Robyn showed me to my room. I had a walk-in closet and my own bathroom. It was a two bedroom two and a half bath. My bedroom was huge, much bigger than my room in my duplex. It was nice, I should be real comfortable here. I unloaded my things out of my car. I had bought a Ford Probe from some mechanic who I felt swindled me out of my tax money. I didn't know why I paid for a car before I saw it. I was cool with the mechanic so I trusted that he would be honest. He made the car seem like it was a cute sports car in good condition. I looked up the model online and thought it was cute, but when it was delivered it was far from being in good condition. The console was missing the radio, the windshield wipers didn't work, and the A/C did not work either! I didn't like it! I didn't want it and the first person I called as Cary. He knew the man and would demand he give me my money back. He told me to let him handle it. He did all right had that man begging Cary to let him get it fixed cause he had already spent my twelve hundred dollars. He was about to be a goner. Cary had much clout and respect and he didn't play when it came to me. He kept his word and fixed everything like he should have done before delivering it.

I put my clothes up and of course set up my bathroom. It was just something about having the bathroom put together. Whenever I moved that was the first thing I did, then the kitchen. Once those were straight the rest of the house was a piece of cake.

I made sure I brought my stereo. I had to fall asleep to music. If it was too quiet I couldn't sleep. Unlike people who slept with the television on that was just weird to me and a waste of electricity.

I had to report to work the next morning at seven at the Marriott and then at three-thirty at Publix. With my schedule and the distance from the house to work I would have to leave at five in the morning and wouldn't get back home until one o'clock in the morning. I never had any idea my commute would be two hours each way. That Atlanta traffic was no joke. I would always get to the hotel by 6:30. I needed to clock in by 6:45 to begin my shift.

I didn't mind. I was meeting a lot of new and interesting people between the hotel and the grocery store. My nerves were bad working at the hotel. With the stress of the commute and working both jobs I began to itch and my legs would break out in hives. I would have to make several trips to the bathroom to pull down my stockings to scratch my legs. I would put cold towels on them to try to stop the itching but it was not working. As I stood at the desk it was as if bugs were crawling up my legs. I would twitch and jerk and look real crazy in front of the guest because at any given moment it felt like I was getting bit and I would scream out or jump to scratch. It was awful. That kept me going to the bathroom to check to see if something was actually crawling up my leg.

I never saw Robyn and I believe that she thought our living situation would be different. We didn't get to hang out because I was working. Why that would upset her I did not know. I didn't come to kick it I came to make money to get on my feet.

My shift started at Publix and my manager pulled me into her office.

"You are doing such a great job, if you leave the hotel I'll give you a dollar more than what the hotel is paying you and guaranteed forty hours." She offered.

I couldn't pass that up. Driving back and forth from Tifton every weekend to see about Nadia was just too much. I hadn't thought about where she would stay while I was at work if I had brought her to Atlanta with me after she got out of school. I turned in my two week notice at the hotel and once I started my new schedule full time things got better. They still allowed me to be off on weekends until I figured out my situation with Nadia. I was so thankful to my new-found God family for keeping her.

I became friends with another cashier Chanel, who was full-time. She was light skinned, her complexion browner tan than yellow. She had big pretty like hazel green eyes with super long eye lashes, her nails were super long in these fancy designs and colors. Her skin was so pretty and flawless she didn't need any makeup just mascara and lip gloss. She wore long curly tresses with bangs. She was a little thicker than me, but a size smaller than my size 11 frame. We worked the same day shift and she also had a daughter the same age as Nadia. We hit it off with no problem. She was from New York and she had stories to tell. She kept me cracking up.

"What do you do with your daughter while you're at work?"

"My daughter stays at home by herself because I don't have anyone to watch her. It's been me and my baby, girl and I teach her everything, she is real independent."

"Wow, aren't you scared something will happen?"

"Girl, my baby knows to go to the neighbor's door. I call her on every break and on my lunch."

"Oh okay, then I guess that works."

"What about your baby, she's in Tifton you say?"

"Yes, my neighbors moved into my duplex so they could keep her for me. It's a long story but now I have to figure something out. I don't have anyone to watch her here." I replied.

"Where's your mother? In California?"

"No, she moved to Washington after I moved to Georgia. She said it was no reason for her to stay since I left and she moved there with her husband."

"Oh snap! Well maybe she can keep your baby for the summer at least until you get on your feet?"

"I never thought to ask her, that's a thought."

There was always a lunch rush from the Businesses Park across the street. There were a group of men that came over from American Express and boy were they fine! It was two that were the cutest but one stood out from all the rest. When he walked in all the female cashiers waited for him to get in line and every time he came to my line. Why did he do that? He made me so nervous. What if my nails were chipped or my hair wasn't right he may think I'm ugly? Every day he came to my line and starred into my eyes and would say hello with this deep voice. I would look up and say "hi" and nothing else would come out.

I mean this man was so gorgeous. He had a bald head, caramel skin, with those funny golden eyes like a lion and there was no way they were contacts. He was six feet tall, so with my high heel sandals we would be the same height. I would have a hot flash when he came in my line and when I went to give him his change I always dropped it.

"Dang! You throwing my change at me?"

"I'm sorry!"

"I'm just messing with you. You have a nice day."

"Okay." I laughed.

When they left, the other cashiers would get together and discuss how fine he was and asked why is he was always coming to my line?

"I don't know. I know he makes me nervous."

A few weeks of that was just too much.

I started training in Customer Service and the same guy appeared out of nowhere.

"I'm on my break, but I wanted to get your number."

I looked up in shock. *He wanted my number*? I had no reply.

"I'm on my break." He said looking at his watch. "Can I

have your number?"

"Oh! You're serious, okay?"

I jumped and grabbed a piece of paper from the receipt roll and wrote my number down and gave it to him.

"Thank you, I'll call you tonight."

"Okay?"

I was still in shock but when reality set in I was smiling for the rest of the day. I never got to tell him my schedule. I was now working 1pm to 10 pm or 10am to 7pm. I loved not having to get up at the crack of dawn anymore and by the time I woke up Robyn was gone. I felt so much better getting dressed knowing she was not at home. I can open my door, play my music and enjoy my morning routine.

School was officially out and it was time to move out of my duplex by the first and get Nadia. I had to bring her to work with me. If Chanel was off she kept her for me and we would hang out when I got off, if not she would hide out in the break room.

I stopped going to Robyn's for the most part. If I was scheduled off on the weekend I would ride down to College Park and stay with Charles's sister. I told her how hateful my cousin was acting. I came home one day and she had separated all our food. She put all my stuff in a separate cabinet and even divided the food in the refrigerator and freezer. I didn't mind buying the food for the house. We would share because I had food stamps but I guess since I was never home maybe she felt I would think she was eating up the food. I don't know she just started to be weird to me. I felt real uncomfortable.

Well you welcome to spend the night whenever you need to she would say, but College Park was at the bottom of Atlanta compared to where I was at the top of the perimeter.

I did the best I could sleeping between her house and

Chanel's with Nadia to avoid that two-hour commute to the house. That whole month the guy was calling and leaving several messages, but I really wasn't taking him seriously. He was too fine and I had too much going on to entertain that. I had also met an executive driver named Ken. He would always ask me out on a date when he came into my line and I would always refuse.

I did need a break from my worries. Chanel would be more than happy to keep Nadia and she wanted me to spend the weekend at her house anyway. I agreed to go out to dinner with him. Somehow me and the American Express guy had gotten our wires crossed. He had left his number on my voicemail. His name was Brandon Hill. He hadn't been in the store, I never called him, and when I thought to call there was no answer. We had gotten the second line double ring thing for me and single ring for her. I didn't have a cell phone only a pager. I had cut it off with Preston. I didn't want to keep leading him on and I felt convicted after realizing he was a married man and he was getting all serious on me. He would page me every day if he didn't catch me on the phone in the mornings. He was not happy with my decision, but I told him it would be best if he just forgot about me and that I didn't think it was a good thing for us to continue communicating with each other. He said he understood but said that wasn't going to make him stop loving me anytime soon.

I started hanging out with the butcher, nothing intimate, he became a good friend and co-worker. He had wanted to roommate but I thought that would be weird with Nadia. Of course, we would have the master but I couldn't see myself doing that. He may have wanted something more serious but I didn't. Although everyone became fond of the girls I didn't know about that. I hadn't spoken to my father since I left and I hadn't thought to call my mother until now. Me and Nadia were sleeping in the car most nights in the parking lot of the store when we had no place to go. If my coworkers saw me I just acted like I was meeting someone or that we were just leaving. Nadia never said a word or complained as long as she was with me that's all that seemed to matter. It was hot during those summer nights so we were never cold. We ate from the deli with our food stamps. Chanel told me as long as the food isn't hot you can use your stamps. So, we weren't hungry. Robyn had asked me to leave and she didn't care if I had a place or not. My stuff was still at her place. I just packed our clothes in the trunk.

CHAPTER TWENTY-SIX

I called my mother and told her what had been going on and how I had to bring Nadia to work with me and everything.

"Send her to me until you get on your feet." She stated.

"For real?"

"Yes, send her to me until you get on your feet. You should have called me a long time ago. I will keep her for a year, that should give you enough time to get settled. I hadn't heard from you so I thought you were fine."

"Hardly! I will check the flights and let you know."

I found a ticket for the next few weeks, but I didn't have enough. I asked the butcher if I could borrow half the money. I told him my mom said if he let me borrow the money she would pay him back. So, when we got paid he gave me the money. I was so grateful it would be a few weeks before Nadia would leave.

So luckily, they had *Bring your Child to Work Day!* What a relief, I didn't have to hide Nadia that day, and at lunch time here they came walking through the door. Mr. Hill and his coworkers. I didn't know what to say or think. Nadia was standing with me at my register bagging what groceries she could lift. So of course, he came to my line, dang!

"Thanks for never returning any of my calls."

"I called you, I never got an answer, and you haven't been in the store so I didn't know what else to do." I replied.

"Oh, my bad. I've been in Chicago. I thought I left you that message on your answering machine?"

"Oh, you did?"

"Yes, I did. I go every year to visit my family, but I see you weren't interested."

My heart sank. "I'm sorry, I just didn't know if you were serious."

"What do you mean? I asked you for your number, didn't I?"

"Well yeah, I guess you did."

"I get off at seven tonight, what time do you get off?"

"I get off at seven too!"

"Cool, then I'll come back up here so we can talk. Is that your daughter?"

"Yes, her name is Nadia."

"She's cute. I see everybody has their kids today."

"Yeah, it's bring your kids to work day."

"Oh, okay well let me get back to work. I'll see you later."

"Okay?"

I was excited to know he really was interested. I had been going out with the butcher, but it didn't feel right. He had taken me and Nadia out. We also had several lunch dates to Red Lobster and Olive Garden. We hung out late nights but I just wasn't feeling him. He was sexy with his shades on, but that's all I will say about that.

Brandon arrived like clockwork. He was sitting at the tables outside when I came out. He didn't have a car so I offered to give him a ride home and that way we could talk on the way.

"Where does your daughter stay while you're at work?" He asked.

"Oh, I hide her in the break room."

"Damn I know she be bored."

"Yeah, when Chanel is off she keeps her for me." I replied.

He lived downtown in some high-rise apartments. When he saw my car, he said he had the same car when he lived in Chicago. I thought that was ironic. He showed me the back street short cuts to his house. When we turned the corner, there were some beautiful new high rises on the right. *I was like awe shucks.* Then he directed me to the left. I stay over here in these. *Damn!* They seemed pretty grimy from the outside, all brick with three levels. But it was still pretty neat looking for what it was worth. I didn't go up to his apartment since Nadia was with me. We said our goodbye. Nadia would be leaving that next week to go to my mom so the next time we got together I would be solo. The next day Brandon came by early for lunch.

"I know your daughter is bored in that break room. I bought her some crayons and a coloring book."

"She is very bored. Thank you, that was sweet."

"You're welcome. I have to get back to work. Call me."

"Okay. Thank you. I will."

I got Nadia off and I was having my first date with Brandon, of course he came to the store and waited for me to get off. I went back to my cousin's during the week. She was gone when I woke up and sleep when I got home so I didn't have to even see her face. On the weekends, I stayed where ever I could.

Brandon decided on dinner and a movie. We went to a

theatre by the CNN building. I never knew there was a movie theatre over there. I loved to go to the movies. It's just something about a movie that put me in a good place. We went to see The Wood. Everyone was talking about that movie. We were not that pleased. It was still warm out when we left the theatre. Brandon wanted to show me downtown Atlanta. We walked to the Hard Rock Café for dinner. He was a vegetarian. That was some news to swallow. He sure didn't look like it. His plan was to stay up all night, but it didn't exactly turn out like that. We strolled through the streets hand in hand. I liked that, I couldn't believe he was so attentive. I was cute, but he was fine! His outside package was unreal, yet he was so down to earth. Brandon was such a gentleman, he opened doors, asked me if I was okay. He just gave off a presence of protection. I felt safe with him. By midnight we were both yawning.

"Guess I'm not used to staying up this late like I thought. All I do is go to work, come home and be in bed by ten. I just wanted to show you a good time."

"Oh, you have. I've enjoyed your company to the fullest. You are so easy to talk to and you're so sweet" I replied.

"Sweet, oh you think I'm sweet? Don't say that too loud out here girl." He said laughing.

"You know what I mean. You are so cool. With your looks, you would think you would be arrogant or conceited."

"My looks, what do I look like."

"You know you look good, don't try to front man."

"Well thank you, I wasn't trying to front. Look at you, you're cute!"

"Whatever man, you're welcome, oh and thank you for my compliment."

"You're welcome, you ready to head back to the car?"

"Do you mind driving?" I asked.

"No, I don't mind."

We weren't too far from his house. By the time we got there we were wide awake.

"I'm not sleepy now, you coming up, right?"

"Sure."

I hope this doesn't mean what I think it means. I don't want to sleep with him on the first date. I hope he ain't playing games. I really like him. He won't have to wait long that's for sure.

He led me down the walk way to the stairs up to the third floor of the building. There were people still hanging out on their balconies enjoying the summer night. He unlocked an iron door to his apartment, and then unlocked another door. I didn't know what to make of his apartment when I walked in. He had a cute spot for a guy. We walked right into the living room, to the right behind the door was the dining area and the kitchen with high counter tops next to the dining area where the table would be if he had one. He had bar stools instead. The living room had a large tall metal computer desk in the corner to the left of the sliding glass door and the opposite wall looked like a library of books and CD's. As I looked there were fiction, non-fiction, books on religion and several auto biographies on different Celebrities. He definitely was a reader. I was impressed.

He turned off the lights and took me by the hand and led me out onto the balcony. The view from his balcony was breath taking. You could see the lights from downtown Atlanta, glares of light from the cars crossing over the freeways. The night was still, all sight, with no sound, the city still alive. It was so romantic, I was just where I needed and wanted to be this time.

We began to talk about our evening. Brandon stood behind me and slipped his hands around my waist. I thought I would faint. I hoped he couldn't feel my heart beating. He was too good to be true and I was hoping he wasn't going to try anything. *Please just be a gentleman.* He kissed me on the back of my neck. I could feel his dick hard as a rock on my butt. *Oh no! Wow it feels like it may be a nice size.* I felt uncomfortable and wiggled myself away from him.

"What's wrong?" He asked.

"Oh nothing, it's just been a long time and you're making me nervous I guess."

"About what?" He asked.

"You."

"What about me?"

"Do you know how good you look?"

"No, how good do I look?"

"Really good and you're so nice. I'm just wondering why you chose to talk to me."

"What do you mean, you ain't ugly!"

"Thank you but you are gorgeous and I'm just having a hard time believing that you are sincere."

"Come hear girl! Quit trippin."

He pulled me close to him and slowly pressed his lips against mine. I kissed him back, as he put his arms around me he went in with his tongue. It was all over then. I was going to make sure he remembered this kiss. I placed my hand on the side of his face as I controlled the kiss, tracing his lips with my tongue, pausing looking into his eyes tracing his lips with my thumb as I held his face slowly kissing him again so softly...POW! Got him! He began to feel on my ass, grabbed my face and was searching for something in my throat. Damn! *I felt his penis again. I better come up for some air before he thinks he getting' some pussy.*

"I better go it's getting late."

"What do you mean? I know you don't think I'm going to

140

let you drive all the way back to Alpharetta this time of night. Girl if anything happened to you I wouldn't be able to forgive myself. You can leave in the morning. I have to work so you can sleep in then let yourself out. My co-worker picks me up when we do over time on the weekends. I usually get my son but his mom will drop him off at my job when I get off."

"You have a son?"

"Yeah, I thought I told you that?"

"No, you didn't."

"Yeah, he's five. His mother and I moved out here to Atlanta together from Chicago and things just went bad. She started hanging with the Seven-day Adventist people, converted religions and everything. So, I wasn't about to leave my son so I stayed instead of going back to Chicago. We been breaking up since he was three, yeah, two years now. So, I get him every weekend and I don't have any females around him until I know she's going to be my wife."

"Oh, that's so special."

"Yeah, it's just me and him. So, unless we decide to get serious I just wanted to let you know up front while we go out, I wouldn't want you to be offended if you never meet him."

"Oh, I understand that." I replied.

I was offended by that statement alone. They say a man knows his wife when he sees her, but it's his business. I can only respect it.

I lay on his couch in the den. I couldn't believe I was here safe and sound in a stranger's apartment. He had offered his bed, but I didn't want to go there. I took the couch and was just as comfortable.

The lights of downtown Atlanta peeped through the blinds so it wasn't as dark as it could have been but I didn't mind. I drifted right off to sleep with a smile on my face wondering if he was thinking about that kiss the same way I was. He had given me some sweats and a t-shirt to sleep in. Now I thought that was cute.

Just when I thought I was asleep and all was quiet in his apartment I felt a presence behind me. I turned to look back and it was Brandon kneeling behind me.

"You sleep?"

"No."

I rolled over to touch his face and he leaned in and we began to kiss. I could feel dick hard against my stomach. I sat up as Brandon stayed on his knees and wrapped my legs around his waist. I didn't know what to expect next. I was anxious to feel him inside me. He lifted up my shirt and began kissing my breasts. He circled my nipples with his tongue. It felt so good I was soaking wet. There were no words exchanged I felt his sweats being pulled off of me. As the sweats fell to the floor I put my hands on his waist but all I felt was skin. He was naked. *Dang he didn't waste any time.* He laid me back and pulled my ass to the edge of the couch as he guided his dick inside me. *This is a nice size, this should be good. He is so fine! I hope this is not a game. He made me feel so good. Why is he smiling? I kept thinking about so many reasons this wasn't going to work. I wasn't paying attention to his skills.*

I was watching his silhouette. I soon forgot all the things racing in my head and I enjoyed this man making love to me. His thrust got harder and harder and faster. Was he about to cum? Was he going to pull out?

"I'm about to cum ..." He whispered.

I pushed him off and he came on my stomach. He went to get a wet towel and wiped me off. He lay on the couch with me, positioning me in his arms.

When I woke up I had a puddle of slobber on his chest. I tried to wipe it before he woke up. Too late, my movement reminded him he was holding me in his arms. We had fallen fast asleep together on his couch. I couldn't believe I actually slept on his chest all night. I guess I wasn't too heavy, barefoot Brandon was actually much taller than me. I stood under his chin, but with heels we were about the same height. I always had a complex about dudes my same height. I need someone I can look up to spiritually, mentally and physically!

CHAPTER TWENTY-SEVEN

I had found an apartment to move into, but it wouldn't be ready until the fifteenth. When I discussed it with Robyn she said she couldn't wait three weeks that I had to move before then.

"Well it won't be ready until then."
"Well, stay at your boyfriends like you've been doing."
"Spending the night is different from moving in."
"Then I don't know what to tell you."
"I just looked at her and walked back to my room."

I met Brandon every day for lunch and stayed at his place most nights for the next two weeks. He had walked up to the Customer Service counter.
"You know your phone is off?"
"My phone?"
"Yes, I called you to make sure you made it home safe and it was disconnected."
"I grabbed the phone while I was behind the counter and dialed my number. *It was off alright.* It's off."
"Man, your cousin is the devil. When we get off let's ride

out there and get your stuff. You can stay with me."

"Really?"

"Hell, yeah you been there every day anyway."

"Okay."

That is exactly what we did. We rode way out there to get my stuff. I introduced him to my cousin and we headed upstairs. Brandon grabbed my stereo and blankets and a few boxes as I packed up my clothes and the bathroom. I handed her keys and she smiled and handed me my mail.

The next day we went to start the car to go to work and soon as we pulled out the axle broke. A loud bang sounded as he backed up to drive out of the parking lot. Wouldn't you know? God works in mysterious ways.

"What the fuck was that?" Brandon asked.

"I don't know? Did something break?"

He couldn't turn the wheel of the car. He got out and sure enough the axle broke. Some Mexicans were outside and tried to help push the car back into the parking space. We just stood there looking at the car thinking what if that would have happened coming from Alpharetta.

"Damn! Thank the Jesus." Brandon stated.

"I know that's right!"

"Well let's get on the train."

"The train?"

"Yeah, girl. How else are we going to get to work?"

He was talking about the Marta train. I remember riding it to Lenox mall with Charles' sister. It was kind of fun, but now not so much. We had to walk all the way to Five Points down Auburn Avenue. There were bums sleep on the street and pissy smells in front of the buildings. *Oh, my God, how far did we have to walk? He did this every day? He must have read my face.*

"I usually catch the bus at the corner. It lets you off at

Five Points and then I hop on the train. What you looking like that for?"

"No reason, I'm just trying to take this all in."

"You cool girl, come on before we miss the next train."

He took me by the hand and we walked swiftly down the street. He paid for me at the gate then we went down to get on a northbound train. This was crazy to me. Eastbound/Westbound. Southbound. Whatever bound? I was confused. We got on and had to stand up, it was packed. He found an empty seat and directed me to sit down as he stood up next to me. That was sweet.

"So, what are you going to do about your car?"

"I don't know."

"There's a Ford dealership around the corner from my apartments."

"Oh, okay. I'll look them up when I get to work and see what they say. I have AAA under my dad. I can have them tow it."

"I was just about to say because if it sits there more than 48hrs they will have your shit towed for you."

"Oh, snap okay. I'll call them."

We rode the rest of the way in silence, kind of rude to keep talking with all those people standing around you. We made it to the last stop at Northside Drive.

"Okay we can walk down the street to the job or we can wait for the bus?"

"We can walk, is it far?"

"No, not really. You'll get used to it."

"I will?"

"You don't have a choice. You got to get to work."

"Oh, I guess you're right."

He took my hand as usual and walked me across the

146

street. He showed me the short cut through the Business Park. I finally got to see where he worked.

"Come on I'll walk you to work. It's just through this parking lot. Just cross the street and there you are."

He was right I could see the big Publix sign beyond the trees. He held my hand as we crossed the street. Almost like you would your child to make sure they made it across safe. He kissed me good-bye and ran back across the street.

"Don't forget to call the dealership." He yelled.

"Ok, I won't."

What a morning. We weren't late. I guess he allotted time for traffic, if we would have drove. Everything calmed down. I went into the break room. Chanel jumped up to give me a hug.

"Hey now sweetie. What's going on?"
"Girl, you wouldn't believe the morning I had."

"Girl, what you mean, you and Brandon?"

"No, my car! The axle or something broke and the tire is bent. It will barely move."

"Shut up!"

"Yes, girl! And we had to take the train girl."

"Girl, I take the train. I hate the train with all those people, but it ain't nothing like the subway in New York girl. You would die if you had to take that nasty subway. Atlanta's is much cleaner. You'll get used to it you spoiled brat. So, what did he say?"

"I moved in with him last night. My cousin cut my phone off. Oh, you weren't here yesterday, that's right."

"Girl, Shut up! For real? Tell me all about it girl." as she pulled me to the table to sit down.

So, I filled Chanel in on everything. It was so much we were talking on the floor. Rushing the customers out our line.

She even came and helped me bag so we could keep flappin' our gums to get all our updates in. I loved me some Chanel boy.

I settled in fine at Brandon's place. Every day he waited for me to get off work and we walked to the train station. If we were running late we caught the bus that came right in front of Publix, other days we enjoyed the walk with each other. Still holding my hand as we crossed the street. That made me feel special. Never judge a book by its cover, this man was so humble and he was my angel.

He let me know every Friday night was our date night. Dinner, a movie whatever I wanted to do that was relaxing to take our minds of the stress of the week. More so for him, he hated those American Express customers. He said they were something else. He would always come home with a story to tell about his day.

I cleaned his kitchen from top to bottom on my day off. I wanted to surprise him. Men can keep a refrigerator so nasty. I'm sure he won't mind me throwing away all the contents with the fuzzy fur on top of it. I rearrange his cabinets, wiping down the shelves. He was sure to notice the difference. I even walked to the store to get a light bulb for his refrigerator.

I told him that I got food stamps every month so in exchange for his kindness and generosity I would buy the groceries and keep his bathroom and kitchen clean. Our first trip grocery shopping he introduced me to the life of a vegetarian. When I went to pick up the bacon he gave me a look like where are you going to cook that at?

"What?"

"Nothing, go on and kill yourself with that pork. Don't say nothing when you get high blood pressure."

"No, he didn't just go there. I didn't know what to think of that statement. He was serious." *Oh, hell no, not my bacon!*

"Put it back. I'll get sick if you cook it in the house."

"Are you for real?"

"For real." He replied.

"Okay." I said with a pout.

He started to tell me about the time he ate a hamburger and was sick for days. I felt so bad.

"What about turkey bacon? I can put it in the microwave."

We agreed on that, but the rest of the groceries consisted of Morning Star products. I couldn't believe I was actually going cold turkey, at least while I was at home with him, but at work I was eating my chicken strips and potato salad!

We loaded up the basket and forgot we were walking.

"Ah, damn! How are we going to carry all this stuff?" Brandon said laughing.

We doubled up the bags and carried three in each hand. *This is awful.* We made it to the parking lot of the apartment and I dropped my bags.

"Sorry, the handles were cutting off the circulation in my fingers."

"It's cool I'll come back and get them." He smiled.

"Thank you, I'm sorry."

When we finally made it to the apartment I had to make room for all the groceries. I had forgotten how small his cabinets were, not to mention the freezer. Brandon grabbed my hand.

"I'll finish putting the groceries up." He stated.

He led me down the hall to the bathroom, when he opened the door candle light shadowed the walls and the tub was full of bubbles. He had run my bath.

"Go ahead and relax while I make dinner."

"What you cooking?" I asked in my ghetto voice.

"It's a surprise, but you will like it."

"Do I get to eat some meat?" I laughed.

I got undressed and stepped into the tub. Ooh the water felt so warm and silky. It even smelled good. He put some oil in the water, and the candles. I love candles. He is so sweet damn! I lay there soaking trying not to think of where this relationship could possibly go. *I know I'm going to do something to mess it up watch!* I was going to take one day at a time and follow his lead. Brandon gave me my privacy for the most part. The door opened.

"Dinner won't be ready for another thirty minutes."

"Can you wash my back please?"

"Sure, do you need me to wash anything else for you?"

"No, I think I got everything else okay." I replied looking up with a smile.

"You sure?"

"I'm sure."

"Okay. Just checking."

Once dinner was ready I got out of the tub and rubbed the oil he left on the counter for me that smelled so good all over my body. I couldn't wait to find out what was for dessert me or him? I walked back down the hall when he called me to the den. He had baked veggie lasagna with cheese. *Thank God for the cheese.* He had TV trays side by side, our plates fixed and two glasses of Kool-Aid. It looked delicious and tasted alright. *Every bite I had to tell my tastes buds there's no meat guys, but we have cheese.*

That night he made love to me so sweet and gently. Brandon was amazing. His soft tongue against my nipples. They stood at attention as his lips shaped them with every suck. I could have cum off his foreplay alone. After a good nut, I needed something rock hard inside me. His penetration felt so good. I thought we were going to go all night. After the third stroke, he came. *What the hell! Damn! Is that it? I wanted some more. We can't be done!*

I tried to act satisfied every time but it became more obvious as the weeks went by. I guess that saying didn't count for this situation, when you're in love the sex doesn't play a big role in the relationship. I dealt with it. I wanted to make him feel special no matter what.

Weeks turned into months and summer was about to come to an end. Brandon and one of his coworkers planned a couple's day to Six Flags. We all got off work early. I was excited about that. I changed and came out from the break room with the cutest short outfit. No one had actually seen me in regular clothes. I got all kinds of compliments when they saw my long chocolate legs. They picked me up and we headed to the amusement park.

We had a great time. I didn't like getting on the rides that made your heart drop. You know the kind that makes your heart beat you to the ground before the rest of your body can catch up. That was the one thing me and Brandon had in common. He didn't trust those rides neither. So, his coworker Chris and his girl were on their own. By the time we met back up me and Brandon were soaked. We had gone on the rafting ride and it got stuck under the water fall right where we were sitting. We couldn't do nothing but laugh.

We made it home by nightfall. Soon as we walked in the door we took off our clothes and headed for a shower together. It's as if we had read each other's minds. We were ready to get our freak on! We had such a fun day together. Brandon ran the water and handed me a new towel and soap and hopped in behind me. This was actually our first shower together. I always lathered my soap from between my legs.

"What are you doing?" He yelled.

"What?"

"Why are you lathering with the soap on your couchie? I gotta' wash my face with that soap."

"What? So, you can eat my pussy and then kiss me in the mouth, but you can't wash your face with the soap? You crazy, but okay Brandon."

He looked at me with a half grin as I put the soap in my towel to lather. Brandon got out of the shower first. He snuck back in the bathroom and laid a sexy navy blue spaghetti strap teddy from Victoria Secret and body spray from Sonoma on top of the folded towel on the toilet for me to see when I got out of the shower.

"What is this?" I asked as I stood at the bedroom door with the teddy in one hand and the body spray in the other.

"I bought it for you?"

"No, you didn't." I replied with a puzzled look on my face.

"Yes, I did!"

"You picked this out yourself?"

"Yes!"

I stood there in disbelief. No one had ever bought me anything so nice without me asking for it. I thought he may have had it for someone else and just decided to give it to me.

"Can you go try it on?"

"Okay..."

I slowly turned around to go back into the bathroom. I looked at the size. It said large. *Maybe he did buy it for me.* I'm sure his other girlfriends were probably petite. I smelled the body spray. Ooh it smelled absolutely irresistible. I sprayed it on my body and some flew in my mouth, Yuk! I better not spray wear he's going to be sucking, that tastes awful. I sprayed the back of my knees and arms. I made sure not to spray it on my neck or my breasts oh or between my legs.

I returned to the bedroom and stood at the door. Well what do you think? Brandon looked up and I saw his whole face expression change. *He liked it.*

"Oh, baby you look sexy as hell."

I never saw him look at me this way, he must have really like it. He stood up and walked over to me. He took my hands and spread my arms out to get a good look.

"Damn!"

He pulled me to him and squeezed me tight.

"Ooh and you smell good too!'

"Thank you for the spray too. It smells so good."

"Yes, it does." As he kissed me on my neck.

He pulled me in front of him as he sat on the bed. He slid his hands up the back of my thighs to my ass as he took another whiff of my sent while he pressed his face to my stomach. He stood up and kissed me while he guided the straps off my shoulders. The silk blue teddy dropped to my feet. Brandon pulled me on top of him. I loved the way he felt so hard and stiff. As I lay on top of him he sucked my breast, holding one in each hand.

Again, we started with the foreplay. Kissing as our tongues traced each other's lips, his hands cupping and squeezing my breasts as I held his hard dick, stroking it up and down. I was so wet as he put his fingers inside me. I wanted him so bad, but in the back of my mind I knew what was going to happen. I hoped it would be different. *Lord, please let this be the*

153

night he fucks my brains out. He would be so hard I couldn't wait to feel him inside me. I couldn't take it. I pulled Brandon on top of me in hopes this would be the night. I felt the tip as he slowly tried to fit it inside me. I loved how he had to force it. He would push harder and harder to put it in as I was soaking wet with anticipation. You feel so good baby I whispered in his ear. Fuck me! One, two, three he was in and it was over. He came. Damn! I tried thrusting against him once more but it was over. He pulled it out and rolled over. Shit! *I want to fuck! Ugh!*

I tried to stay calm doing them exercises in hopes to give myself an orgasm. Nothing! I got up and went into the bathroom and sat on the toilet. I began to rub myself in hopes of my own pleasure. It was right there waiting to explode. I rubbed harder and harder making sure my middle finger was gliding right over that spot. I started to aspirate. I spread my legs further apart with my eyes closed so tight as I stroked myself faster and faster. I felt all my energy coming to my spot and then it was ready to blow. My toes curled as I held my breath. It was coming, I was cumming. I was stuck in that one position, the stars were spinning as my eyes we shut, I was cumming so hard. I tried not to make too much noise but I had to catch my breath as my orgasm came to an end. My pussy was throbbing, still pulsating again at the thought of the pleasure I just gave myself.

Shit! I leaned back to catch my breath holding on to the sink. I reached for the toilet paper to wipe myself. I stood up to wash my hands. I hated to flush the toilet, it might wake up Brandon from his coma then he might ask me what I was doing in the bathroom so long.

I tiptoed back to the bedroom. Brandon liked for us to sleep naked so I left my teddy on the floor and climbed in the bed and scooted behind him. I wrapped my arm around his waist and he took my hand and held it on his chest and wrapped his feet around my ankles and we drifted off to sleep.

When morning came, I could never figure out how I ended up on the other side of the bed laying on my stomach and Brandon on his back starring at the ceiling when I lifting my head up trying to get my bearings. It was our late day to go into work which meant we would both be getting off at seven.

"Good morning." He said as he turned on his side.

"Good morning. What time is it?"

"Seven, we have a little time."

He always like to for us to lie together with me on his chest. We never usually have time. We didn't have to be to work until ten. That meant we could enjoy the walk to Five Points station instead of catching the bus. He always paid my fare. If he didn't have enough we would walk. That was sweet. I had to insist if I wasn't up for the walk.

Later that day a lady came through my line. Dark skinned, short hair wearing scrubs. She was short a penny.

"Oh, baby can I bring it right back, I have some change in my office next door." She said

"Don't worry, I got it." I said as I pulled a penny out of my pocket.

"Oh, that's sweet darlin'! I'll bring it right back."

"No don't worry about it." I insisted.

That was my good deed for the day. I must have made a good impression on that lady. She started coming through my line whenever she came in the store. Wasn't until a few weeks later that she introduced herself.

"How you doing today darlin'?"

"Just fine! How are you?"

"Blessed. What's your name? She asked as she tried to read my name tag."

155

"Danielle."

"I'm Brenda. I'm the manager at the Dentist office next door and I need a receptionist."

"Really?"

"Yes, darlin'. Come talk to me on your lunch break."

"Okay I will!" I said surprised.

Wow a job offer from a customer.

I walked down the walk way until I saw the Dentist office. Okay its right next door and Arby's is right across the way. I hate Arby's. The guy in Customer Service had asked me out when I first started working. Said his brother was on vacation and he was staying at his place while he was gone. Of course, I said thank you but no thanks. He was not my type and he was nothing compared to his brother. His brother was the GM at Arby's and he was fine too. He had the prettiest brown eyes against his dark skin, another like Wesley Snipes black. He always came to get change. Now he could get it if he asked me!

Here it goes. I went in the office. I stepped to the window.

"Hey darlin', come on back. Again, my name is Brenda, this is my office and I need some help. I need a receptionist bad. Someone to confirm the patient appointments, answer the phone, check patients in and make deposits to the bank. There's so much stuff I got going on on this side. I just don't have enough time in the day. Let me have you fill out an application. How soon can you start?"

"Start? Just like that. You really want me to work for you?"

"Yeah, I'm serious girl."

"Well let me see if they will let me work nights."

"How much they paying you? This position pays nine dollars an hour. Monday through Friday 8 to 5."

"Seven fifty."

"What? Well I think you'll like this job much better. Definitely."

I couldn't wait to tell Brandon. I started in the next two weeks. Publix let me work part time in Floral. It was cool as long as I didn't have to do it every day. I worked the weekend so I would have a place to be during the day. I stayed at Chanel's on the weekend since Brandon kept his son. It was always a pleasure to stay over there. We always stayed up cooking and telling stories about our past. That kept us up all night! She could not understand why I hadn't met Brandon's son yet. I told her it was fine. I respect his reasons, I ain't trippin.

"Okay girl, whateva."

One thing about Chanel she was down for our struggle together. She also had an empty two bedroom. The gas was off and she used the oven to heat up the apartment. We camped out in her room most of the time doing our nails or hair. Me, Chanel and her daughter slept together on a queen size blow up mattress. We never complained we just rolled with the punches, putting our food stamps together when one of us was short or hungry. She was the sweetest person and she taught me how to always see the good in any situation because people had it way worse than we did.

CHAPTER TWENTY-EIGHT

By September it seemed as if I had been working in the Dental office for months. I got along with all my coworkers and the Dentist and everyone knew who Brandon was.

After learning about my teeth, I decided to go to school to be a Dental assistant. Then they talked me into getting braces. The school hours would not work with my schedule so I learned there was an Ultrasound Diagnostic School right across the street. I was still considering braces, but I went to register for school at night. It would be perfect. The next classes would start in January. When I called to check on Nadia I told my mom I had registered. She thought that was wonderful news.

A young lady had walked by the office a few times. I noticed her because she was carrying a guitar. She wore her hair natural somewhat curly. She ended up inquiring about a new patient appointment. She seemed sweet with a free spirit. No makeup pretty complexion. I gave her a patient information sheet and scheduled her appointment a couple months out. I read her name as I completed the chart, Chasity Bennett. I thought that name fit her appearance and personality, real sweet and carefree.

The next few weeks Brandon was acting different. When I went to clock in at Publix I realized I hadn't heard from Brandon all day. That wasn't like him not to call me. Most days I couldn't keep him off my line in the Floral Dept. with his prank calls because he knew I was the only one in the department that would answer the phone. He was supposed to be leaving for Chicago for the Labor Day weekend with his son. Surely, he didn't leave without calling me or coming by the office to say goodbye. I called his extension and there was no answer. I called the main line and they stated he had already left for the day. I quickly hung up and called the house. No answer. My heart sank to the pit of my stomach. Why didn't he call me or come by to say he was leaving?

I had had the place to myself and couldn't sleep. So, I ended up calling Shelise to fill her in on all that was going on.

"Have you talked to Daddy?" She asked.

"No, I haven't talked to anybody since I been here."

"You probably should call him because he thinks you're living in a shelter."

"Wow I've been here six months and he hasn't tried to contact me but he's okay with thinking I'm living in a shelter. Whatever, I'm good. My mom has Nadia. She is keeping her for the whole school year until I get settled. They wouldn't even keep her the last few weeks of school. I had to leave her with my neighbors."

"Oh Damn! That's not cool. I feel you. Well as long as you're fine, I mean you're grown."

"Yep, I'm good. I'm starting Ultrasound school in January. Everything is fine with me and this man here is real sweet to me, and he's fine too. I wish you should meet him."

"Well I'm glad you cool. Keep me posted."

"Okay, talk to you later, bye."

I couldn't really sleep. The phone rang. I was hesitant to answer it. I never answered his phone, but no one ever called. It stopped ringing and then rang back again. This time I answered it.

"Hello."

"So, you are answering my phone now?"

"No, I just figured it was you since it rang back twice. Why didn't you call me to tell me you were leaving?"

"Oh, I forgot. I was rushing with my son."

"Oh okay."

"Are you going to Chanel's?"

"Yeah I'll leave in the morning. I didn't think I had to go over there tonight did I?"

"No, you cool."

"Well okay, glad you made it safe. Do you think you could let me know when you make it home?"

"Yeah, I won't forget to call you."

"Okay, talk to you later. Enjoy your weekend."

"Alright."

He hung up. Wow. That was weird. I forced myself to go to sleep. I would get up early to go over to Chanel's. We had a full weekend planned. Of course, to talk about all the crap that was going on and window shop as always.

The next few weeks Brandon started going to the gym. I didn't think anything of it although it was something new for him. He would always let me know ahead of time if he was going because he would get dropped off by a coworker and I would know to catch the bus with Chanel and we would go our separate ways on the Marta at the Lenox station. She would go east and I would go south.

Brandon met me as usual. We walked across the parking lot but didn't bother to walk to the corner to the crosswalk instead we just shot across between cars to cross. As we stepped of the curb to run across I reached for Brandon's hand. This time his hand wasn't there when I looked up. Brandon had already crossed the street without me. My heart sank. He never allowed me to cross without taking his hand. Believe me this was big. He would never do that. What was going on with him?

When we got home, Brandon would hop in the shower without me, he would fix himself something to eat, not even bother to ask me if I wanted something or even fix my plate. We sat in silence while watching television which would force me to just go to bed. If I woke up in the middle of the night I would find him asleep on the couch and the television would be off which also meant he had intended to sleep on the couch. I started to feel sick. What did I do? Why the sudden change in patterns? I was too scared to confront him so I just dealt with it hoping the problem would surface and he would initiate the conversation. He has been acting different ever since his trip to Chicago. Brandon had also purchased us Kings of Comedy tickets for the following month in October. *Would we be broken up by then, things just haven't seemed the same.*

My day was just about over. I called Brandon's work extension to see if he was almost ready to go. I now walked over and met him at his job and it was easier to just cut through that parking lot to the Marta station.

Brandon was ready to get out of the office. The calls were driving him crazy.

"Hey peoples I'm about to go home, you'll cover my calls?"

"Sure." They replied.

Brandon thought he could go to the gym, workout and

161

then go home and crash. He didn't bother calling Danielle. *I'll call her when I'm done before she gets off.* It was around one in the afternoon, Brandon headed for the bus to go to the gym. He had a good work out and lastly walked on the treadmill. He began his time as he looked over he saw a thin girl, cute shape, natural hair, nice complexion. She smiled and he smiled back, and they kept walking.

"So how long do you walk?" She asked.

"Forty-five minutes"

"Oh okay! That's good."

Forty-five minutes had passed and she went into the shower. She passed the desk...

"Hey fellas..."

"Hey Chasity, they all responded as she walked by. Always having them take look at her ass in her shorts.

Brandon gathered up his things, on his way out he runs into the same girl from the treadmill on the way out.

"All finished?" She asked.

"Yep, about to head home."

"Oh, where did you park?"

"Oh, I got dropped off, I don't live far."

"I can give you a ride if you like."

"Oh, cool okay, sure."

She stepped to the car conveniently parked in front of the gym. They chatted on the way as he directed her through traffic to his apartment.

"Can I see your place?"

"Sure, but it's not much to see." He replied.

"I'm sure it's a bachelor pad."

"Yeah, pretty much."

She walks in and Brandon leaves the bar door open. She admired his CD Collection.

162

"Oh, somebody loves Sade I see." She stated.

"That's my girl!"

"So how long have you been going to the gym?"

"Not long. I just started going a few weeks ago."

"I was wondering because I've never seen you there before, and I would have remembered you."

"Is, that, right?"

Yes, I've been going there almost a year. It's almost time for me to renew my membership.

"Oh! That's cool."

"Yeah maybe we could work out together. Let me give you my number and if you ever need a ride call me."

She grabbed a piece of paper from the desk. Brandon picked up the letter I left on the desk for him. He picked it up, read it and crumbled it and tossed it in the trash, but he missed it landed on the floor. Chasity Bennett, 404-555-6121.

"Here you go. Call me, now that I know where you stay."

"Thanks for the ride. I'm about to hit the shower I'll call you."

"Okay, I'll let myself out."

Brandon didn't think to lock the bar door behind her. He looked at the time it was four. *Danielle won't be home until after six.* I'll take a shower and chill. When Chasity left, she locked the bottom lock and closed the bar door. She didn't know it would pop back open if you didn't lock it from the inside.

He jumped in the shower, when he got out it was still so hot he laid at the edge of the bed on his back naked trying to cool off under the fan. *She had such an attitude lately, I ain't feeling it. It might be time for her to get her own place. When she moved in it was only temporary and it turned into months later, she is my girlfriend but she been tripping lately.* With his mind racing, Brandon had drifted off to sleep. The phone was ringing...no answer. I called the main line...

"Hey this is Danielle is Brandon away from his desk?"

"Brandon left early today."

"Early? Okay thank you."

My heart raced. *He's cheating on me. I know it. Damn! What did I do wrong? He would never get off early and not come and tell me. Just like when he left for Chicago and didn't even call to say good-bye. I remember checking the bathroom for his toothbrush when I got home. Gone! Then I went into the closest, his bag gone too! He hadn't even called to say he had left or that he made it safely.*

I hung up the phone and called Ken to come a pick me up. Ken was that guy who had been asking me out for a date ever since I started Publix. We did hang out on the weekends I had to leave Brandon's. He would ride me around between clients and drop me off at Chanel's so I wouldn't have to catch Marta.

When he picked me up I immediately started telling him what was going on. He was a good listener and he gave good advice. The closer we got to the apartment I got butterflies in my stomach. We got to the top of the parking lot and he pulled over to let me out.

"Don't call me talking about you need me to bail you out of jail girl!"

"Shut up man! Bye."

I climbed the stairs to the third floor quietly. My heart was pounding again like bass in a Chevy. When I approached the apartment, the bar door was open. I looked with alarm, we never leave this door unlocked. We always lock it behind us because that is the only way it will close. When I went to open the door the bottom lock was locked, but not the deadbolt, which means someone, had to have let themselves out.

I got my key and quietly unlocked the door. I just knew

he was in here with another woman. I had left work at four it was four forty. I turned and locked the bar door. My heart was still pounding. *He was going to wonder how I got home so fast. Oops I hadn't thought about that. Then he would ask me why I got off early. Then he would know I must have called his job and that they told me he left early. Then he was going to make a big deal about why I'm being sneaky. Wait a minute! He can't turn this on me. He's the one that left work early without telling me, leaving me to ride the bus and the train by myself.*

Where's the note I left him? I wonder did he read it. I had to be to work earlier and I started leaving work before him so he would always get up with me to walk me to the bus stop to make sure I got on the bus safely. I was responsible for opening up the office early so Ms. Brenda wouldn't have to leave home so early. She stayed an hour away and it was only a thirty-minute difference for me. I was more than happy to help. She treated me just like a daughter.

That morning I couldn't bring myself to wake up Brandon, he was sleeping so good so I left him a note...
Can't wait to see you tonight, I miss you already.
Danielle

When I looked for my note I saw a piece of paper with a phone number. I picked it up. Chasity Bennett 404-555-6121. What the hell? Chasity, Chasity, that name sounds familiar. The girl from the office? Couldn't be? When the hell did they meet? She must have been here. I knew it. I knew a woman had been in this apartment. There was a crumbled-up piece of paper by the trash can. I opened it, it was my note I left Brandon. Damn! It was so quiet I tip toed down the hall to the bedroom. There he was sleep naked on top of the bed. He must have had sex. Every time he has sex it knocks him out. I didn't make a sound. I didn't want him to know I was home or had gotten off early to try and catch him with another female. I went into the den and turned the television on mute. I took out two veggie lasagna's trays and placed them in the oven for dinner.

I lay on the couch wondering what I did to make him start acting different towards me. I had an attitude cause he was changing his patterns. It was time for me to get my own place before he put me out. I couldn't wait to tell Chanel this crap! Within the hour and thirty minutes you could smell the lasagna. I heard his footsteps coming down the hall. My heart started to race. I heard the oven door open. He peeped in to see what was cooking.

"It should be about done."

"What's up?" He asked as he walked into the den.

"Hello how was your day?"

I wondered if he was going to tell me he got off early or claim he went to the gym after work.

"It was cool."

"You went to the gym after work?"

"Yeah."

"You could have called me and let me know I was waiting around for you to go home."

"Oh, I meant to call you but I fell asleep."

"Yeah, I saw that. I didn't want to wake you, you looked real tired."

"What time you get here?"

"I don't know exactly, Ms. Brenda dropped me off. That lasagna should be almost ready."

"Yeah, I just checked it."

"Well I guess I'll go jump in the shower." I added.

I had bought a cute two-piece short set to sleep in that Brandon liked. I put on a few pounds so it might not be as cute anymore. I went in the bathroom and turned on the shower and stood in front of the mirror and started to cry. I was pissed. His ass been fucking and going to act like he ain't did shit.

When I got out of the shower Brandon had our food and Kool aid set on the TV trays. I was surprised to see he fixed my plate and he didn't forget my cheese. I wanted to talk after dinner but my anger wouldn't let me say a word. We ate in silence. When we went to bed, we slept on separate sides both thinking of the day's events falling asleep without so much as a goodnight.

I got up with my normal routine not wanting to wake him up and have him walk me anywhere, as soon as I touched the door knob he was calling my name.

"Danielle wait for me."

I walked half way back down the hall.

"No, you stay sleep. I'll be fine."

Before he could respond I was out the door running down the stairs so if he had attempted to come behind me I would already be gone. I wanted him to feel guilty for treating me so shitty these last few weeks.

When I got to work I immediately told Ms. Brenda what was going on and she told me to run over to Publix and pick up an Apartments for Rent book.

"You need to get your own place." She said with that motherly look.

We began to look at different areas that would be close to the office since I didn't have a car. Ken had called to let me know he would be stopping over for lunch and to hear the details of what happened. He walked in at 1 o'clock just as I was about to lock up for lunch. He had Arby's and I was not hungry at all. Whenever I worried or stressed I couldn't eat. I told Ken what happened when I got home and it dawned on me to look up that new patient chart and see if that was the same chick. I jumped up and pulled her chart and there it was Chasity Bennett 404-555-6121. Bitch! I wanted to call her and let her know I found her number on my desk when I got home.

"You better not call that lady, ain't no telling what ol' boy told her. Especially since he let her come up in y'all pad." Ken advised.

"Yeah, I guess you're right. I know these days it's the guys that don't tell the truth or the whole story."

"I'll help you find a place. You shouldn't have moved in with him in the first place."

"I didn't have any where to stay remember?"

"Oh, yeah that's right." He frowned.

He took me to a few complexes that day on our lunch. Just to see what they looked like. You know I'm very picky so I have to make sure the places were nice enough for me to live in. I stopped going to Brandon's. I told him I was looking for an apartment and I would stay some nights at Chanel's and other nights Ken would get me a room at the Residence Inn next to the office. He would buy dinner and keep me company until he had to pick up another client. He had the hook up on suites so I even stayed two nights. I had to show Brandon I had other options. When we did discuss what had happened in our relationship he said I was mean.

"Mean? I am not mean! I am sweet, you just started changing your patterns and shutting me out. You have never been this distant from me so I was being defensive not mean. You leave work without telling me, when before you would always come and wait for me to get off. I wouldn't even have to call you. Then you have been going to the gym. You've never even asked me if I wanted to work out with you. Oh, and don't forget you don't even hold my hand when we cross the street, you would always make sure we crossed the street together."

I found myself doing all the talking. It's okay. I'll get my own place. I found a complex I liked in Roswell on the bus line and it dropped me right off in front of the office. I could move on the first. When I arrived at work the office gave me a house warming luncheon. Ms. Brenda gave most of the gifts. She was so sweet.

I was excited to finally be moving into my own place, but sad that Brandon didn't want to continue our relationship. Those four months seemed longer when you live together. I received a call from the apartment manager at work.

"This is she...really? But can't I just pay a higher deposit? Well you verified my employment. I don't have a place to stay. Okay thank you." I immediately called Brandon.

"The apartment manager just called and said I can't rent the apartment because my credit is too bad." I could barely talk from crying.

"I'm sorry. It will be okay. Don't cry."

"It's not going to be alright. You don't want me at your place and I don't have anywhere else to go."

"Let me call my manager and ask her if there is anything for rent where I stay. I'll call you back, and quit crying!"

"Okay."

I was so hurt. I just knew I would be able to move in. Brandon called me back.

"My manager said come fill out an application and she will work with you."

"Okay."

That made me feel a little better but how would I feel, us living in the same complex and not be together. Then to top it off he was being all nice.

CHAPTER TWENTY-NINE

I was able to move in the by fifth of October. Ms. Brenda advanced me my deposit so I wouldn't have to wait. I called Michele. I hadn't spoken to anyone since I left. She said the same thing Shelise said about my father thinking I was probably staying in a shelter. He knows I was working at Publix he could have called at any time to check on me. Oh brother, that's why I left in the first place to get away from them. Judging me and never helping me with my daughter, but her son is always over there, but whatever it doesn't even matter.

I was called to ask if she and my brother in law wouldn't mind bringing my furniture up out of storage. It had been in storage since I left. The weekend I was moving was the same weekend Brandon's mother came up. He and his sister had said I looked like their mother. So, that explained why he was attracted to me. He was used to chocolate girls being raised by one. I was actually four years older than Brandon. I was twenty-nine and he was twenty-five.

When I arrived home, I saw my sister waiting in the parking lot with all my stuff.

"We met your man, he's a cutie."

"Thanks." I replied.

I didn't bother to tell them that we had broken up.

"He just left with his mom and his sister."

I tried not to show my disappointment. I would never even get to be introduced as his girlfriend to his mama.

"Oh, okay then let's get started. I sure appreciate you guys coming to help me."

While my brother in law unloaded the truck, I still had my key I asked my sister to come with me to Brandon's apartment to get the rest of my stuff and so she could see where I had been living.

I got the rest of my clothes and other belongings. He must have forgotten that was my microwave and toaster because he didn't have either unplugged.

"Oh well sorry for ya brother." Michele said and grabbed both of them.

We went into the bedroom and got my stereo and speakers. I felt bad about taking my television out of the den too. He'd just have to go buy one. His place looked rather empty now.

When we went back into my apartment the electricity wasn't on yet nor the water. What in the hell? We called Georgia Power and they said it would not be on until Monday.

"I guess I'll go stay another night at Chanel's. I'll just stay and unpack while it's still daylight."

My brother in law suggested we run up the street and get a flash light and some candles. They dropped me back off and headed down the road to get home. I unpacked and put everything in its place threw the boxes away and I was done. I lit the candles and it was peaceful for the most part to be in my own place. I just had butterflies at the thought of me and Brandon's relationship ending.

I couldn't get a phone in my name either. They didn't turn my gas on for another week. I had no hot water and no way to take a bath. I told Brandon and he didn't even offer for me to come to his place to take a shower so I heated up a pot of hot water on the stove and took a hoe bath out of the sink. He hadn't even been over to see my place and I was right in the next building. My feelings were hurt. I made no attempts to bother him at all at that point.

The Kings of Comedy show was coming up. The verdict was still out on that date. I waited to see what that would be. I changed my whole route to work so I wouldn't have to run into Brandon. I woke up every morning at 5:45 to pray for fifteen minutes, I watch Creflo Dollar from 6- 6:25 and was out the door thanking him for my job. I started going to church with one of the dental assistance at the office. Her name was Kelly. We quickly became friends. She was young in her late twenties and living with a sixty-year-old white man. I didn't find out he was white until she invited me over for dinner after church. I didn't ask any questions on that arrangement. It was none of my business.

I was now the office manager at the Dentist office. Ms. Brenda slid me right in her position so she could become a manager with another company making twice as much. Now if that wasn't a blessing. My regional was black and they made me office manager before they both left the Company, now I was salary averaging twelve dollars an hour.

Instead of leaving at 6:47am to catch the 7:06 am bus

that Brandon and I always rode on, I caught the 6:43 am bus right in front of the parking lot to Five Points Station. I was scared to get on at that station. It was so many crazy people that rode the train so I always took my bible and read that on the way. I got a call from Brandon at work.

"Are we still going to the Kings of Comedy?"

"Sure, if you're sure that you still want to go with me."

"Well that would be rude to take someone else."

"Okay well sure then we can still go."

I made an appointment that Saturday to get my hair done. I wanted something real cute with some color tresses added. I went to the Salon that the girls from Escape went to. I heard that they were really good. I showed a picture to the stylist of a real cute wrapped style around the face with color. The picture next to it showed the back view and it was tapered at the neck. I showed her the front profile and told her that is what I wanted. I never indicated that I wanted the back profile of the hair style. She washed my hair and the first sign of horror was when she cut my hair when it was wet. I hate for my hair to be cut wet if I don't know your skills. Then the second thing she did was whack off the back of my hair.

"What are you doing?" I screamed.

"The back of the hair style is tapered."

"Yes, but I showed you the front, I didn't say I wanted the back of my hair like that. I wanted it in a full even bob at my shoulders with color added for fullness."

I was pissed I didn't know what my hair was going to look like now. She turned my chair so my back faced the mirror. When she finished, it looked nothing like the picture it looked more like Megan Gooden's hair style. She chopped all my hair off!

"This just cost me one-hundred and twenty dollars and it

looks nothing like the picture. I am not pleased with this at all and I will make sure to tell everyone not to request you!"

Kelly picked me up. I hated for her to address me as her boss, we were friends and what went on at work stayed at work.

"Your hair looks so good. Oh, my god that is pretty, it has so much body and the color in the back. I love it!"

"Exactly you're supposed to see the color in the front around my face? I hate it! I am pissed she cut all my hair off."

"You didn't want your hair cut?"

"No, this is not even close to what the picture looked like. I wanted to look cute for my date with Brandon! I wanted everything to be perfect. Maybe he would change his mind about our relationship."

"He is going to love it watch and see."

When I got home I went over to his place to make sure we were still keeping our date.

"You better go get ready girl." He said as he opened the door.

"I just wanted to make sure our plans hadn't changed."

"No, we going out! I'm ready to get my laugh on. Hey you cut your hair. It looks good. I think short cuts are sexy. What... you got some highlights going on up in there? What are you trying to do rub it in my face that you ain't my woman no more?"

"No, not at all, just trying something different. What time are we leaving?" I laughed.

"Just be ready by 6:30. It's 5:15."

"What? Okay it starts at 8?"

"We need to hurry up. I rented a car."

"You did?"

"Yeah, we are going dancing after the show."

"For real? Where?"

"I don't know we'll find some place to go."

"Okay, let me go. I'll be ready!"

I ran out the door and down the stairs to the next building. I put my hair in a shower cap but I didn't want to sweat. I did like how the front of my hair feathered swoop over my eye. I took a quick bath. I had to pee bad. When I wiped myself, I saw my ugly friend Mary. Awe Damn! I started my period! Of all nights, I just knew this night would end with some sex! Damn, damn, damn! If he did want some now I couldn't give him none anyway.

I got dressed and brought an extra tampon in my purse. I hated to carry a purse when I went out. They were always in the way. I didn't want him to know I was on my period. I at least wanted him to treat me extra sweet at the thought he might be getting some that night.

The comedy show was too funny! I just wasn't comfortable. I was on my period. My hair wasn't right *so I thought.* I was glad he liked it, and I had on the wrong bra! I had on some cute black stretch Guess pants with a cute red fitting top to match my lipstick showing too much cleavage. He didn't know any different. The night was actually going great. Brandon was a perfect gentleman. This was the man I knew. After the show, we drove to Buckhead and went to Club Royal. Brandon brought us drinks to loosen up and the music was off the hook. When we finished our drinks, it was a wrap.

"I want you to shake what yo mama gave ya!"

"What, you so crazy!"

"Come on drink up! I'm ready to get you on the dance floor." He yelled in my ear.

We danced all night. He could dance. Damn! All that bumping, grinding and getting our groove on, he couldn't keep his hands off me. I felt over dressed with my tight pants since all the other woman in the club were half naked. I watched his eyes and he never took them off me. He held me tight and we grinded to the rhythm of the music. He kissed me as we slow danced, that was so nice. I couldn't have asked for a better night. The club was closing. It was two in the morning already? We decided to leave before the crowd. Brandon took my hand and lead us though the crowd.

"You want to go get breakfast?"

"Are you hungry?" I asked.

"Hell yeah, all that dancing we did I worked up an appetite."

"Okay sure I can eat."

We went to IHOP on Peachtree. It was packed but worth the wait.

"I'm getting my monies worth tonight shoot!"

"Well thank you this night has been the best night ever!"

Once we ate I let Brandon know my time was running out for my pad and the tampon I had was done.

"You started your period?"

"Yep."

"You didn't bring a tampon. I used it already, and I left my purse at home."

"Well go put some toilet paper on it and I'll make sure you straight from the back."

I stood up. He let me know I was straight. I was actually okay. It was more sweat than anything else, but it was time to go while I was still safe. Brandon was waiting outside the door.

"Are you okay in there?"

"Yes, I'm good."

"Okay well we can go."

"Thank you." I said as I came out of the bathroom.

When we got in the car Brandon looked at the time on the

dashboard.

"Damn it's four in the morning."

"I see, and I still have to take a shower when I get home."

I knew he wasn't going to stay the night, but it would have been nice to lie in his arms. We made it home and Brandon walked me to my apartment first. He walked me in to make sure I was safe. He followed me in to the bedroom as I kicked my shoes off and turned on the lamp.

"Okay well goodnight get some sleep the sun will be up soon."

"For real! Good night thank you again for a wonderful date." I stated as I walked him to the door.
I locked the bar door and closed the door behind it.

That next morning Kelly picked me up for church and I told her all about our date. I was still on cloud nine in hopes of us reconciling our differences. Not happening. I just knew Brandon would be knocking at my door. He had never asked if I had a phone and I never volunteered the information that I didn't. He didn't come by and I stayed home all day after church just in case he had decided to come see me, but he didn't.

Brandon had woken up thinking about what a good time he had with Danielle last night. I just know she should be coming over to talk about last night if she isn't still asleep. I really had a good time, too bad I couldn't get me some. I'll put in Sade on the computer and lay on the couch in the den. He opened the door so he could hear if she came up, but she never did.

He never came by and he never called my job. Since Brandon hadn't called me I never got a chance to share the news about my promotion. That would be my excuse to call him. He didn't seem as thrilled as I thought he would be.

Certainly, he wasn't jealous. I was making more than he was and he did just put me out. Oh well I was happy on one hand and I was still heartbroken on the other.

"Let me take you out Boss." Ken stated.

"Take me where?" I asked.

"Out to dinner, I have a taste for a juicy steak."

"Sure, I can go."

We left from work. I stayed late to the office doing charts until he picked me up around seven. I always carried an extra bag of clothes with me. I guess it was habit from always staying here and there but now I did have my own apartment. We went to Ruth's Chris Steak House in Alpharetta. I was impressed. We had plenty of conversation. I really enjoyed Ken.

"You want to stay with me tonight. We can go to this nice hotel."

"Hotel and do what?"

"Man, don't play you know a brotha' been wanting you. You're single now."

"You are crazy, but sure I'll stay with you..."

"What in the hell? We staying here?" As I looked out the window to the top of the hotel.

We were at the Renaissance Hotel, it was nice! He had great connections from his clientele. He kept looking at me some type of way as we rode in the elevator.

"What is you looking at me like that for man?"

"You so hood. You my girl, shoot I can't look at you?"

"You know what you lookin' like."

The room was to die for. The robes were snow white and plush, felt like I was wrapped in a blanket as it absorbed all the water off my body from our shower. We did the anticipated. He was an undercover freak. I didn't know if I liked that side of him. It was almost weird. He had me up all night. I was dry as a bone! That morning we got up and got dressed. There was no time for breakfast. We walked to the car to put our bags in the trunk and the windows were busted out of his car.

"What the hell happened?"
He checked his voicemail and all I heard was a woman's voice screaming on the messages. Evidently there were several messages left.

"Damn, is that your woman? You had a girlfriend this whole time and you never told me?"

"Don't trip I can handle it she's my boy's mother."

"Boy's?"

"Yeah I have two sons. Oh, wow you ever told me about any of this. You scandalous! She must know all you clientele spots."

"Let me drop you off so you don't be late."
He dropped me off at work, and I wished him well.
"I'll call you later."

"Don't call me! You better call you boy's mother." I said as I got out of the car shaking my head.

By the end of the week my leg was so sore and swollen I could barely stand on it. I left work early and walked to the Emergency room down the street. I had gotten a spider bite and it was bad, must have gotten bit in that hotel room with Ken. They put me on bed rest for a week and gave me an antibiotic. I could not stay home for a week, but I stayed in the weekend with my leg up. That was so boring not being able to go anywhere. Ken picked me up and dropped me off until I was able to walk.

He brought movies and said he was going to make me his famous Buffalo wings and fries. I let him have the kitchen as I posted on the couch. I never knew how they prepared them. It looked fairly easy and they were delicious!

"You think you a chef boy." I teased.

"Shoot girl my wings are the bomb. You're going to be asking for the recipe so let me just tell you now." He said laughing.

"So, you not going to tell me what happen when you got home huh?

"She put me out."

"What are you serious?"

"I slept on the couch. I pay the bills up in that joint and my boys are there so she can't put me out of nothing!"

"You crazy! Your stuff would have been on the lawn, wet when the sprinklers came on if you didn't bring your butt home!"

We laughed and started talking about old relationships. I told him about Charles when I put his stuff on the lawn and I ended up telling him about my past. He couldn't believe it.

"I knew yo' ass had some ghetto in you. You straight hood girl!"

"No, I am not!"

"Man, you did some time? Were you scared?"

"No! Well at first but I got through it. I don't want to talk about it. I told you enough."

"You good girl! I'm messing with you. We all make mistakes. It wasn't like you meant to kill her."

"I know but it is still something I have to live with for the rest of my life. And when I get close to someone I feel like I'm not being honest if I don't share my past with them."

"Well you still my baby. You can't get rid of me. So, don't trip."

"I know, I know. Thank you."

CHAPTER THIRTY

I spent the next month dating myself. It looked like it was going to be a long winter. Every Friday night I went next door to block Buster and rented their date night special, two movies, popcorn, candy and a drink for ten dollars. Yep, that was my routine for the next six weeks. I snuggled up every Friday night with my movies and snacks and cried myself to sleep. I watched the same movies again all day Saturday without even getting out of bed.

The Perimeter office had scheduled their new Holiday hours. We would be closed for the week of Thanksgiving to return for one week and closed for the whole month of December. I had no plans for the Holiday. Kelly dropped in to check on me for Thanksgiving and brought me a plate. I thought that was so sweet of her to think of me.

It was time to get back on the grind. Every morning I still woke up at 6 am to watch Creflo and out by 6:25 with earmuffs, scarf, hat and gloves with my black wool Trench coat I was out the door like clockwork in the freezing cold praising God for my life, health and strength and to get through this breakup with Brandon. Several nights I would sit in the staircase in the dark waiting to see if he would get dropped off by some chick or if he would stay out for the night. Well if you look for it you will find it. I made sure our paths never crossed. We hadn't seen each other since the night of our Kings of Comedy date.   Well that silence was broken. A car pulled in the parking lot and Brandon came out of the next building with his overnight bag. My heart dropped to my stomach and it was pounding. I ran in the stairwell so the light wouldn't reflect on my figure in the dark as the car backed up out of the parking lot. I went back to my apartment, I walked in the bathroom and starred in the mirror. It was really over and he had moved on. I could feel the tears surfacing. I tried to hold back as I put in Kirk Franklin. Lord, I can't take it. I laid on the floor crying,

"Lord please send me my husband. I can't go through another heartbreak Lord I can't take it." I was all alone, I was hurt and I was broken at what I saw and felt. *Please help me get over this. Please send my husband.*

CHAPTER THIRTY-ONE

*L*ord *please send my wife, who is God fearing, loving, sensitive, compassionate, and wants the same things in life, my life partner, loves kids, and the ones I already have, willing to build a family business.*

These were the requests Marquise wrote on his tablet while he sat in his manager's meeting. He was tired of dating and wanted to be married. When the meeting was over he wrapped it up for the day and made plans to go home. It was Friday and he was ready for the weekend to relax. Take it easy everybody, if you need me call me on my cell. He headed out the door to his car. There were some movies in the passenger seat. *I forgot to take those back to Blockbuster.* He grabbed them and headed across the parking lot.

"What's up man?"

"What's up Black?" The clerk greeted as he came in the door.

"Here are some movies I forgot to bring back."

"Oh, no problem." He stated as he received the movies from behind the counter.

I approached the counter. The guy stepped aside to let me make my transaction. *It was my co-worker's brother, Marquise, chocolate with the pretty eyes.*

"You all set Ms. Danielle?"

"Yes, sir, you know me it's my date night. I got my M&M's and my Lemonade!"

"Ready to cuddle on that couch?"

"You know it!"

That was Derek and every Friday he teased me about having a date night with myself.

"Okay Miss Lady ten seventy-three."

I reached in my jacket pocket and realized I had forgotten my wallet.

"Ah shucks I did it again. I left my wallet in my desk. I'm sorry let me run next door and get it. I'll be right back."

"Just put it on my account."

"Oh, no that's okay, my office is right next door."

"No, I insist. Just say it's an early Christmas present."

"You're serious?"

"Yes, go ahead. Man, put it on my account."

"Well okay thank you, I owe you one."

"No, you don't. Enjoy your date."

"I will." I laughed.

"Here you go." Derek handed me my bag.

"That was sweet, thank you again."

"Merry Christmas."

"Merry Christmas to you too." I said with a smile as I went out the door. *That was sweet.*

"You ain't slick boy."

"Nah, nah, I'm just being nice, 'tis the season."

"Yeah, whatever. She's single. She comes in every Friday and buys 2 for $10. She says that's her date."

184

"Serious?"

"Serious."

"She have any kids?"

"I don't know all that. I know she's the manager of that Dentist office next door. I'm telling you boy you better check it out."

"Maybe."

"Okay."

Marquise made his way to the door.

"Take it easy man and Merry Christmas."

"You too Black, you too."

I cleaned off my desk and locked up the office. The Perimeter office was officially closed the month of December for the Christmas holiday, not to return until next year, the year 2000. Everyone had their own predictions of what would happen to the world once the clock struck twelve. I heard rumors of people buying up generators and water, stocking up on can foods. Thinking that the world would stop functioning, and computer data would not transfer over. Some even thought the world was going to end. *"But about that day or hour no one knows, not even the angels in heaven, nor the Son, but only the Father."* Mark 13:32. No one can predict the future and our God is bigger than any situation or circumstance.

"Merry Christmas!" I said as I turned the key. Everything seemed so quiet and cold. I headed to the bus stop to go home.

CHAPTER THIRTY-TWO

Since I had become manager I was split between two office locations. On Monday, Tuesday, and Thursday I worked out of the Buckhead office and on Wednesday and Friday I worked at the Perimeter location. The Buckhead office would still be open the month of December.

I changed my look as well. I dressed in skirt suits with boots and classic slacks with button up dress shirts most days or I just kept it simple and wore my scrubs at least one day out the week. I couldn't take doing that short hair cut in this winter cold. I had laid my own tresses. I wore a part down the middle wearing 18 inches of that new Urban Beauty. I looked like a black Pocahontas with my naturally long eye lashes. I have a nice grade of hair so I can rock the silky straight. Almost even looking like a black Cher as the hair just hung over my shoulders.

I liked working at the Buckhead location. I would get off at the Lenox station and walk down Peachtree. The office was in the Kroger plaza behind Rooms-To- Go. The Dentist was a black fine light skinned brother with braces. I soon learned he had the lowest self-esteem in the world as he put others down. He was the victim in his own abusive relationship, go figure. I enjoyed working with my Buckhead staff. They made working fun. The office was much bigger and we had the televisions on in the back for patients to watch and we also listened to satellite radio. He would treat us to lunch as a group at the restaurant in the same plaza. I had wished Brandon could see this office. It was really nice.

The rapper Mase had come into the office as a patient. I couldn't resist asking him for his autograph for Nadia on the back of my business card. He signed his name with the "S" as a dollar sign. He noticed my bible on the side of my desk.

"Is that your bible?"

"It sure is."

"What church do you attend?" He asked.

"I'm not a member of any church yet. I have gone to a few, but I faithfully watch Creflo Dollar every morning at 6."

"That's good. You're real pretty. Do you think I could get your number, maybe we could go out to dinner or something this weekend?"

Damn, I didn't have a phone yet. I only had a pager with a 229-area code. I would always run to the phone booth down the street in the back of the apartment complex. I have to get a phone.

"Sure, here's my number. Call me."

I gave him my pager number. I hope the 229-area code doesn't throw him off. I scheduled his next appointment, but we didn't enter personal information in the system for Celebrities. I didn't tell him it was a pager number. Maybe I should have because he never called me or shall I say paged me.

The phone rang.

"You want to meet me after work?"

To my surprise, it was Brandon. My heart raced at the sound of his voice. I tried not to smile, he would hear in it in my voice.

"Where?" I asked.

"I could come to your office."

"Okay, you'll have to get off at the Lenox station..."

I waited and waited for Brandon to arrive at my office and he never showed up. I finally locked up the office and left. I began to wonder if something happened as I walked to the train station. *Is he walking there now and I missed him? Did I leave too soon? I waited long enough and I was going home.*

As I stood up from the platform to catch the train a voice yelled my name. I turned around it was Brandon, he was on the train.

"What happened to you?"

"I didn't get off in time."

"Well you could have called. I just left the office. My appointments ended an hour ago."

We both hopped back on the train. I was disgusted by now, he could fall off the tracks for all I cared. We had to stand up, Brandon had his earplugs in and didn't say a word to me the whole ride. *What was the point of meeting me in the first place, it was his idea?*

There were two things I could do. Stand and ride the whole way to Five Points or get off on the next station after midtown and leave his ass on the train. I could catch the bus and it would drop me off right in front of our apartments. The station was next I started sweating and had butterflies in my stomach. That must have been my conscience because I was about to be ugly. Yep I chose ugly, I jumped off the train at the last minute so he wouldn't have time to ask me where I was going. He wasn't paying me any attention anyway. I had tapped him on the shoulder to get his attention, he was being a weirdo. I made up my mind I was done with that.

When I came out of the station the bus was waiting right in front. *Good.* I will beat him home and won't answer the door if comes to see why I got off the train. I stepped on the bus and the bus driver said,

"wait before you pay this bus is broke down and I'm waiting for someone to relieve me."

"For real?" I asked in surprise.

"If I'm lying I'm flying..."

I knew I shouldn't have gotten off the train. That's what I get. I sat down to gather my thoughts. He reminded me of somebody but I couldn't think of who? The more I stared at him he reminded me of a cuter version of Alf. (*laughing to myself.*) He had pretty Chestnut eyes but they were close together like Alf. He was cute though. His mouth was even cute the way he had a little over bite. We started casual conversation as I sat across from him. I had decided to wait and see how long it would be before his relief.

Forty-five minutes turned into two hours. We talked the whole time and never realized so much time had passed. His name was Glen. The phone on the bus rang.

"They are going to have to have someone replace me?" He stated with great irritation.

"What do they mean replace you? Then what are we supposed to do?"

"I don't know what everybody else is supposed to do but we're going to dinner."

"Dinner, who is we?" I asked.

"Me and you! It's the least I could do for making a pretty lady wait."

"Sounds like a plan, but how are we going to manage that?" I said with a smile.

"Whoever comes to replace me I will just take that

vehicle back to the yard to get my car because technically my route is over?"

Well he meant what he said he drove the Marta van back to the yard and we had good conversation the whole way. It was a good ways out.

"Wait here pretty lady. I'm going to go clock out and get my things out of my locker." He instructed.

He had parked on the curb by the gate. I waited in the van until he returned, but he sure was taking a long time. *What the hell am I doing out here with a man I don't even damn know. It was getting late I know that. I wonder what Brandon is thinking? Did he even go to my apartment? Wondering why I still wasn't home. I don't even care so why am I thinking about it.* Why was he taking so long? Now I'm really feeling stupid sitting in this company van. Just as I was about to panic he and another guy walked out the door. One guy went back in and he walked toward the van.

"Sorry I took so long my boss had me writing up an incident report about that raggedy bus."

"What time is it?" He asked.

"9:51"

It had only been twenty minutes but seemed like another hour since my mind was going 90 miles a minute.

"Everything will be closed. Are you still hungry?"

"I guess."

"What do you have a taste for?" He asked as he opened the door to let me out of the van.

We walked to his car in the parking lot. He had a nice clean shiny car. I looked at the back to see what kind it was. Oh, it was a Cadillac CTS. It was Black. He must make some good money. He opened the passenger door for me, I got in and he closed the door. *This was a nice car and it smelled good too.*

We headed out of the parking lot through the gate. We

drove around trying to find a place to eat.

"It's been a long day. We don't have to go to a restaurant. I will be fine with some chicken."

He took me to some store that sold food in it. I don't know what part of the game this is. I didn't know what part of Atlanta we were in, but by the looks of it I knew we were in somebody's hood. The loud music, and the cars on 22's and 24's. All I saw was dudes everywhere. He was in the store for a minute too. *What the hell was he doing now?*

I had lost my appetite by now. I was definitely not eating any chicken and fries out of a convenient store. That was just nasty. He came out of the store with a brown paper bag. He handed me a bottle of Hawaiian punch.

"Didn't know if you were thirsty and I figured you can't go wrong with Hawaiian punch."

"Thank you, that was sweet."

"They're some chicken wings and fries in the bag."

"No, thank you. I lost my appetite."

"Well okay, so what's next?"

"It's late."

"I know you want me to take you home or you want to stay with me?"

"I can stay with you. There's nothing at my house."

"Okay cool. You sure have a pretty smile, I know your boyfriend is gonna wonder where you are when he finds you not at home." He said with a cheesy grin.

"Please, if I had a boyfriend then I wouldn't be here with you now would I?"

"You sure about that?" He asked with what looked like a big question mark on his face.

I still didn't know where we were. I just knew we made a whole bunch of turns into this big subdivision. We pulled up at this big dark house. Dark meaning no lights were on outside. He didn't pull his car in the garage. It must have been full of junk or else why would he leave his CTS in the driveway. When we entered the house, I could see it was a fully furnished house. He didn't turn any lights on, just the lights in the hall way leading up the stairs.

"Follow me dear."

"Okay." As I followed him up the stairs to his bedroom at the top of the stairs.

"We can chill in my room. Excuse the mess. I didn't make my bed."

He moved some magazines, the newspaper, and a pile of clean work shirts that needed ironing or to be taken to the cleaners.

"Would you like some sweats and a t-shirt to sleep in?"

"Yes, please."

"If you like I can throw your scrubs in the washer. There's a laundry room downstairs next to the kitchen. There's a bathroom down there too if you'd like to take a shower?"

"Yes, that would be fine."

"There are some towels in the dryer. Let me go and set them up for you and get you a new bar of soap. Just toss you clothes out when you get in the shower and I'll put them in the washing machine." He added.

I followed him downstairs to the laundry room for the towels. He handed me a new bar of soap. He showed me to the bathroom and waited for me to toss out my clothes.

"Thank you."

I got in the shower. There was a knock at the door.

"Yes?"

"Here is a shirt, it should be long enough and my eyes are closed."

"I see that, thank you again." I laughed.

I peeked out of the shower to make sure his eyes were closed as he backed out the bathroom with his hands over them. When I came out of the bathroom I took a quick glance around the house. Yep a woman with horrible taste lived here. Touch flower lamps, wallpaper and silk flowers everywhere. Yuck! Who does that? I could not picture myself in any part of this house. So, to keep it real I may never be back after tonight.

When I returned to Glen's room he was changing the sheets on the bed. Oh, this would be good, clean sheets and a crisp pillow case. I climbed in his bed while he took a shower. He came out of the bathroom wrapped in a towel. I watched him closely with a seductive eye as he searched for something in his drawer. He knew I was admiring his tall athletic build. Here we go with these shoulders and that damn chest. I love a man who is naturally muscular with thickness. And his butt looked firm wrapped in that towel.

What was he doing? He had some ancient vibrator. Was he crazy? First all the damn flowers now he trying to freak me with some rusty device. No way man.

"What do you think you are doing with that?"

He found some batteries that didn't work. Okay is he a weirdo or what? Put that mess up and let's go to bed. We have to go to work in the morning. Glen jumped on top of me in hopes to persuade me into playing. He started kissing me on my neck and slid his hands straight between my legs. I could tell he was smooth. He went right to my spot and tried to kiss me in the mouth. I turned my head as if to enjoy the moment. I don't know about that kissing in the mouth business. Too many germs. I learned a lot about your teeth and your mouth since I had been working in the Dentist office. I couldn't help that feeling though, the back of my legs started to sweat. I could feel an orgasm about to come down. Damn! He was good. I was enjoying the sensation and he rolled on top of me and began to direct his penis inside me. I jumped thinking about a condom, but he was already inside of me.

"Don't worry about a condom, I have one on. He whispered"

Did he just read my mind?

"Oh, so you knew you were getting some."

"No baby, I was just hoping you gave me some." He said as he slowly enjoyed the wetness inside me.

He was smooth, not the bang bang, I want to bust a nut type, he was more like yeah, I want this to last a minute type.

That morning I took another shower.

"The phone kept ringing when we were sleep, you didn't hear it?"

"Yeah, I heard it."

"Well why you didn't answer."

"It was my wife."

"Your wife?" I replied in shock.

"We're separated. She took my kids and moved back to her mom's in North Carolina." He replied.

That explains all those ugly flowers downstairs. I didn't get a good vibe from this house anyway. I had no plans on returning. He explained his marital situation on the way to the train. He was dropping me off so I could ride it into work. I asked him where we were. He said North Atlanta at the beginning of the train route. So, I had to ride south all the way into Atlanta about 45 minutes to work. What the hell? He gave me a hand full of tokens to use.

"Thank you."

"You're welcome, have a nice day at work."

"You too." I replied.

The train ride was pretty long, but at least I could ride for free for a few days.

CHAPTER THIRTY-THREE

I talked to Glen into the Holiday season. I always made him think I was too busy for us to get together. I had no intentions of sleeping with him again or returning to that house of his, but we did become good friends. He became someone I could rely on for advice, comfort and transportation on his days off. He would offer to pick me up from work just to spend some time with me, but by the time we pulled up to my apartment I always had some excuse as to why I couldn't come over or why he couldn't come in.

Glen asked me to keep his car and pick him up from five points after his late-night routes. Thinking he was going to get to spend the night. Not a chance brother! He gave me his spare key and I was to pick him up at eleven at night from Five Points. This time he would play like he was too sleepy to drive home just to see if I would offer for him to stay.

"No, not at all, you better roll that window down to keep

yourself awake. Call me when you get home so I know you made it home safe."

"Are you serious?"

"Serious as a heart attack, Mr. married man!"

I went into my building with a smirk on my face and didn't even look back to say goodbye.

We talked over the phone a few more weeks. He shared a story with me about his past and his days in the streets. He had got hit in the face with a bat and got his grill busted. Damn! *No wonder why he never talks showing his teeth.*

I talked him into coming to my office to get his teeth fixed. After his consultation, I asked him to take me to Target. I had already picked out an entertainment center for my living room. I wanted to see if he would get it for me for Christmas. I had a certain charm about me. Men just wouldn't tell me no. Or I made them feel hella cheap if I didn't get what I asked for and of course dudes don't want to seem cheap when they are trying to impress you.

When we arrived at Target I knew exactly which entertainment center I wanted I just didn't remember how much it cost. We looked at different styles and the cheapest one was still on sale for one hundred and forty-nine dollars.

"I didn't know it would be that much. I was looking for one like eighty-nine dollars. I don't want to spend all my money?" I stated aloud.

"I'll get it for you."

"Are you serious?"

"Sure."

"For real, ooh thank you." I screamed as I kissed him on the cheek.

"Don't say I never gave you anything."

We had to find room in the back seat and partially

between the front seats. When we got back to the office, we put the box into Alexis's car. She was the Dental assistant at this office. She was a sweetheart. I loved her spirit and we hit it off right away. We also hung out after work and on the weekends. Alexis was really smart. She was going to school to become a Dentist. She was peanut butter color, wore braces and had long pretty black hair. She was a little shorter than me with a cut shape and hips. No weave and not mixed. She was a natural pretty black girl.

I didn't talk to Glen much. He made sure he checked on me though. I never saw a future in our friendship since he was married. I was convinced never to get involved with another married man after Preston. He had given me another big jar of tokens when I shared with him that it cost so much to wash clothes in our complex, and no, that I was not going over to his place to do my laundry or spend the night. He told me that the tokens worked in the washers and dryers, that the machines couldn't tell the difference in the tokens from the quarters.

When I went to do laundry downstairs from my building I mixed to tokens with quarters in the washer. Hot damn it worked! I put all tokens in for the dryer and it worked! I started to laugh. I tried to hurry and wash as many loads as I could. I had a big jar full of tokens, had to be like a hundred dollars' worth. Are you kidding me free ride and free laundry? You know I felt a little guilty so I would at least put one quarter in with the tokens.

Funny thing, it came to mind to share the news with Brandon and give him a few tokens. I hadn't seen him since the day on the train when I met Glen. I remembered how we had to go make change to get quarters to wash and that it cost almost twenty dollars. You had to pay double for the dryer because the cycle was so short it forced you to spend more money to make sure your clothes were dry. Just as I was putting my clothes in the dryer, I saw Brandon walking by. I couldn't believe it, he must have been coming from the bus on the way to his apartment. I ducked behind the dryer, I had butterflies flip flopping in my stomach. I made it a point to avoid him and I never saw him out anywhere. Even when I would try to run into him I wouldn't. Life had changed our patterns.

I couldn't help the thought of sharing my tokens with Brandon so he would be able to wash his clothes too. I didn't know why I was being nice even thinking about him. That was taking away from me, but he was good to me and I never had to pay for my bus fare with him either. I wanted to share in spite of the situation between us. It was hell getting change up to wash all those loads of clothes. I went to get dressed to make myself presentable maybe even a little tempting before heading over to his apartment. My heart was pounding as usual I'm such a scary cat, I hate getting my feelings hurt. I hadn't called before popping up, I just hoped he didn't have company by now.

I knocked on the bar door, my hands were all sweaty I almost dropped the jar. I hoped he would hear me without me having to beat on it. He opened the door and looked at me with a smirk on his face.

"What's up? He always said so nonchalant as he invited me in.

"Nothing," I replied as I followed him through the door. He walked back into the kitchen and I sat on the bar stool.

"I just wanted to share something with you." I placed the jar on the counter.

"Oh, yeah what's that?"

"Tokens."

"Oh, for real? How you get all those?"

"I got them from one of the bus drivers, but check this

out."

I placed a token next to a Quarter.

"Look."

"What?" He said as he leaned over to see what I was showing him.

"The machines in the laundry room can't tell the difference between the token and the quarter."

"Shut the fuck up!"

"I'm for real! I've been doing my laundry with them."

"No shit?"

"Yep, so I was coming to give you some."

"Girl stop."

"I'm for real you don't want any? Okay negro! All you have to do is put one quarter in with the three tokens and wash your clothes."

I left him twenty dollars' worth of tokens. He ain't no fool. He better use those tokens. I felt a little lonely walking back to my apartment. I missed him but I had to get over it. He never called me to let me know if he used the tokens or not. If he didn't I know he used them for the bus.

CHAPTER THIRTY-FOUR

December was a cold month. I still didn't have a car but I still woke up every morning to watch Creflo and head out walking to the bus stop with my gloves and scarf wrapped around my face with my bible under my arm. I made sure I read it on the train. One as a deterrent, two because I had a long ride to the Buckhead office, I could read a chapter, and third it kept people from talking to me. I was thankful to God as the wind whipped me in the face that I was able to go to work, blessed with this position to make this money. I've never been a manager before, but I was always a leader. I fit the part and loved what I did.

Me and Glen had gone to the mall to do some Christmas shopping then and he dropped me off. We pulled up to my apartment and there was Brandon coming out of the laundry room in some sweats and a holey wife beater. I paused as I was about to open the door, that's him.

"Him who?"

"My ex-boyfriend."

"And what's the problem?"

"I don't want him to see me with another man."

"Oh, that makes me feel real good."

"What? He doesn't need to know my business!"

Glen was really offended but I didn't care. I didn't want Brandon to see me with anyone I was not serious about. I waited until he was out of site before I got out of the car.

"You can come in Glen."

I know he was staring at me like *what the hell*? I was probably all kind of selfish names as he followed me into my building. He was admiring the entertainment center I had swindled out of him. I had bought me a 5-disk CD changer to go with my receiver and speakers. I had to rock my Gospel!

Glen handed me a box, Merry Christmas pretty lady. I had no idea what it could be.

"You got me a gift? Why did you do that? We never said we were exchanging gifts."

"I know, I just thought I'd get you something that I know you really needed." He replied.

As I opened the box, it was a cell phone. The kind you added minutes to.

"Oh, my god, you got me a phone!" I said with excitement as I jump to give him the biggest hug.

"Yeah, I thought you could use that. You travel on the bus and the train. I can't get to you and you're always alone. It's not safe for you to be out with no way to call anyone in case of an emergency."

"This is the sweetest thing anyone has ever done for me. Thank you so much."

202

I gave him another big hug as he felt me up and he gave me a kiss on my forehead.

"You're welcome. Let me get on out of here. I set it up for you and I got you some minutes on there already. I already locked your number in my phone. You can go to any track phone station and get some more minutes."

"Oh, my goodness, okay, I'm so happy!"

I walked him back out to the car. Now I didn't care if Brandon saw him or not and his nice Cadillac. I'm so dirty. The Lord is fixing me though.

CHAPTER THIRTY-FIVE

*S*he should be back in the office today. The sign said the office would open Monday January 3, 2000. I'll go and introduce myself. Let me write my number on the back of my card. Marquise headed down the stairs of his Condo and hopped in his car.

The Holidays were over and it was time to get back to work. I got off the bus across from Publix this time. I didn't feel like walking. I arrived early so I could get all my charts in order. I stopped at Publix and got a dozen donuts for the ladies. I sat at my desk and felt the base of a car coming through the parking lot. *Who was that? If they don't turn that music down* as I walked to the door to see who it was. Oh my! It was Marquise. He drove a black mustang. It was sharp! He had the beat up in there too. My office windows were rattling. I laughed and shook my head and sat back down after I watched him back into his parking spot in back of Arby's. I should go over and formally introduce myself. I grabbed my business card and wrote my cell number on the back. I'll go buy an orange juice.

I waited a little bit to let him get settled. Once my staff got in I asked if anyone wanted coffee or juice from Arby's. I didn't want to seem too obvious. As I walked in he was there right at the counter.

"Good morning what can I get for you?"

"Two orange juices please." I replied.

"Coming right up!"

"Thank you." As he handed me the two cartons.

"Anything else I can get for you?"

"No, that's all. Thank you."

"Oh, take my card!" We both said simultaneously as we handed our cards to each other showing our cell numbers on the back.

We both laughed and read our cards.

"Okay I'll call you." I replied as I smiled and walked out the door.

I would be starting Ultrasound Diagnostic School today. I no longer worked evenings at Publix. Did I mention that already? Class started at six, so I would be walking right across the street from Publix into that office park. Not the same one Brandon worked, this was on the opposite side where the bus stop was. Classes lasted until ten and I would jump on the train leaving the Perimeter Mall all the way downtown and take the bus that dropped me off in front of my apartments.

I quickly made friends in my class and I was so excited to start school. I had it all mapped out. I would finish school in 18 months and I would apply for a private OBGYN and schedule my appointments Tuesday thru Thursday. I loved my Fridays and sleeping in on Mondays. Sounded fool proof to me.

Those next few weeks I kept missing Marquise's calls. Once I got out of class I would check my voice mail and there his voice sounded.

"Hey, Danielle this is Marquise just checking in with you. Don't

bother trying to call me back, by the time you get this message I'll be asleep. I will try to catch up with you tomorrow. Have a good night."

I hadn't spoken to Marquise at all since we exchanged numbers. I don't think he knew that I didn't have a car and he definitely didn't know I had started school. I would see him leave work around 3:30 but he never stopped by my office and I didn't see a need to bug him at his place of business either. We had a new full time Dentist at our office so there was no need for me to go to the Buckhead office anymore. I was relieved of that.

When we finally caught up with each other he asked if we could get together on the weekend. Said he had a grand opening at another store and would be getting together with some friends to play spades after. I agreed to accompany him.

That Saturday the spade game had been somehow cancelled and Marquise asked if he could take me to grab a bite to eat so we could talk and get to know each other.

He called and said he was pulling in so I went out to meet him. He walked up the drive way with his face painted. That was cute. They had that and other things for the kids at the opening. We decided to go to Applebee's on Memorial Drive. That was fine with me. We were seated and admired each other's features. I could still picture him coming into Publix to get change for his store. He was a cutie! His eyes were still so brown against his dark black skin. Yeah that pretty black, with a fat bald head. I was always attracted to those meaty head dudes. The waitress that came to the table asked if we were interested in any drinks as she showed us the alcohol menu. We both immediately replied,

"Oh, I don't drink." We looked at each other and laughed.

"I'll have lemonade." I replied.

"And I'll have a sweet tea." He added.

"So, you don't drink?"

"Nope or smoke." He replied.

"Me either, that's a good thing!" I smiled.

"Yes, that's a big plus."

We enjoyed dinner and talked about our personal desires and goals. I was excited about the possibilities of a relationship. We got on the subject of God and churches in Atlanta.

"My Grandfather has a church."

"Really?"

"Yes, he's a Pastor. You'll get to meet him."

"Okay." I said hesitantly.

"Would you like to go to church with me tomorrow?"

"To church?" I replied almost choking.

"Why not you're going to meet my family sooner or later anyway?"

"Sure, that would be nice. Where do they live here in Decatur?" I asked.

"Yes."

"Where are you from?"

"I'm originally from California. I've lived south of Atlanta two hours away in Tifton since ninety-six."

"Oh, so I got a Cali girl huh?"

"Yes, you do." I said with a giggle.

He didn't say much about his personal life just yet, but he was passionate about his job. I watched his facial expressions and his proper speech. I was infatuated by his whole being. *Lord is this my husband?* I tried to eat slowly so I wouldn't seem so greedy. I was used to eating fast. Normally I would have inhaled my steak and bake potato. I get the same thing every time I go to Applebee's, Bourbon Street steak with baked potato and fresh vegetables.

We finished up and Marquise drove me home. He was able to pull up to the entrance of my building. It was a glass door and down a long hallway were rows of apartment doors.

"You don't have to walk me in. Thank you for dinner I really enjoyed you."

"You're welcome. I'll call you."

The phone rang.

"Hello?"

"Just making sure you made it in safe."

"That was sweet yes I'm in."

"So, I'll pick you up around ten-thirty eleven. Sunday school should be ending by then."

"Okay, I'll be ready. I'm about to jump in the shower so call me and let me know you made it home safely."

"Okay."

I jumped in the shower and set out my sage and cream small checkered pattern skirt suit. It was my favorite it was a short-fitted skirt with a short Jacket. Not too short, it stopped right above my knee, and I had matching sage pumps.

Marquise rode down 75 North. Music loud windows rolled down. His heart was free. God has sent his angel. *I know she is just what I asked for. I forgot to ask her if she had any kids. I hope she loves my kids.* Marquise had two girls age five and three. *Yes, that would have to be the subject on tomorrow's list.*

Marquise had called me that morning. He forgot to call me to let me know he made it home.

"I'm on the way. I should be there in about 45 minutes."

"Okay, I'll be ready."

I was half dressed. I saved my jacket for last. I wanted to take my time to put on my makeup without sweating from anxiety. I straightened up my place and put on Kirk Franklin low so I could still hear the phone. It was ringing.

"What is your apartment number?"

"23."

I was dressed I just had to put on my jacket and brush my hair. I was still rockin' my Pocahontas look. There was a knock at the door. When I opened the door, he looked surprised. I could tell he liked what he saw.

"I'm ready I just have to put on my jacket."

As I stood in the mirror by the door I brushed my hair one last time as he watched before placing it in my purse. *She is sexy. Look at her hair.*

"Do I look okay?" Knowing he was admiring me.

"Yes, boy do you!"

"Okay, I'm ready." I gave him a side glance and smiled.

I grabbed my bible, turned the stereo off and we headed out the door. He smelled so good. He had on some jeans, a nice button up shirt and a black leather jacket. I loved a man in a leather jacket. That was so sexy to me. He was sexy!

When we arrived at church I noticed he didn't have a bible. I didn't say anything I just made sure I persuaded him to follow along with the reading from my bible. I motioned him to look over as I held it for both of us to read.

I was nervous to be in church with him. When it was time for offering, we were directed to stand and bring it to the altar. I started to sweat. I didn't have an offering. He handed me a five-dollar bill and pulled out a hundred-dollar bill and dropped in the offering bucket.

After service was over Marquise wanted to introduce me to his Grandfather. He had already noticed me because he was actually walking towards us.

"Who is this beautiful lady?" He asked as he reached for my hand.

"Hello Darlin'. How are you?"

"Fine Sir. How are you?"

"Well I see you're fine. How do you two know each other?"

"She works in the same complex by my store." Marquise replied.

"I want to see you more often okay?

"Okay." I said with a smile.

"Marquise you better hold on to her."

We walked back towards our seat and my co-worker approached us. It was the guy in Customer Service that asked me to come over while he house sat for his brother.

"How you hook up with her?"

"What do you mean?" I interjected.

"You know my brother?" Marquise asked as he walked off.

"That's your brother?" We worked together at Publix." I added.

"Oh, okay."

Oh, lord! What is he going to tell Marquise? He better not lie...good thing I declined his invite. He was driving a F150. That must have been Marquise's truck he was flossing too. Yeah, he was not my type and he kept trying to get me to come with him for the weekend. I hope he wasn't offended. Looks like he may be now, seeing me with his brother. Next on the list was his aunts, he introduced me as they walked up.

"Ooh Marquise has a pretty girl in church. This is a first. He has never brought anyone to church. She must be special Marquise?" They said smiling.

I was flattered, and I think their comments embarrassed him. I thought it was cute.

"We hope to see more of you." They added.

That was his mom's sister and his uncle's wife. I didn't see his mom in church. We all headed out the door. Marquise drove me home. I thought he may have had something to do since he didn't ask if I wanted to grab something to eat. Oh, but he did just take me to dinner last night. Maybe he figured if I wanted to stop somewhere I would have asked him not insinuating for him to pay though. I didn't show any concern I just wanted to spend more time with him.

"Thank you for allowing me to come to church with you. I'll see you tomorrow hopefully."

"I'll give you a call later this evening."

"Okay, talk to you later then."

"Okay, bye."

I hated to walk to the door because I just knew he was watching me walk. When I got to the door I turned around just in case. *He wasn't even there!* I laughed to myself.

I took a shower, washed my face and got comfortable on my couch. I forget I still had two movies to watch. I rented LIFE with Eddie Murphy and Martin Lawrence. I had never gone to see it. That movie was so sad. *That could have been me, in jail for the rest of my life.* I began to cry with tears running down my face. Lord thank you Jesus for sparing my life. Thank you, Lord! Oh, God I screamed as I dropped to my knees. My heart was hurting with sorrow. I cried out to the Lord uncontrollably,

"Oh, thank you God! Thank you for saving me. Oh, Jesus Thank you! Thank you!"

I lay on the floor until I had no tears left to cry. I was all cried out and wanted to go to bed. I had given myself a headache. I got up off the floor, turned the TV off, and straightened my pillows on the couch. I grabbed my blanket and turned out the lights. I placed the cordless phone in the bed with me in case Marquise did call. I haven't felt like this in a long time. I could have still been in jail. That wasn't nothing but the Lord. The thought had not crossed my mind in a long time. I was always told once you repent you are forgiven and to forget about it. But how could I just forget? I never thought I could forget but I would always be thankful. Seeing where I could have still been, my circumstance could have ended another way. The ladies I met in the facilities are still there for the same crime I committed.

"If it wasn't for the blood of Jesus covering you, you could still be in jail. If it wasn't for the blood of Jesus covering you, you could have been dead from that gunshot..."
Creflo's voice came to mind... I knew that message was for me. I was saved by the blood of Jesus. I lay there and cried myself to sleep.

Hours later the phone rang...
"Hello?"
"Danielle?" It was Marquise.
"Hey Marquise."
"Where you sleeping."
"No, just lying here."
I didn't want him to feel he was interrupting me and tell me to go back to sleep. I wanted to talk to him to find out where his head was and how he felt about us attending to church together. He talked about his family's opinion of him bringing me to church. They felt that it said a lot for him to bring me to church. I was happy to hear that. We talked about a few other goals we had. I told him that I had started school across the street for Ultrasound and that I had one child who was eight years old living with my mom for the school year until I had settled in my routine. I also shared with him how I worked three jobs to be able to transfer to Atlanta.

Marquise shared his College experience stating that is was too much on him to work, go to school full-time, and take care of his family which consisted of his mother, brother, and sister coming to live with him out of state. I didn't understand what that was all about but I didn't want to pry. I let him know I understood his load and reasoning behind quitting. That is when he told me he had two girls age five and three. One by an encounter during Freak Nik! He didn't find out until months later that the girl was even pregnant. His youngest daughter was by a white girl. That didn't sit too well with me because that meant all women could be a threat not just the sistas'.

Freak Nik was the wild days in Atlanta a few years back. I remember coming up to hang out with my friend April for the weekend. Evelyn and Shonda had also come up. I left my husband that week for sure without any regards to how he felt for a wild weekend in Atlanta.

I had no comment to his story. I continued t0 listen and he hoped that I could meet them one day. We talked until 1 am. That was a good sign. We realized it was late and we both had to be up at six in the morning. I couldn't believe he hadn't wanted to hang up.

"Okay I'll talk to you tomorrow."

"Okay."

I waited for the phone to hang up. There was silence.

"Hello?"

"Yes." Marquise replied.

"I thought you were getting off the phone?"

"I was. I was just waiting for you to hang up."

"Oh okay. I was waiting on you to hang up."

We both laughed and said goodnight.

CHAPTER THIRTY-SIX

I did my usual spying out the window once I heard the bass hit the parking lot. My heart could just leap out of my chest as I watched Marquise like clockwork pull up, back into his same parking space, turn off his music, lean back in his seat and pile all his files and top out with his bag in his arms and walk into his store.

I noticed on the phone he had a cold and a stuffy nose. Said he felt like crap. I asked him if he had taken any medication for it and he said no. I made it my business to go into Walgreens and get him a cold and flu care package of medicine and I also ran to the mall once it opened and bought him a Ralph Lauren winter hat. Like a ski cap that fit snug over your head. It was smoke gray with the POLO logo in the front. I put all the medications inside the hat and left it for him at his store.

He surprised me that afternoon as he walked into my office wearing my gift.

"Hey Danielle." As he walked in.

"Come on through." I signaled.

Marquise opened the door and sat down at my desk. I noticed it was a much smaller space behind the door. There was only one patient left and the staff was cleaning up in the back.

"Ah, I see you got my care package. It looks nice. Make sure you wear it so you don't catch Pneumonia!"

"Yes, thank you."

"So, you have class tonight?"

"Yes sir."

"How are you getting home?"

"The bus as always."

"Well I'll pick you up."

"For real?"

"Yes. The forecast said it's supposed to snow so I don't want you to freeze on the way home." He warned.

"Serious, it snows here?"

"Yeah, just flurry's, they don't stick, but one year we had like two inches of snow. We hadn't had snow since."

"Oh okay, I get out of class at ten."

"Okay, I'll be there."

I was watching the clock during class. I didn't have any minutes on my phone and I didn't know if Marquise was trying to call me to say he wouldn't be able to pick me up. Once class was over I waited out front with the rest of my class mates waiting to be picked up. It was going on 10:30 and he was still not there. I was the only person left waiting. I hope he didn't forget. If he called I could hear the ring I just couldn't answer it. It hadn't rung.

I was disappointed, and then I became angry. It was going on eleven so I started walking to the bus stop. I waited on the curb just in case Marquise still showed up and I could still see the bus coming down the street. I started seeing little white pedals falling from the trees. When I looked up it was falling from the sky. Was that snow flurries? Oh, lord it was snowing just like he said. He really didn't come and pick me up. Just as my lips were about to touch the bus stop sign across the street I saw the lights of the bus coming down the street. Then I saw a black mustang coming out of the parking lot on my right. It was Marquise. I felt stupid for still being there waiting but the bus ran every hour so that was not my fault. I walked around and he reached over to push open the passenger door.

"I'm sorry. I fell asleep and didn't hear my alarm."

"Oh wow! I tried not to show I was pissed. I was thankful I didn't have to catch the bus."

"Are you cold?" He asked as he turned on the heat.

"I'm freezing! The bus doesn't run but every hour after ten."

"Do you mind if I crash on your couch. I don't think I can drive   all the way back home."

"Are you serious?"

"Yes, do you know what time it is woman?" Marquise said laughing.

Okay that broke the ice. I wasn't mad anymore. When we got to my apartment he had his bag and his clothes from the cleaners hanging in the back seat. *He was really planning on staying. What if I would have said no?*

Marquise watched my routine. I dropped my bags at the door, went into the bathroom to run the water for my bath. I hadn't bothered getting a shower liner since I liked taking baths instead of showers. I grabbed the blankets from the closet and placed them on the couch.

"I want you to get a good night's sleep. You can sleep in my bed and I will sleep on the couch." I insisted.

"I couldn't do that."

"No, I insist! You are my guest, and I appreciate you picking me up. Now go and get some sleep. The alarm is next to my bed, and there's a television in the too."

Marquise went into the bedroom and I closed the door. I had a one bedroom apartment and it was an open space with the kitchen off the living room. The bedroom was right across from the bathroom off the entrance way. I made it look as cute as possible with curtains and border mid wall level around the living room. I placed a tree in the corner next to the love seat with hung pictures of me and Nadia.

I hated the shag green carpet. I got used to it. I wouldn't dare walk barefoot in my apartment. I always wore socks. When I got out of the bath I made my way to the couch. I couldn't believe that gorgeous man was in the next room in my bed. I was so excited I wasn't sleepy, but I had soon drifted off before I knew it and I was awakened by that gorgeous man kissing me on my forehead. He was so black I couldn't see him so I just reached out to feel him.

"I can't sleep knowing you are out here on the couch. Come lay with me, I'll make sure I stay on my side of the bed."

"Okay." I agreed as I got up from the couch and walked in my room.

We both climbed into bed. I didn't know what to do with myself. Did I turn and face him or lay on my comfortable right side facing the door? I decided to lye facing him, but I still couldn't see him, dang he was really that black.

He pulled me by my waste, as he guided me to him I responded by tracing his silhouette with my fingertips, down his jaw bone to his lips. I gently brushed his lips with mine. Once our lips met he pulled me close and began to kiss me so passionately, I just fell right in with his rhythm. Ooh he was a good kisser. Good Lord you can always tell what kind of sex you will have by the intensity of a kiss. I loved to kiss and from what I saw so did he. I could feel his body against mine. I was so excited at the possibility of having this man to myself. His body was so thick, not fat and not skinny. Just right and solid. We kissed each other with so much passion making up for the sex we weren't going to have. If we did I would see rockets and fireworks. We then both realized it was way too soon for sex.

"We better get some sleep."

"Yes, I agree. We have an early day tomorrow."

I turned over on my right side facing the door. Marquise followed my body, scooped me close to him putting his arm around my waste. I thought that felt nice. Before we knew it, we were knocked out and morning came.

I woke up and like clockwork and got up and turned on Creflo. I placed a face towel for Marquise and put his toothbrush on the counter with toothpaste. I went back in my bedroom.

"Good morning...time to get up." I whispered.

"What time is it?" He asked as he rolled over.

"It's 6:15."

"Oh, okay"

"I put your bag in the bathroom, with a wash cloth."

I didn't tell him I put his toothbrush out for him. I had already washed my face and brushed my teeth so he could have the bathroom to himself. I would get dressed in the bedroom. When I came out Marquise was dressed tying his tie in the mirror. I admired him as he hooked up his tie. I made sure everything was in place, made my bed and we headed out the door.

As we pulled into the parking lot the first thing I thought about was who might see us riding together so early in the morning. Would they figure we spent the night together, even though we had? Oh well, we both got out of the car.

"Thank you for the ride."

"Thank you for letting me sleep in your bed."

We both laughed and went in separate directions.

CHAPTER THIRTY-SEVEN

I was enjoying Ultrasound school. So far so good, I made friends with my classmates quickly. Valentine's Day was approaching and I couldn't wait to see what Marquise had planned.

We had talked a few times this week, but hadn't spent much time together so I knew he would have something planned. When Valentine's Day came, it was just another day. No candy, no flowers, no call from Marquise at all. He was at work but didn't even come across to my office to say hello. I was so sad. I love Valentine's Day. I hoped he would at least call me once I got out of class. I felt bad I had to catch the bus home on Valentine's, while my classmates were talking about their after-class plans.

My sadness turned to upset when he never called at all. I didn't answer his call for a whole week after that. He had left so many messages I thought I'd better answer the next time he calls. When I finally answered, I tried not to seem upset, but did make it around to asking how he spent his day.

"Oh, I went and played basketball with my boys and then I took my mom out to Red Lobster."

I know he doesn't expect me to believe that crap!

"Your mom?"

"Yeah my dad passed away last year so I try to fill that void when she gets depressed."

"Oh, my goodness that is so sweet. I'm sorry to hear about your dad. Was he sick?"

"Yeah, I'll tell you about it one day."

"Ok. I would like that. Whenever you need to talk I'm here to listen."

"I appreciate that."

That softened me up to mush. *How could I be so selfish and inconsiderate?*

"What are you doing tomorrow after work?"

"Oh, the usual getting my movies."

"Well you want to come to my place and we can watch them together after I take you to dinner. I'll let you pick the movies."

"Okay but let me warn you I like white romantic comedy."

"That's not a problem. I like all kinds of movies." He laughed.

"Okay then I'll see you tomorrow." I replied.

"I will come over to the office once I'm finished at the store. I have a few errands to run and deposits to make."

"Okay, talk to you then."

"Okay Goodnight."

"Good night."

I didn't know if I would be spending the night or not. Should I pack a bag or should I just come as if I didn't have any intentions on staying over. I thought I would play it safe and wear something comfortable but cute to work instead of scrubs.

We left the office and went down 285. He lived three exits up, but then he got on another freeway that went a ways further until the exit to his house. The restaurant was actually around the corner. It seemed odd to have an Outback in this small plaza. He handed me one red rose from the back seat once we parked.

"Thank you, how sweet." I added as I smelled it.

We had more depth conversation over dinner. Marquise shared his family history with me, how he was raised and how his father passed. His life wasn't easy growing up that's for sure. I could see why he was so driven and compassionate about his family. We had total opposite lives. I was spoiled and we had plenty of money, and the only thing I remember about my father's habit was that he had a shot of Jack Daniels once he got home from work every day. That was the extent of his activities. I know now how blessed I was to have my father in my life now and growing up. I'm certain Marquise's father would be proud if he were still alive.

Dinner was great and I was stuffed. We pulled up to a huge gated community.

"This is where you live?" I asked in surprise.

"Yes!"

"These are so nice! So, when you pick me up and take me home you have to ride all the way back out here? No wonder why you didn't want to drive back home. I sure appreciate you picking me up when you did."

"No problem. I didn't mind."

We entered through the gate by waving some sort of card over a key pad. We drove down a long steep hill then around a stone wall and pulled up to a two-unit condo. I was impressed. I took in the surroundings as I got out of the car. I followed Marquise up the stairs, entering into a small ceramic tile foyer with a coat closet. You walk around a wall to the right to a huge living room with the dining area off the kitchen.

I could see myself in this place. Marquise settled out of his clothes while I made myself comfortable on the couch. It was dim, I could see the light over the stove. The phone rang. It was on the wall in the kitchen.

"Your phone is ringing." I yelled around the corner as I peeked in his bedroom.

"Can you get it for me?"

"Oh, okay." I replied.

I ran to catch it before it stopped ringing.

"Hello?"

"Hello? Can I speak to Marquise please?" A woman's voice sounded in my ear.

"Yes, one moment."

"Who is this?"

"This is Danielle."

"Oh, hi Danielle, this is Marquise's mother Randi. How are you doing sweetie?"

"Oh, just fine thank you."

"My son told me about you..."

"Oh okay, it's your mom." I said with a smile as Marquise walked up.

I continued to listen as he snatched the phone from my hand.

"What you talking about woman?" Marquise laughed as he teased his mother.

I went to sit on the floor as I pulled the DVD's out of the bag. *"Message in a Bottle" with Kevin Costner.* I loved him and I had been waiting to see this movie since I missed it at the theater. I didn't know what Marquise was going to say. He told me to get whatever I wanted. We settled in on the couch. I was on the slim side these days.

"Make yourself at home, anything here is yours. If the phone rings you can answer it."

"Okay." *Is he serious?*

He put the movie in and turned out all the lights and joined me on the couch. He lay behind me and placed his arm around my waist. Towards the end of the movie I heard someone putting a key in the door. *Who was that?* Marquise didn't move a muscle. He kept his arm around me.

"Black?" A voice sounded along with a guy coming around the corner from the foyer. He stopped in his tracks when he saw two bodies cuddled up on the couch.

"Black what's up man? What ya'll watching?"

"Message in a Bottle."

"I'm going to come back when my boy returns because I don't know you right now." They both laughed.

"This is Danielle man."

"Hey Danielle it's nice to meet you, and what have you done with my friend?"

"Nice to meet you too, I haven't done anything." I laughed.

"I'll check you out man. You two enjoy the rest of the movie."

That was sweet. When the movie was over Marquise asked if I was ready to go.

"I have to get up early for another Grand opening, but you're more than welcome to stay. I mean there's nothing at your house that's not here. I have food if you want to eat. You can sleep in and make yourself at home."

"Are you sure?"

"Of course, and I can take you home tomorrow or Sunday if you wanted to stay the weekend? I have some boxers and a t-shirt you can put on."

"It's supposed to rain, isn't it?"

"Most likely."

"Okay then I'll stay."

I got the t-shirt and boxers. I wanted to take a quick shower. I hadn't planned on giving up my cookies but I wanted it to be fresh in case he wanted to rub his fingers in the jar to see what they might taste like. I didn't know if he would even go that far, but you never know.

I took a shower in the hall bathroom, so he could take a shower in the bathroom in his bedroom. When I returned, Marquise was on the edge of his bed waiting for me. His bed was against the wall and he slept on the right side next to the nightstand. I climbed in on the other side which meant I would be facing the wall. When I turned on my side he immediately put his arm around my waist and scooped me into his arms. As we lay there together our bodies felt like the perfect fit.

Marquise kissed me on the side of my neck. That was all I needed. I reached back to touch his face with my hand and he directed my whole body to turn to him. We started kissing again with the same passion as our last encounter. I was soaking wet. I was on clouds again he kissed so good. All I could think about was being able to enjoy this man whenever I wanted. He felt so good and I felt him strong and hard against my thigh. I wanted to feel him inside me, but we had not even discussed having sex. It had only been two months. I had just been screened for HIV at the hospital clinic down the street from my apartments. The doctor stated that Aids testing were only for homosexuals and prostitutes. What an idiot! I'm not a prostitute but I had been surely active in my life. A physician should never discourage anyone from knowing their status.

I didn't know what to do. I didn't want to seem like a hoe

and give it up my cookies. I wanted to take this relationship slow and make no mistakes. He lifted up his t-shirt and began to kiss my breast. His mouth felt so soft against my nipples. I held his head with my hands as he enjoyed them both. We might as well have been having sex through our clothes. When I did get some, I knew it was going to be good. I didn't want him to stop but I didn't know how to tell him we needed to.

CHAPTER THIRTY-EIGHT

O ver the next four weeks I spent every weekend with Marquise. I would pack my bags on Friday and ride into work with him on Monday morning. We still hadn't had sex so we spent time getting to know each other in different ways.

I had filed my tax return and the first thing on my list was a car. I also made an appointment for my braces after talking to the hygienist about the health of my teeth. Those three weeks Marquise had taken me around to run all my errands. He took me to the grocery store. As we walked down the aisle a lady stopped and told us what a beautiful couple we made and asked how long we'd been married. We both looked at each other.

"Oh, we're not married!" We blurted.

"Well you make a lovely pair." She added.

We looked at each other and thought how ironic.

"We've only known each other what not even a full two months?"

"Well I guess that's a sign" He stated.

"A sign for what?"

"For us to get together and make plans to get married."

"Are you serious?"

"Hell, why not? I want a new relationship based on friendship without the sex. We already know that part will be good. I want the other part without the lust. My goal is to be married, buy a house and have a baby by my wife. I made GM in less than a year. I've been manager of the year three years in a row. You're in school. Once you complete that you'll have your ideal job making three times your salary now."

"True, true."

"So, let's get a house."

"Okay, if you say so?"

I had never thought about that, buying a house but I did know something about credit. I knew mine was bad. Marquise had made an appointment with a realtor that he met after church a few weeks ago.

My car was still at the Ford place. I had no way to pay for it to be fixed and I was not even trying to get it out. I had made friends with one of the salesman. I contacted him to assist me in finding me a finance company that would finance a loan for a new car.

"I found a company to finance you. Why don't you come on down and see what we can find you?"

"Serious? Oh, great I'll be on my way around lunch time."

Of course, Ken was waiting to drop me off. When I got there, he pulled my credit report. Good this is just what I needed to show Marquise what I had to work on. When the salesman took me outside to look for a car, we passed all the good cars and went to the last lot in the back where all the old used cars were. My smile quickly turned to a frown.

"Can I at least get a cute used car?"

"Sorry sweetheart I'm trying to get you financed. This will help boost your credit score and if you pay on time you can always come back and trade it in for something you like. You got to crawl before you can walk babe." He added.

We walked up to a white Ford Contour.

"Are you serious? This is so ugly! Do I have to get this one?"

"This is the best car out here, low miles, clean interior, and one owner. You're not going to be in it forever. We'll do a loan for 18 months and you can trade it in."

"18 months that's a whole year and half of another one!"

"Trust me darling. You won't be in it long and you come back here and get you anything on this lot. I promise you."

I reluctantly signed the loan papers. The only good thing was the 18 months. That should go by fast. Once I paid it off it would make my credit score go up and I could trade it in. I got the keys and was on my way back to work. I definitely didn't want to show Marquise, but oh well I had my own transportation. No more catching the bus and I could leave right after class and not have to wait for a ride.

The next day I walked over to Marquise's store to let him know I would be leaving work early to my Orthodontist appointment, I would be getting my braces. When I walked up to the counter he handed me a key.

"This is for you." He stated.

"What is this for?" I asked.

"I asked my mom to come over so she could take care of you. Your mouth is going to be real sore so I got you some cans of soup and Motrin."

"Are you for real? Your mom is at your house?"

"Yes, just let yourself in and if you need anything she'll be there to take care of you."

"That is so sweet. What if she be like I don't know you?"

"My mom is cool. I told her all about you."

"You did, well what did you say?"

"You don't need to know everything woman! You'll be fine. Just go over there and chill."

"Okay, just let her know I'll be there around three."

"Okay I should be there around six."

"I'll be waiting. Thank you, Marquise."

"You're more than welcome."

I couldn't believe it over the past few weeks I had been spending a lot of time with Marquise. Now I was meeting his mother. Boy he was right. I was so excited to get my braces, until the pain actually set in.

I pulled up in front of the Condo. I was a bit nervous knowing that once I turned that key his mother would be on the other side of the door.

Randi had dozed off on the couch watching General Hospital. She heard the key slide into the lock and the deadbolt turn. That must be Marquise's girlfriend. She got up off the couch to walk towards the foyer.

"Hello..." I yelled in hopes not to startle his mother. As I turned the corner Marquise's mom was there to greet me.

"You must be Danielle? I'm Randi Marquise's mother." I extended my hand, oh baby we hug in my family. She pulled me in to give me a hug.

"How are you feeling baby?"

"I have a headache my mouth hurts so bad."

"Well make yourself at home. Go lie down if you need to, do you have some aspirin? I believe Marquise bought you some Motrin. My son likes you. He bought you some soup and juice and told me to warm it up for you if you wanted something."

"Okay." I chuckled.

"I think I'm going to take some Motrin and try to take a nap. Marquise said he should be home by six."

"Oh, he called and said he was going to get off early so he could come home."

"Oh okay." I said with a smile.

Marquise came home early alright. When he walked up to the stairs his mom was smoking a cigarette.

"Your princess is taking a nap. She's seems to be a sweet girl. She said her mouth was sore and she had a headache. I gave her the Motrin's and told her to make herself at home. She has been in there sleeping for over an hour in your bed."

"Ok, thanks."

Marquise headed up the stairs anxious to see Danielle asleep in his bed. There she was sleeping peacefully. He didn't want to wake me up so he got undressed and took a shower in the hall bathroom. Once he got out he went to lie on the couch and visit with his mom.

I laid down in hopes to avoid the pain. When I woke up it was after six. I was wondering if Marquise had made it home. The bedroom door was closed. I got up and washed my face. My mouth was so sore. I kept a cold wash cloth on my mouth and walked into the living room. Marquise was actually on the couch asleep. His mother must have gone outside. I kneeled down beside him and lightly kissed the side of his face. That even hurt. That woke him up.

"Hey, how's your mouth?"

"Sore." I said through the wash cloth.

"Let me see."

I removed the wash cloth to show him my tracks.

"Oh wow, you look cute with braces."

"No I don't. I think it makes my mouth look bigger now and I can barely close my lips."
I placed the wash cloth back over my mouth. I have to do my homework.

"Are you hungry?"

"I am starving, but sorry I don't want any soup I want some food."

"My mom fried some chicken, mashed potatoes and corn." He laughed.
I couldn't resist the thought. I may be able to nibble. He fixed me a small plate. My mouth was so sore.

"It feels like my teeth are going to fall out of my mouth if I take another bite."
Knowing that made me even hungrier.

"Would you liked me to fix you some soup?" He asked with a smile.

"Yes, please."

CHAPTER THIRTY-NINE

That next week was Marquise's birthday. I hadn't been home all week. I would just go straight to Marquise's after class. I hated to come in so late and disturb him but he insisted I come. We still hadn't had sex, almost 90 days' shy of three weeks. We pacified each other with our kisses and spooning, agreeing with one another that we wanted to build this relationship on a friendship.

Marquise had a dual alarm clock. His set for six and mine set for seven. I hopped in the shower quietly and slipped into my side of the bed trying not to wake him, but he always turns over, puts his hand around my waist and scoops me up under him without saying a word and we fall fast asleep.

I had planned a family get together with his mom. I wanted to surprise him with a huge cake with his picture on it. He would be turning twenty-five and I would be turning thirty a few months after. I had to make sure the ladies in the bakery didn't spill the beans about his cake. I didn't know if they knew I had snagged him, so I had to let that be known. Everybody loved Marquise. My old coworkers loved me being with Brandon too, but that was no more. Marquise was sent to take his place.

After work I went down to the Underground to do a little shopping for some gifts for Marquise. I wanted to go to Foot Locker and get him whatever new tennis shoes were out. I knew nothing about sports. I just knew he loved to play basketball, and whatever player was hot he would have the newest Nike shoe out.

I placed the shoes with a matching shirt under the bed in the shoe box, and I bought Marquise three bottles of cologne, Kenneth Cole, Armani, and Calvin Klein. I placed them on his dresser that night while he was asleep with his birthday card. That morning I watched him get dressed and he instantly noticed the bottles on the dresser.

"Happy Birthday Baby!" *I was still not comfortable with pet names but I was forcing myself to say them.*

"Three bottles damn, thank you baby!"

His favorite ended up being the Armani. I acted as if I had misplaced one of my K-Swiss under the bed.

"Baby can you look under the bed to see if my shoe is under there."

He pulled out a gift-wrapped box. He looked back at me and smiled. He ripped the paper off and saw the shoe box. He held up the shoes and laid out the shirt.

"These fire baby! Thank you, but you didn't have to do all this. It's just a birthday."

"Your birthday is the most important day of the year, besides Christmas and Easter." I laughed.

I got on my knees and put my arms around his neck and gave him a big kiss.

234

"Happy Birthday baby!"

That afternoon I tried to beat Marquise to the Condo so I could hide his cake. I rang the doorbell. My hands were full. His mother opened the door.

"Hey baby!"

"Hey, wait until you see this cake."

I hadn't told anyone about the cake. I set the cake on the table and opened the box for Randi to see.

"That's bad! I ain't never seen no shit like that. Marquise is going to trip the fuck out!"

I smiled in agreement.

Marquise came home early with a Bar BQ grill that needed assembling. He loved his cake. That was also his first time seeing a picture on a cake. His family started showing up that evening. Everyone was engaged. The food was on the grill. His brother and his mom were handling that. We made our way to the bedroom to get cleaned up. I got in the shower first, after I lathered my body I was washing my face and felt a breeze of cold air. Marquise had opened the shower door. I was startled as I felt his skin against mine as he grabbed my waist. I turned around wiping the water from my eyes. He grabbed me in his arms and started kissing me.

"Can I make love to you?" He whispered as he kissed my neck down to my breast.

"I thought we were going to wait?" I whispered as I rubbed his head.

"I can't. Please I need you."

I kissed Marquise back and led him between my legs. He grabbed my ass and lifted me up against the shower wall. *Oh, shit he's strong.* I wrapped my legs around him as he thrust his dick inside me. The water sprayed over our bodies. I couldn't believe he actually picked me up, controlling every movement of our bodies and his dick was big, fitting me better than a glove. I was sliding from the water. I turned the shower off and Marquise carried me out of the shower onto the bathroom counter between his and her sinks. He put my legs on his shoulders. He had a clear runway to the bottom of my stomach. He was pounding at my wet walls. It felt so good and hurt at the same time.

"Am I hurting you?" He whispered as he kissed my neck.

"Yes, but it feels good."

"I'm sorry baby..."

"No, no don't stop its okay."

When I said that he squeezed my whole body tight, it was as if he released all the love he had built up for me in those past two months.

We returned to the party fully dressed. They had started a spades game. It was really nice. The food was good and everyone was enjoying themselves. His brother was there with his wife and children. He ended up being a nice guy, still no comparison to his brother. I met his sister. She brought the alcohol and before the night was over everyone had a red cup but me. I had actually made my spot on the floor lying on Randi's lap. She was really sweet to me and treated me like her daughter. They were fired up on that card table. They even convinced Marquise to have a drink for his birthday. His sister poured him his third cup of gin.

"This one's for you baby!" He said as he tilted his glass in my direction.

His cousin was drunk and somehow ended up in Marquise's bed hanging over the edge directly over my K-Swiss tennis shoe where he had conveniently thrown up in! The party was definitely over. Happy Birthday Black!

CHAPTER FOURTY

We were starting labs in my class two nights per week. I was excited. This was the introduction to hands on with the ultrasound machine. This was the fourth month into the semester. Labs would consist of ultrasounds that we would perform on each other.

We were told to get in groups of five and the instructor would demonstrate the ultrasound procedures, all the evaluating measurements and different organs. I was asked to be the first gunny pig, but I didn't mind. I lay on the table and the instructor applied gel just as they do at the doctor's office. She started to examine different organs. I watched the screen as the instructor toured my uterus. As the screen clearly showed my empty uterus there was a little pea shape in the corner. It took my instructor by surprise.

"What's that circle over there?" my class mate blurted out.

"I'm not a doctor but I've seen plenty of ultrasounds to know you need to make a trip to your OBGYN." The instructor replied

"Why? Am I pregnant?"

Oh, my goodness! I hadn't kept up with my cycle. I was so surprised. It hadn't even been two months. His birthday! Oh snap. That was the only time we had sex, and we haven't had sex since.

"Did you know you were pregnant?"

"No, we've only had sex one time on his birthday."

"Well happy birthday!" They teased.

I was real cool with my classmates. Everyone knew my relationship was new and they listened to my updates as we spent more time together.

Marquise was spending the night over at my place this time. I made my way to my apartment. I put my key in the door I was happy to see him on the couch eating a bowl of cereal.

"Hey baby!"

"Hey, how was class?"

"Very interesting."

Let me go get in the tub. I walked in the bathroom to run my water, but before I flicked on the light switch I saw candle light flickering from behind the shower curtain. I pulled back the curtain and saw my bath already drawn with plenty of bubbles. I walked back into the living room over to Marquise with a smile.

"Thank you, that was so sweet." I said as I kissed him.

There was a knock at the door. I had an iron screen as well. The knock actually scared me. I looked at the time. Who could that be this time of night? I hesitantly opened the door. It was Brandon. What in the world? He has never been over here since our Kings of Comedy date. Wouldn't you know? Negros always a day late and a dollar short.

"What's up"

"What's up?" He replied as he peaked around my

shoulder and saw Marquise on the couch with the bowl of cereal up to his mouth.

"Oh, my bad, I see you have company."

"Yeah."

He walked off without saying another word. I slowly closed the door not really wanting to turn around to see Marquise expression.

"Who was that?"

"Oh, my ex, he lives in the next building. He has never come over here before since we broke up last year. He must have smelled you." Marquise just laughed.

That next day I called Chanel from my desk.

"Are you sure you're pregnant?"

"Well yeah aside from what my instructor saw. I haven't had a period since before Marquise's birthday."

"There's a Planned Parenthood on Roswell Road, go there and make sure you let me know what they say mama."

"Okay, I'll call you when I get back."

I was so scared. I went after work instead of on my lunch. We closed at four. I rode down Roswell Road searching for the famous clinic. There it was. I pulled into the parking lot and sat there for a moment hoping no one would see me.

CHAPTER FOURTY-ONE

I waited in the room shaking my leg from nervousness.

"Well Ms. Manning your test was positive"

"Really?"

"Yes, it was."

Here we like to have you speak to a counselor and have prayer and give you information of any support systems you may need.

"Would that be something you're interested in doing?"

"Yes, ma'am, sure."

She took me into another room and introduced me to a counselor and she gave me a book about Jesus Christ. I thought that was a bit forward, although I was a Christian. I listened and received the prayer and thanked them politely as I could before I left.

When I made it to my car I sat there for a few seconds before I rushed to Walgreens where Chanel worked. I shared the news.

"Girl, I'm glad it's you and not me. Now you gonna be having to buy diapers, formula and bottles, girl." She laughed.

Chanel was running the list down in her New York

accent. I was more concerned with how Marquise was going to react. I went looking down the aisle for baby items. I picked up a cute silver rattle and a card to give to Marquise as a way to break the ice. I showed Chanel.

"That is so cute, girl. Tell me what he says."

When I arrived to Marquise's I placed the box and card on his dresser. I chilled on the couch waiting to hear that bass as he pulled up. It was very distinctive. The door shut and his body appeared.

"Hey baby."

"Hey! How was your day?"

"Great! How was yours?" He replied as he untied his tie.

"Oh, I think it was good."

"You think? What happened" He asked as he took his shirt off heading into the bedroom.

I got up off the couch and followed him into the room. I lay across the bed and waited for Marquise to notice the box on the dresser. He got in the shower and never even noticed it. I kept quiet wondering what was going on inside of my body at this point. When Marquise returned to the side of the bed, he reached for the lotion which was on the side of the box, where I had conveniently placed it so he couldn't help but notice. The suspense was killing me.

"What's this?"

Marquise opened the card first. It read...

"A precious new baby will come from above, to live in your hearts and fill them with love..." Congratulations!

Marquise looked at me and smiled as he opened the box and saw the little silver rattle.

"You pregnant woman?" He asked with a smirk.

"Yes, are you mad?"

"No, of course not. You know we got to get married now right?"

I gave him a puzzled look.

"My aunt ain't gonna go for me having another baby out of wedlock." He said with a big laugh.

"Oh!" I said with a laugh.

"We were planning to do it anyway. Pay your rent next month and turn in your 30-day notice. If we are still getting along great you can move in and we can get married on your birthday."

"Are you serious?"

"Yes!"

"Okay!" I agreed.

CHAPTER FOURTY-TWO

I t was my birthday month. I turned in my notice when I paid my rent. Everything seemed to be going well. I couldn't keep my eyes open and I started eating everything in sight. Class wasn't going as planned. I was flunking Physics. My birthday was in less than 20 days away, but no mention of getting married.

We went to our first Dr.'s appointment. I spoke with the doctor privately before inviting Marquise into the office. I never discussed my past with Marquise and we actually never had any personal conversations about anything else. I had not shared being married or divorced or even the fact of how many abortions I had had or my miscarriage. We hadn't even talked about all my drama and abuse I suffered.

Marquise joined us in the office. He answered all the questions concerning my pregnancy, my last menstrual cycle, how long they usually last, how frequent I had been going to the bathroom.

"Has she experienced any nausea or fatigue?"

"Yes, fatigue not sure of any nausea."

"No, no nausea." I answered.

The Physician was impressed at Marquise's responses as well as me. So, he has been paying attention. When the appointment was over we went to have lunch at Applebee's. This was my favorite place to eat right about now.

Once I moved in we combined checking accounts. We had met with a realtor and advised us both of our chances of purchasing a home. Marquise having a better chance than me, my credit was shot, and at least now he knew. My credit needed a little work. We decided to sign another lease at the Condo and work on my credit.

My birthday was soon approaching. No word of a party or surprise wedding so far. I met up with his mom and aunt to pick up his sister from work. She worked at Marshall's. We all decided to go get our nails done. I also needed a pedicure.

"So, do you think you guys will be ready by next month?" Marquise's aunt asked.

"So far so good, I don't think we will be getting married on my birthday like he said at first."

"Well he needs to marry you and settle down. He can't keep having babies and not get married." She replied.

"I already know you're my daughter in law. Anytime my son pimp me to take care of a female I don't know, you're the one!" His mom laughed.
I laughed at the thought when we met.

"Yes, thank you for that, I was flattered. Speak of the devil." I said as my phone rang.

"Hey."

"Hey" I replied.

"Where are you?"

"With your mom and your Aunt getting our nails done,

waiting on your sister to get off work."

"For real?" He asked surprised.

"Yes, sir."

"Don't listen to nothing my mama say about me unless it's something good!" He laughed.

"They are really sweet. I'm getting hungry though, are you off work?"

"Yes! Where are you guys going after you leave the nail salon?"

"I don't know. Marquise wants to know where we going when we leave here."

"Tell Marquise he can come to the house because I need to start my dinner for my husband for after church tomorrow."

"Your aunt says meet us over her house."

"Okay, I'm going to jump in the shower then I'll be over there."

"Okay baby see you then. Hey, have you eaten?"

"Yeah, I had a couple roast beef sandwiches."

"Okay."

I wasn't really worried if he had eaten I just wanted to know where we going to go out to eat. I need something to eat now and later.

Once Marquise mentioned marriage I spent a day to myself going to different Bridal Shops. I ended up at David's Bridal off of Roswell Road. I found the perfect dress, but I didn't even know why I was there. I couldn't really imagine being married. Something would go wrong, it always did. Everyone in the store thought I looked so beautiful in my dress. It was so real that the possibility of actually getting married didn't fit. I admired myself in the mirror and how beautiful I looked. Then left feeling more depressed. Things seemed different. He hadn't mention getting married on my birthday and I didn't want to ask.

I couldn't have been any more than eight weeks. Had I gotten that big all ready? I didn't have anything to wear to church. I had planned on wearing my favorite sage suit I wore on our first date to church.

"Can you help me zip my skirt?"

"Sure baby. It won't zip. It's too small."

"I've gained that much weight?"

"Looks that way."

The jacket even felt two sizes too small.

"I'll be right back. I have to run to Target to find something quick."

"Just wear something else."

"I don't have anything else to wear if that doesn't fit. I'll just grab an extra larger skirt outfit."

There he was trying to sound cheap. He had not shown me any compassion since I became pregnant. We had not even had sex. He never offered to bring me breakfast in the morning and I was always starving. When I asked him he said it would be stealing from the company. I thought of all that food you must throw away when breakfast is over. I couldn't stand the smell of his clothes when he came home. It made me nauseous. I always craved McDonalds and there was not one on the way to work anywhere.

When I got to Target I tried to hurry but nothing fit. *Oh my gosh are you serious?* I hadn't noticed since all I wore was scrubs every day. I finally found an outfit in the maternity section, of course. I was in denial! I put it on and put the tags in my hand and handed them to the cashier. I had tried to make it back as fast as I could. When I pulled up Marquise already had the car running.

"We're late." He replied as he came down the stairs and unlocked my door.

"I'm sorry." I apologized as I hopped in the car.

That day still no mention of getting married. *What happened in these few weeks?*

On my birthday, there was a card left under the door at the office when I returned from lunch. I picked it up as I unlocked the door opening the office back up. I sat at my desk and opened the card.

May this be a very special day for a very special friend, Happy Birthday- Brandon

I could not believe he remembered. My heart fell to my stomach. Now he wants to be nice. I hadn't told him about the pregnancy. When I got home I tossed the card on the dresser just to show Marquise I was still being thought of by my ex.

"Oh, he got you a card?"

"Yeah it was under the door at my office."

"Oh, that was cool I guess?"

"Whatever." I replied acting nonchalant. Knowing it made me feel good.

That weekend Marquise took me to the outlets to let me pick out whatever I wanted for my birthday. We ended up at the mall it was so hot at the outlets that was a bad idea. I still was in denial and refused to wear maternity clothes. Marquise had a Lane Bryant account and ask me to find something in there. That was a good idea. I ended up getting five dresses. We went into Macy's and I got a watch and a foot massager and two pair of comfortable shoes.

We returned home with a bunch of bags, tired feet and I was hungry again. Marquise didn't eat much and he didn't like spending money to eat out. That was one thing that started to be a problem. I was always craving different things all day long and I spent all my money on fast foods.

"Where my gift?" Randi asked as we walked in.

"It's her birthday."

"Oh, happy birthday then."

"Thank you."

I felt bad the way Marquise replied to Randi. We hadn't been on good terms either. I know it was the pregnancy. Everything got on my nerves and I stayed hella grumpy I admit. I took all the bags to the bedroom. I couldn't wait to try my massager. My feet were on fire. He filled it up with water as I got comfortable and soaked my feet. Marquise had put some bubble bath in the water not knowing the bubbles would run out everywhere! We laughed

"Oh my gosh! Stop, Stop! The floor is going to be soaked. You need bath salts baby not soap."

"Oh!" Marquise laughed and emptied the water out into the shower. He put oil in the water instead. That was a nice touch.

"Thank you, that feels good."

Later that night we got dressed to go out to dinner to top off my birthday! The strangest thing happened over dinner as we sat face to face. We had no conversation. The restaurant was rather empty and I hadn't even heard of this particular restaurant before. This was not the evening topper. Marquise didn't order anything to eat. I couldn't even think of anything to talk about. We sat face to face with nothing to say to each other. Maybe the day's event of spending money had Marquise over whelmed. He didn't like spending money, but it was my birthday.

"So, my birthday has come and gone. We haven't talked about getting married any more. Have you changed your mind?"

"Not exactly I just want to see how things progress over the next few months."

"Progress, that doesn't sound too good."

"Well you know it's a few things to consider now."

Oh okay." I replied. *Whatever that meant, he had changed his mind.*

CHAPTER FOURTY-THREE

Things got kind of routine for me and Marquise. I wrote out all the checks from the check book from his account. He bought groceries for the house. He never asked me to contribute or pay anything. It never dawned on me to ask if he wanted to go over a budget and assign certain bills for us to cover separately. I was secretly trying to pay off my credit and with my eating ten times a day I was broke.

I was too embarrassed to discuss it with him. I am guilty of not totally opening up to Marquise. I still had my pre-paid phone because my credit was too bad for a contract.

I was added on his car insurance policy to lower his rate. Either one of us smoked, that gave an additional discount. The morning comments started as I got dressed and put on my MAC makeup.

"Why do you put that stuff on your face? It makes you ugly."

What did he just say to me? It makes me ugly? I was pretty enough to attract you, but now I'm ugly? He also started talking about my tresses and me getting my nails done. What the hell is going on here?

"You shouldn't put fake hair in and you should just get a manicure and look more natural with clear polish."
What? I guess the pregnancy was affecting him too because I was starting not to like him right about now and he was showing the feelings were mutual. We still hadn't had sex. Where they do that at? I thought all men like pregnant pussy! He is trippin'.

I went to get my nails done after work. They were taking forever. I had them remove the acrylic and put on a gel over lay on my own nails which were pretty long now. I wanted to call Marquise to tell him where I was but I didn't have any minutes on my phone. If I called, he wouldn't be able to call me back. Marquise arrived home and his mom was sitting on the stairs smoking a cigarette.

"Hey son, how was your day?"

"Oh, my day was great."

"Did you get to see Danielle today at all while you were at work?"

"Not really. I guess I could have walked over but we were so busy I didn't bother."

"You think she's the one huh son?"

"I did. I'm not sure now."

"I see I haven't heard about any more wedding plans. You change your mind?"

"No not really. Just may need a little more time."
Marquise checked his phone, no missed call. It was almost six. He checked his phone a few more times, still no call.

"What's the matter son?"

"Nothing."

Randi knew he was wondering where I was. I hadn't called and I'm usually home before six. Marquise went outside to clean his car. He took it over the hill to wash it. When he returned, he ran up the stairs he had left his cell phone on the couch.

"It hadn't rung son. You talk to Danielle at all today?"

"No."

"Did you call her?"

"No, she probably had some errands to run."

Marquise didn't know what to ask if he were to call me. *Where you at woman? You were supposed to be home hours ago, He didn't want to say anything.* I pulled up and Marquise was cleaning out his car.

"Hey." I stated as I walked over to him.

"Hey."

"What are you doing cleaning your car?"

"Yeah."

He stood up and I leaned against him to give him a hug, letting my stomach be the first to make contact.

"I've never seen you clean your car out, are you okay?"

"Yeah."

"Well I'm not."

"What's wrong?"

"I'm scared."

"Scared of what?"

"I see what's happening. We are not getting along anymore, and I know I'm going to end up raising this baby by myself."

"Give it to me."

"What do you mean? I'm not going to just give you my baby. What about me, that is so mean!"

"No, it's not I've always wanted all my kids with me."

"Well I don't think this is how to go about it. Let me go change my clothes. I'll be right back. Your mom home?"

I peeked my head into the living room to speak to Randi.

"Where you been?"

"Oh, I went to get my nails done. Marquise said he didn't like fake nails so I had them put gel on my real nails. Why what's wrong?"

"He got his nerve. They look nice though, nothing's wrong I just know my son couldn't sit still wondering where you were. I can tell you make him happy." She said with a smile.

"Oh, that's good to hear, but I don't think that's the case now. He hasn't talked much lately. I was beginning to wonder if he was having second thoughts. I'm so scared I'm going to end up raising this baby by myself." Marquise walked through the door.

"Everything okay?"

"Yeah, everything is fine. I went to get my nails done. Is this natural enough?"

"Yes, those look nice are those your own nails?"

"Yes, the just have gel over them so they don't break or chip. When you're pregnant your hair and your nails grow you know."

"No I didn't know that. They look nice. Now you don't have to waste money getting them done."

I could feel myself compromising a few things for Marquise. The nails I could deal with but the hair and makeup now that was just ridiculous. Now he had me feeling self-conscious every time I wore makeup and did my hair. No tresses are you kidding me. His mom came and never left. I loved her but with this pregnancy I wasn't feeling her at this point. She was the free-spirited type, no rules no bars! No worries. She started having male company over which meant I had to be fully dressed every time I came out of the room because they were camped out in the living room. I started to feel smothered, coming home to that condo just made me sick, but I didn't have anywhere else to go. I gave up my apartment and I should have listened to my brother and kept it until we got married.

The next day I received a call from Brandon at my office. I was surprised to hear his voice sound in my ear.

"How are you doing?"

"I'm doing okay."

"I miss you."

"You do?"

"Yes, I do. Something wrong with that?"

"Well, I don't know. I haven't seen or heard from you in months."

"Well the last time I came over to the apartment you had some nigga sitting on your couch with a bowl in his hand."

"Well you never bothered to ask me for my number, so sorry for the inconvenience! Oh, and on another note, I'm pregnant!"

"I hadn't planned on having any more kids."

"What do you mean? It's not yours!

"Are you sure?"

"Um yes I think I would know that. I'm like three and a half months. You do the math!"

"So how are you feeling?"

"I feel okay, a bit over whelmed these days. I moved out of the apartment and moved in with Marquise."

"Marquise? The manager dude from the restaurant across from your office?"

"Yes, that would be the one."

"Oh wow. So, you sure you are doing okay?"

"Yes, I'm fine just hungry all the time."

"Why don't you come over after work and let me cook you dinner."

"Are you for real?"

"Yes, I miss you and I want to see you."

"Okay."

"Call me when you're on your way and I will give you directions to my new spot."

"Okay."

I was ready to get away for a few hours, anything better than going home to the Condo, of course I had to call Chanel to let her know my plans for the evening. I had needed to talk to her any way about the way I've been feeling. I don't know what is happening? Or do I with these darn hormones and this pregnancy. I was feeling so confined.

It had begun to rain on my way to Brandon's or was it my tears I wouldn't let fall. I had Marquise's second phone. He let me use it so I didn't have to waste time adding minutes to my prepaid. Marquise had called twice already. I didn't want to answer and answer any questions he might be asking. I just wanted a few hours of peace. I looked at the phone and turned it off.

It was raining even harder and Brandon was waiting in the breeze way for me to pull up. He walked to my car with an umbrella. I grabbed my purse as he opened my door.

"Hey."

"Hey." I replied.

He invited me in. I looked around admiring his new place. It was much nicer than the apartments we used to live in.

"Make yourself at home. Do you mind spaghetti and garlic bread? I have cheese."

"Okay that will be fine thank you."

"So how do you really feel? I could hear in your voice something was bothering you."

I feel smothered and we really don't talk much. He is like a robot. He is respectful but he is not affectionate, compassionate, or anything. We haven't had sex since I've been pregnant, well maybe once or twice and he doesn't like to kiss. I'm dying over there! His mom is staying over there too. It's all just driving me crazy. I know it's my hormones but it's too much. I already feel I'm going to end up raising this baby by myself cause he is going to hate me by the time this is over. He's called me twice already and I just turned the phone off. I don't feel like being bothered, and I know that ain't right. I'm always tired in the morning and starving all day. I was standing in the door way of the kitchen while Brandon was preparing our dinner.

"Go relax, you need to put your feet up and try not to think about anything."

He went to his room to grab a pillow and led me by the hand back to the couch and propped my feet up. Relax and chill until the spaghetti is done. He handed me the remote to the television. I was relaxed now. My mind was free of the thoughts that were pounding my head about Marquise. We enjoyed dinner, more conversation and the sound of the rain that turned into a thunder storm.

"You know I can't let you go out in that weather. You can stay here with me tonight can't you?"

"Yes, I'd love too."

I didn't give it any thought. I took a shower and climbed right in the bed next to Brandon. I lie on his chest, as a tear fell from my eye he rubbed my baby bump and wrapped his arms around me giving me a kiss on the forehead just like he used to do. I looked up at Brandon as our lips met we invited the most passionate kiss you could ever imagine. We missed each other, but we knew we could not go back to that place. Just for the night we didn't mind. We lay in the comfort of each other's arms letting tomorrow worry about itself.

"Everything will be alright, you'll see."

CHAPTER FOURTY-FOUR

That next morning I woke up, we got dressed and headed out of the apartment going our separate ways. I went home to catch my breath before going into the office. I called Marquise once I got to the Condo to let him know I was home. I hadn't bothered to explain where I had been.

"Are you coming into work?"

"Yes, I'm getting dressed now."

"Okay."

"Okay, see you in a minute." I replied as I pushed the talk button as I held the phone in my hand pressed up to my chin.

The office was closed for the day but I had reports to run and deposits to make. Marquise came through the door.

"Hey." I greeted as he walked up to my desk.

"So you decided not to come home last night?"

"No, I actually fell asleep at Christy's."

"Sure you did."

"What you don't believe me?"

"No."

"Why not? Where else would I be? I didn't know it mattered if I came home or not?"

"Well now it doesn't."

"What do you mean by that?"

"Just what I said, nothing from this point matters to me. My feelings are out of it."

"What do you mean your feelings are out of it? It seemed to me your feelings were out weeks ago. You haven't even touched me since I've been pregnant."

"Like I said."

I got up from my desk and walked into the lobby to look at Marquise in the eyes.

"So, what are you saying?"

"I said it, nothing you do matters anymore. I'm not putting anything into this relationship. You haven't even apologized for not coming home and you didn't call me. I called my damn cell phone about a hundred times thinking something had happened to you in the rain. I drove up and down 75 crying making sure you weren't stuck on the side of the road or in an accident."

"I had no idea you cared that much about me. I am sorry if I hurt your feelings by not coming home. You never ask how I'm feeling. You never even offer me breakfast from your store, hell we haven't even had sex since I started showing, but you say you were concerned when I didn't come home. I didn't even think you cared.

I just needed some space."

"Well now you have it, take all the space you need I'm done."

He walked out of the office not saying another word. Damn, I really didn't know he cared that much. He never touched me, or kissed me. Marquise would sleep with his arm around my stomach but that was all. All these thoughts started running through my head. I've fucked up my relationship and now he is going to make me pay for it. Shit!

I stood there in shock. *He might as well have slapped me in the face. Damn! I am always able to talk my way out of situations but this one was not happening. Damn robot! That's just what he acts like a robot with no emotion. Ever since I started showing we haven't even had sex. What was that all about? But you say you crying driving up and down the freeway. My shock became shitty. I may be wrong but if you didn't see me then it wasn't me.*

I knew exactly where I was going after work. Straight to Chanel's to digest what really just happened.

CHAPTER FOURTY-FIVE

Things remained the same between Marquise and I. He expressed to me again how he searched for me in the rain. Praying to God I was okay. I didn't know what to say.

"I understand what you're saying but the issue is what led up to me needing space."

"What can I do to understand how you are feeling?"

"Communicate. Ask me. You never ask me anything. I'm always hungry in the morning and you never even send anyone over with breakfast for me from your store. There are a lot of emotions that come along with a pregnancy and if you are not compassionate about understanding how I feel that just makes me a pregnant woman bitter!"

He didn't get it though. He had already checked out emotionally and there was no checking back in. I came home after work and Marquise mom was sitting on the steps. I spoke as always but this time I was too tired to sit with her and chat. When I went inside Marquise had met me in the foyer.

"You have a long day?"

"Yes."

He was kind of blocking me from walking in the bedroom.

"I have company over."

"Okay."

I looked at him strange and walked around him. When I walked into the room there was. There was a light skinned chic sitting at the edge of the bed.

"Excuse me, what the hell are you doing in my room and sitting on my bed?"

She looked at my stomach in plain view.

"Can you get the fuck out of my room! What the hell? Marquise you have lost your damn mind!" I stated has I through my bag on the bed and kept walking into the bathroom."

They both headed to the front door and I followed them out the door screaming to the top of my lungs,

"You might as well go with that bitch cause your ass ain't coming back in here!"

Soon as I got those words out Marquise turned to run up the stairs to the door and I slammed it just in time and locked it. My heart was racing. I couldn't believe it. *Damn that nigga ain't playin' ol' bastard! He did that one ol' mothafucka'!* Marquise continued to ring the doorbell and bang on the door. I went into the room and closed the door to the bedroom and locked it. I took off my clothes and jumped in the shower. Marquise just stood there ringing the doorbell.

"Oh, she ain't fixin' to let you in no time soon. I told your ass not to have no other girl up in ya'll house. You don't do that son. I'm surprise she ain't beat both of you, cause if it was me I would have killed you." Randi warned.

When I got out the shower I got dressed and got my keys and his keys and put them in my pocket. I went out the front door and ran down the stairs as Marquise went into the house. I ran down the stairs to jump in my car because I knew the first thing he would look for was his keys. As I started the car he was running down the stairs. I hurried and pulled off trying not to hit him as he tried to stop me.

I went straight over to Chanel's as usual. I had nowhere else to go and I was furious. I could see my past flashing before my eyes if I would have whooped that girl's ass. Nothing phases Marquise. He doesn't argue and he does not curse. So, I would be fussing and cussing with myself.

"You won't believe what just happened?"

"What girl what happened?"

"I came home and there was some chic sitting at the edge of my bed."

"No! You are lying to me girl! Marquise ain't playin' boy, and you know what I woulda' did? I would have gone tanzmanien devil on both they butts girl shoot! That is so wrong!

"What you do girl?"

"I didn't do anything but told that girl to get the fuck out of my room. Then when they walked out the door I told him to stay with her cause he wasn't getting back in the house. Then he thought about it and ran back up the stairs and I slammed the door and locked it. I let him stand out there with his mama while I took a shower then I got dressed and came over here with his car keys in my pocket. He knows I have his keys, he ran right back down the stairs trying to jump in front of the car."

"And I would have run his butt over too! I'm so sorry you have to go through this. I don't want no dirty low down man girl! I went through the same thing with my kid's father. Girl, I ain't got time to be playin' no games shoot!"

"Man, and it's a wrap now, and I'm going to be going to get Nadia from my mom while I'm on vacation for two weeks. It ain't no telling what he will be doing while I'm gone."

When I got back home Marquise was in the bed and

didn't say a word. I had nothing to say as well. As I changed my clothes I was throwing stuff down trying to make noise so he knew I was still pissed. He didn't care. He didn't budge.

I was six months, it was July, time for my vacation. I contacted HR to make sure of my time off and whatever else I needed to do before leaving. Nadia would be graduating from the sixth grade. I was going to surprise her and bring her back to live with me.

Marquise had asked a few months back if he could come with me to meet my mom and Nadia, at the time I thought it might be too much to take in all at once. Him and a baby I didn't think it was a good idea. When I reconsidered, and asked him to come with me he said I had plenty of time to think about it before I told him no so now he didn't want to go and he didn't.

Marquise dropped me off at the curb at the airport. No kiss good bye no anything. I didn't know what to think of that but he did say he wasn't putting anything else into the relationship. I walked to the gate when I looked back Marquise was nowhere in sight.

I arrived in Seattle Washington. It was like a dream. I haven't seen my mom in four years. When I did visit California, she had already moved to Seattle. My mom was so happy she kept telling me to pinch her.

We made it back to my mom's and waited for Nadia to come home from school. It was almost time. Once the bus dropped the kids off on the corner you could hear all the laughing and screaming. Nadia would soon be coming through the door. I was so excited to see Nadia. I hid behind the door and my mom got the camera to capture that Kodak moment.

As I stood behind the door, Nadia didn't know I was pregnant, so that would be the second surprise. She walked in and as soon as she closed the door she jumped so high she almost lost her balance. Everyone was so excited to see each other it really did feel like a dream. I noticed my daughter was wearing a nappy pony tail looking like a boy. I would have to fix that right away. We made plans to go to the mall and get her some summer outfits and of course pick out her graduation dress and give her a relaxer.

My mom made all my favorite dishes. We talked about everything we could imagine as if I would not be there for thirteen more days and planned on taking a trip to Sacramento for the Fourth of July to see the rest of the family.

We spent all day at the mall. Nadia did not like anything I picked out. She kept going to the boy section. Oh, my goodness. Girl! I remember when I was her age and didn't like anything my mom picked out for me, but this is crazy. She did not like one single item. I picked out the cutest Capri outfits from Limited Too and her lips were poked all the way out to the food court.

"Nadia, you cannot wear boy clothes! What's wrong with you?"

"I don't like those pants."

"What's wrong they are Capri's. You can wear these outfits your last week of school and the shorts when we go back to Atlanta."

"Well I don't want to wear that dress."

"Well then wear this skirt outfit."

"Never mind I'll wear the dress, but I don't like pink."

"Then what about lavender."

"I like the blue one."

"Oh, my gosh! Okay, okay get the blue one. Is it your size?"

"No."

"Then lavender it is. Sorry Charlie!"

On Monday morning I did Nadia's hair. She had hair just like Chase long and thick. It was past her shoulders to the middle of her shoulder blades once I put the relaxer in. That bushy ponytail turned into long silky hair. I wrapped it and parted it on the side and combed her hair behind her ears. It was so cute. She hated it! She wore her new Capri outfit and sandals. She walked to the bus stop as usual and me and my mom ran to the window to see the other kids' reaction. It was so quiet, they didn't even recognize her. Nadia had to tell the kids who she was. They all yelled and the chatting began as they told her how different she looked. Me and my mother just laughed. She was such a tomboy.

The next two weeks seemed like months away from Marquise. I called him every night before he went to bed but the conversations only left me in tears and frustrated then I was taking it out on Nadia. How could I be doing this again. Letting my emotions get the best of me and now I'm spazzing out. My thoughts immediately went to when she was four and I would slap her with the brush when she wouldn't keep her head still. Oh, my God! I am a horrible mother and now I am pregnant with another child that I will raise by myself. I again could not bring myself to say I was sorry once I realized what I had done.

That was that frog in my throat. I tried to apologize by smoothing the situation over and talking softer. I was trying to get her to talk to me to make sure she wasn't hurt or upset. She was still so quiet. I'm certain that was my fault too. I was always yelling at her when I was frustrated.

CHAPTER FOURTY-SIX

A fter Nadia's graduation, the three of us got on the road to Nevada to go visit my grandmother then on to California to see my family in Sacramento. They were having a big celebration over my Aunt Jean's house. I was happy to see all my family again. I thought to myself how nice it would have been to have Marquise with me along with my belly. He would have enjoyed all my cousins. I always ended up putting my foot in my mouth. Now he didn't care about me or my family.

Of course, I had to see Juelz. He heard I was in town. He pulled up right on the corner from my Aunt's house.

"Now you know you wrong."

"What do you mean?"

"You know that's supposed to be my baby."

"Then you should have asked me to come home and showed me that you couldn't live without me." I pleaded.

"Man, you know you my nigga man."

"I only know what you show me, and you haven't done

too much of that. When your uncle died, you could have easily let your mama know you wanted to keep the house and I would have had a spot to come back too, but you too busy fuckin' around with that same dumb ass female. So, it's evident who you choosing. So, save it for David."

"Aww nigga! You left me what was I supposed to do? And you ran off with all my money."

"I know you are not about to start that conversation again."

"Alright, alright, I'm gonna squash it. You still got love for me though?"

"Yes, me and my baby crazy. I'm actually due on your birthday."

"No shit?" Juelz laughed.

"Yes! Now that's crazy."

"Where your baby daddy at? He didn't come with you? When you going back?"

"No, he did not and we leaving tomorrow."

"Well damn, how long you been here? You ain't called me."

"We drove with my mom from Washington. I flew there for Nadia's graduation. She has been living with my mom for the past year. So now she'll come back with me to Atlanta."

"Oh, is that right. Nadia, my little nigga. She looking more like Chase now?"

"Yes. That's funny. He still locked up?" I asked.

"Yep. Oh sucka."

"Wow. Well let me go back inside."

"Well it was good seeing you mama."

"Yeah you too."

"I don't get no sugga?"

I leaned over as Juelz hugged me and rubbed my belly. I

269

looked into his eyes and began to cry. Damn here I go. He didn't care about no tears, but maybe this time he would be a little soft on me.

"Don't cry mama, everything cool ain't it?"

"It will be. I'm fine."

"You sure?"

"Yes, I'm sure."

"Ok. Get my number from Evelyn and call me sometime. Let me know if you have the baby on my birthday."

"I will try my best not to!" I smiled.

I went back in the house and joined Evelyn and LeAnn in the kitchen. She was pregnant by another child hood sweetheart. He was locked up most of the years when her and Marquise were together after high school but he claimed his prize when he came home with no hesitation. They loved them some Evelyn. She was due any day and I was due in November. So, our kids will be the same age!

"What Juelz talking about same ol' shit" LeAnn asked.

"You know he was. Danielle, you know you my nigga man..."

Evelyn laughed.

"What he say when he seen your big ol' belly?"

"Talking about I'm wrong and I know this supposed to be his baby."

"There he go!" LeAnn replied as she rolled her eyes.

We all just laughed. That nigga had a lot of nerve. What's done is done. We took more pictures with the family. It was time to head back to Washington that next morning in order for us to catch our fight back to Georgia. Randi had moved into the second bedroom before I left so I didn't know what the next plan was as far as everyone's sleeping arrangements. Had she planned on moving out or what?

We had packed and headed to the airport. My overall trip was aggravating with my pregnancy and everything else that was going on. Now I had to return home in hopes that Marquise missed me even a little bit and that everyone would receive Nadia.

When we made it off the train and up the escalator to baggage claim I called Marquise and instructed him to us as he came through the doors of the airport. When I spotted him we made our way through the crowd. He was there waiting. I expected a hug but only got assistance with my bags and an excited greeting for Nadia.

"So, you're Nadia?"

"Yes sir."

"Sir? I don't look that old do I? Glad to have you join us."

I smiled and we proceeded to the car. As soon as we were settled in and on the freeway Marquise handed me a letter.

"You have some mail."

"Oh, I do. What is it?" I asked as I read the envelope.

It was a letter from Cobra Insurance. Why would they be sending me this, as I opened it I read information giving me options to apply for insurance. It read, since your request to voluntary resign from Coast Dental we are extending the opportunity to continue medical coverage to you...

"What in the hell? So, they fired me while I was on my vacation? This makes no sense. I just talked to her about my benefits before I left. This has got to be a joke!"

"Just call them on Monday to find out what's going on." Marquise advised.

When we arrived home, there was a card on the dresser from Marquise with my name on it. He was excited to have me back and have Nadia join us, but he felt guilty. He had been spending time with one of the managers from another store.

Yes, there was a new female on the scene.

She indeed worked her way to her position. Probably harder than Marquise considering he made GM within his first year, both having so much in common with broken homes and drug abuse. She was dating one of the other managers, and she only had one son.

Marquise was definitely attracted to her. I placed my bags on the floor in the bedroom and Marquise looked on as I opened the card. It read...

I wish I could keep all the good feelings that you've ever given me safe inside a bottle. Every time I needed a smile, a joke, a hug, all I'd have to do is take the lid off, and experience all your caring ways you've shared with me. It would be my very own treasure of sweetness and tenderness. It would be like holding our friendship in my hand.

I thought that was so sweet of him to take the time to pick that card. He wasn't really big on expressing his feelings. I guess that's why I took our lack of communication as lack of caring. Once he says something he means it no matter what his actions show. He was like a robot, no need to ask any questions or need to know details. Everything was at face value. What you see is what you get.

I introduced Nadia to Randi. They hit it off. Randi always made us feel welcome and loved. She tried to stay out of me and Marquise business for the most part. We settled in fine. They took turns sleeping on the couch. Whoever fell asleep in front of the television the other got dibs on the bed.

First thing Monday morning I called the Human Resource department and spoke to Kim. The same person I had spoken with before I left on vacation.

"I received this letter from Cobra regarding insurance. May I ask why this letter was sent to me?"

"Well it shows you voluntarily resigned."

"Resigned? What do you mean? I went on vacation and I'm six months pregnant, why would I resign?"

"I don't know we have it here in your file."

"I just spoke with you before I left on vacation and I did not mention anything about resigning then. This is absurd. Who do I speak with regarding this situation? I am six months pregnant!"

"I'll put a message in to our director and someone will give you a call."

Those sneaky heffas! They just didn't want me in that management position because they didn't hire me. They know I slid right in under their noses before my regional quit. I called Ms. Brenda to let her know what they had done.

"Honey, that doesn't surprise me in the least, but that's okay God don't like ugly honey and he ain't too fond of pretty either. Just go down and file your unemployment and get your money."

That didn't help me too much but after they gave me the run around, that was my only resort. Once I went through the whole process at the EDD office my claim was denied. I did not want to go through an appeal process although I should have. I hadn't even considered applying for another job with my big belly. Who would hire me pregnant? I would be due in three months.

Everyday Marquise came home I would act like I had been out or busy. Fully dressed so he wouldn't think I had been asleep all day, which I had. He always asked if I had been out looking for a job. What was that about? We lay in the bed in total silence.

"So where have you applied?"

"All the stores around here, I applied at Target, TJ Max, and Publix. I don't think anyone will hire me this late in my pregnancy. I'm due in like three months."

"Well you need to move because you are getting on my nerves."

"Move? What do you mean move? You told me to give up my apartment."

"Just go stay somewhere for a few months until the baby comes. I'm paying all the bills."

"And what does that mean?"

"It means you are selfish and you never even offered to help."

"Well you never asked me to split the bills. You asked me to move in with you. I told you I would work on my credit so we could buy a house."

"Well I shouldn't have to ask."

"So, I'm pregnant with no job and you want me to move out? And where do you suppose I go? I don't know anyone I can stay with."

Right then my life flashed before my eyes. I really didn't have anywhere to go. Tears began to fill up in my eyes. *He don't want me no more...* I thought back at that movie *Baby Boy* when Taraji was sitting in the car with her friend and started to cry.

"Don't cry."

"What do you suggest I do? How do you think I should feel?"

I got out of the bed and went to lie on the couch in the living room. My anger kicked in. This mothafucka'! I went into the kitchen and called Sunny.

"Hey girl, what's up?"

"I need a place to stay?"

"What you mean?"

"Marquise wants me to move out because I don't have a job."

"What?"

"Yes, girl he says I'm getting on his nerves and wants me to move out."

"Well did you ask the mothafucka' where the hell he suggests you go?"

"Yeah. My dad is on vacation. You think I could ask your mom. I know my sister ain't going to want me to stay with her and I don't want to anyway."

"Let me call mama and call you back."

The next morning I woke up. Marquise was gone to work. I began to pack. I just carried all my clothes out of the closet on hangers and laid them in the trunk of my car. Up and down the stairs I went. I emptied out all the drawers in the dresser and put my other clothes in garbage bags. I let Nadia know to get ready because we would be leaving, and that we would be staying someplace else until the baby came. The phone rang.

"Hello."

"Mama said your key will be under the mat. I told her what happened and she said you don't even have to ask."

"Oh wow! Thank God. I just finished packing everything in the car hoping that you would be calling. So, we're about to leave in a minute then."

"Have you talked to that asshole?"

"No, I'm just gonna leave his key on the dresser and be

out. There is no sign of me here."

I took my pots from the kitchen, and anything else that I might have bought. My furniture had been in storage at his God mother's house. It was only my sofa set and my mattresses. I had left Nadia's bunk bed in the closet at the apartment by mistake. It was just too much to deal with so maybe who ever found it could use it.

I placed the key on the dresser and took one last look at the room and thought back... *the bed used to be by the window and I slept against the wall until I had trouble climbing in and out of the bed with my belly to go to the bathroom ten times a night. Marquise had rearranged the bedroom on his own. The bed was on the opposite wall and I slept on the same side closer to the bathroom. I thought that was so sweet of him to surprise me. He had left me a note on the dresser that night...*

Hate I missed you. I'll be at my uncles playing cards, can't wait to see you. -Marquise

I walked out the room and out the front door. It was real I told myself as I looked back at the front door. We traveled down 75-south. It was a two-hour drive at 90 miles per hour, three hours doing the speed limit. I felt a sense of peace once I made it to my little Mayberry town. I exited South Central and headed down Martin Avenue. My god sisters were outside waiting to welcome me back.

CHAPTER FOURTY-SEVEN

I settled in and unpacked my things. We sat outside and talked about all the mess that went down and what I was going to do to get back on track. The first thing I needed to do was find a job, but I didn't know how long. They told me to go apply for aid and food stamps. When all else fails, they will put me on the Work Works Program they created to help people get off of welfare. As long as I was actively seeking employment they would approve me for aid. They only gave me two hundred and thirty dollars. My car note was two hundred and eighteen dollars. At least I was still on Marquises' car insurance.

My father had returned from vacation and I had also been by Michele's apartment to fill her in on my situation. No one even offered to let me stay with them if I needed to. I didn't desire to stay either place but it was the principal of the situation to allow me to impose on strangers said a lot in itself. It was no difference than when they allowed Ms. Marie to keep Nadia that time when I had transferred to work in Atlanta.

I ended up getting a job at Kmart. Heaven worked there and referred me for hire. I would start once I completed orientation that next week. I started before I was able to get a relaxer. I hadn't realized how much new growth I had. I had trained on the floor with a girl named Kim. She was a little darker in completion than I was. Nice length hair about the same as mine, pudgy with smaller eyes. She seemed to be a regular girl, no assets like pretty full lips, or big brown eyes with long eye lashes. No big pretty white teeth with a sexy smirk when she smiled. Like the one I was often told I had. Through the course of the day she asked me all sorts of questions, basically making sure I didn't know her man or any of his friends. I assured her I was only visiting from Atlanta and that my baby daddy has never even heard of Tifton, the nerve of her insecure ass. I played it off nice and innocent. Not even telling her my age, she was clearly in her mid-twenties. I turned thirty this year. That whole week she and I held conversations and she helped me on the register. This store was so unorganized, every item was either priced wrong or in the wrong section requiring a price check.

Ms. Marie offered to put a relaxer in my hair. My hair must have really looked nappy for her to offer to do my hair. That sure made me feel loved, she had never done my hair before. It gave us a chance to talk and for her to minister words of encouragement to my broken spirit.

We had a connection. She loved me like a daughter and a sister. We weren't too far apart in age. I was like the big sister to the girls. They went to the club and I liked staying home with Ms. Marie having heart to heart talks talking about the Lord.

"Honey when men treat you wrong ..."
Marie wrapped my hair and I anticipated another day of work.

When I clocked in I greeted everyone as usual and signed in on my register. I spoke to Kim and she walked over.

"Who wrapped your hair?"

"I did."

"You put your relaxer in?"

"Heaven's mom actually put it in for me."

"Oh, it's pretty, is that all your hair?"

"Yes, thank you." I said with a smile.

The rest of the day I worked in silence. Kim never spoke another word for the remainder of our shift, nor did she visit me at my register like she usually did when it got slow. *Wow is she really not speaking to me today. Was it something I said? I can't imagine what.* The rest of that week Kim didn't speak to me at all and I felt no need to entertain her foolishness by asking questions.

I was asleep in peace and quiet. It was my day off and everyone was at work or school. I was content resting for a few more hours when the phone rang. I didn't want to answer it but I thought it might be important.

"Hello?"

"Hello may I speak with Danielle?"

"Speaking."

"Danielle this is Alan were you coming into work? You were scheduled today."

"Oh, I thought I was off the schedule. I can come in, give me like ten to fifteen minutes to get dressed and I'll be right there."

"Okay, thank you."

I got dressed so fast and I was on my way. I just knew I was scheduled off. I whizzed through the store when I arrived and clocked in and signed onto my register. Kim was in her normal place. She didn't say anything to me. *How retarded is that girl?* I finished my shift and clocked out.

Alan came over to the registers as Kim stood on the end of the isle.

"Hey Kim."

"Hey Alan."

"How's it going?"

"It's going."

"The new girl gone home?"

"She left earlier."

"Okay, so how is she doing?"

"I don't know, seems to be okay. She has a lot of price checks."

"Oh yeah, she was scheduled but didn't show up. When I called she thought she was scheduled of but she came on in."

"Yeah but she had an attitude."

"What do you mean?"

"She told me ya'll were lucky she even came in because she knew she was off today."

"Oh really?"

"Sure did. I don't think she likes working here."

"Well we can fix that."

Alan went and spoke to the store Manager Ms. Cathy. She was the hiring manager that interviewed me. The next day when I came in to work she called me into her office from my register. I knocked on the door.

"You needed to see me?"

"We're going to have to let you go."

"For what reason?"

280

"You've had too many price checks and although that may not be your fault we just fill you're not catching on quick enough. Just turn in your badge and you may clock out and go."

I couldn't believe that I was asked to clock out. So how do you get fired from two jobs for no reason within two months' time? That's all Marquise needed to hear. I didn't want him to think I couldn't keep a job and would not think I was reliable as a mate. I went to pick up Nadia from my father's. I wasn't in the mood to visit so I knocked on the door and asked if he could send her out.

"How's the job going?"

"It's not. I got fired."

"That figures."

"What do you mean that figures? I didn't even do anything."

"You have a nasty attitude. I knew you wouldn't keep that job."

"Why would you say something like that? I don't have an attitude, but I have every reason to be disturbed. I'm homeless living with strangers, with no money no food and no job. Not to mention none of you have even offered to help me and I'm pregnant. No one has even offered for me to come to dinner. So, no I don't have a nasty attitude my feelings are hurt."

Nadia walked out of the house and I motioned for her to get in the car as I followed. I didn't have anything else to say. A few weeks had gone by before my father called over to Ms. Marie's.

"I have some files I need filing down here at the office. I can pay you twenty-five dollars a day if you want to put some time in and answer the phone?"

"Yes, I would love to. What time do you want me to come?"

"Whenever you get up and dressed will be fine. Have you had breakfast yet?"

"No."

"Well come by and pick up a few dollars and go grab us a bite."

"Okay!"

I got dressed as quickly as I could. I was starving, so knew my baby was hungry too. I wanted a McDonalds Egg McMuffin and my dad wanted a chicken sandwich from Checkers with those spicy fries he loved so much.

I typed up a few labels for the client files between answering the phone. I wish my dad would get a computer and put all the client data in the system. Then the labels could be created much easier. He was still using a type writer and handwriting everything. My father's home number appeared on the caller ID as the phone rang.

"Good morning Citywide Bail Bonds Danielle speaking, how may I help you?"

"What you doing at the office?" A squeaky irritating voice sounded in my ear.

"Answering the phone?" It was my step mother...

"Oh okay. Is daddy there?"

"Yes ma'am, hold on one moment."

I tried to be so nice to that lady in spite of how she seemed to always treat me. I swear she was always so sweet until she married my dad. After the wedding, it seemed like the next time we saw her she was a totally different person.

I used to visit my new found sisters when I was fifteen. My father had taken us all out to dinner. We didn't know we'd be meeting our sister. Apparently, she felt it was time to tell her daughter who her real father was now that she was eighteen.

We arrived at the Rusty Duck and there was a lady and a young woman with a baby seated at the same table we were being seated. Me, Shelise, and Khrista looked at each other in confusion. Who were these people and why were they at our table?

My father made a story of an announcement. I was always loving and accepting at that age. I was happy I had a new sister three years older than me and she had a baby! I loved babies! I took to my niece quickly. She was so cute! That summer I would pick her up and keep her for the weekends. I loved to comb her hair. It was long and pretty. She was like my own live baby doll.

I spent a good part of the summer over their house with my new found siblings. That's when I met Michele and the other two sisters. Michele had a baby boy and I was still pregnant at that time. After twelve weeks, the baby died of SIDS and my pregnancy was terminated. I didn't really connect or realize what had actually happened but I know I was sorry for her loss.

Once we turned eighteen we were both pregnant again. I had a girl and she had another boy. They were four months apart. Within a year's time is when I went to jail and Michele went to war in Dessert Storm.

Back at the office I knew my step mom would be coming down to the office. She acted as if she couldn't stand for me to be alone with my father, and sure enough by lunch time she came strolling in. I was packing up just in time to leave for the day. The next thing out her mouth was...

"If Danielle getting twenty-five dollars a day then I want to start coming down and help out in the office too."

Are you serious? I'm pregnant and homeless with no job and you want to take my time at the office away from me? She act like she hates for my dad to do anything for me, and he is so accommodating.

My duties at the office didn't last long between paying me and my step mom. That was just ridiculous. I was just able to pay my car note with TANF. Michele was on call at night writing bonds for my dad and she didn't even offer to let me write one or give me a few dollars. Her last bond was two hundred and fifty dollars. *Can a sista' at least get fifty bucks, Damn!*

I was actually mad at Michele. I was hungry and of course I had no money. She always seemed so sincere and caring, but I couldn't figure that one out. I wrote bonds before. We could have split the calls.

I let it go and we stayed the night over her house anyway. I slept in the living room on the comfy couch of course Nadia was in the room with her cousins. I hadn't been getting peaceful rest at the other house. They had mice and not to mention the break in. Yes! Someone had broken in the house...

I woke up to a man standing at my bedroom door. I slept in the front room and I felt someone standing there. I opened my eyes and looked toward the door and saw a male silhouette.

"Who is that I yelled?"

He ran out the door through the kitchen. My heart was pounding. I tipped out of the bed and peaked out the door way and ran down the hallway to Ms. Marie's bedroom to wake her.

"Ms. Marie! Someone broke in the house!"

"Hmm?" She moaned in disbelief.

"Someone broke in!"

She jumped out of the bed like a cat to the ceiling!

"What? Jesus! Lord have mercy!" She yelled running down the hall turning on all the lights.

Sunny came running out of her room.

"What happened?" Hearing the loud footsteps down the

hall.

"Girl someone was in the house. He was standing over my bed in the doorway."

"Oh my god! Mama come in the house!" She screamed. Ms. Marie was all outside in the dark. She come running back in the door.

"Call the police Danielle! Where's my purse?" As she headed down the hall into her room. Ms. Marie's purse was outside in the driveway, all the contents on the ground with no wallet.

The police arrived and took a report from me. They informed Ms. Marie they would be in touch with her regarding any leads on the burglary...

The next morning I woke up and Michele had walked into the kitchen.

"Good morning, good morning!"

"Good morning."

"How did you sleep?"

"I slept well."

"I know, I came in and prayed over you. You looked so peaceful."

"Yeah I don't even remember moving. It felt good just to sleep   with no interruptions..."

It was August I still had three months before the baby was due.

There was a general manager's meeting being held at Dave and Buster's. Marquise thought it would be a good spot to mix business and pleasure. He teamed up with the other GM's. Marquise sensed a little tension between the two. It was lady and another male GM. After the meeting was over they both ended up at the bar for a drink after the meeting.

"Everything okay? You seem upset" He asked.

"I'm upset alright. Just having a little disagreement with Bryan and actually I'm so ready to go home."

She shared that they were seeing each other and a little of what was going on and that they had rode together. By the end of the story and two shots she had the courage to ask Marquise for a ride home.

"Can you give me a ride home?"

"Sure. No problem."

She lived on the East side of Atlanta. That gave them plenty of time to talk. Marquise thought she was a real nice girl from their brief encounters during store drop offs or pickups. They were always able to lend store items if they were short before delivery.

She favored me, same complexion, and similar frame. She may have seemed to have a sweeter demeanor. Like me in the beginning of our relationship. They seemed to have a lot in common.

"Would you like to come in?"

"Sure, the night is still young why not."

She didn't waste any time in her feelings and Marquise didn't think twice to stop her. A kiss can tell a lot and all it told Marquise was that he needed some pussy.

CHAPTER FOURTY-EIGHT

I t was now November. I had three weeks left of my pregnancy. It was time for me to start looking for a place. I didn't know where I could stay with no job and no money. During my doctor's appointment, we discussed scheduling to induce so I wouldn't have to spend Thanksgiving in the hospital. Then I thought of my due date being on Juelz' birthday.

Okay, that was not a factor right now. We agreed on the 17th to ensure I would be home rested in time for the all the food and family. That's the same day as Evelyn son's birthday. There was at least three more birthdays in November in our family, all those Scorpio's! Not to mention a few of us had the middle name Marie after my mom's sister that passed.

I hadn't had a name picked out yet for the baby. I had wanted to name my baby Chanel, but I would have to run that by Marquise first. He started calling every evening before he went to bed, that made me feel good to know he was concerned and thinking of me. I had asked him had he slept with anyone,

      "...I won't answer that question in your condition."

That went right over my head, but I never asked the question again.

CHAPTER FOURTY-NINE

T hat Sunday Sunny and I decided to go to church with Michele. It was a church we had heard about in the neighborhood. St. John Baptist Church. A few people had spoken of the Pastor, so we decided to go. Before the end of service the Pastor called me out of the pew to the altar. I was embarrassed.

"I want to pray for you my daughter and anoint your head and feet with oil. When are you due?" He asked.

"In two weeks."

"Do you have a place of your own for you and your baby?"

"No."

"God told me to tell you not to worry. He will give you a place to stay and this child will want for nothing. I anoint the crown of your head to the soles of your feet. Everything you touch will turn to gold and you will have favor. Do not worry. God has everything in store for you!" He added.

I began to cry and my sisters surrounded me. I felt a

burden lifted off my heart. I knew God would not leave me. I felt blessed staying with my god family. I know God sees all.

With that blessing I got a call for an interview with Bath and Body Works in the mall the next day. I had planned on working up until I had the baby. I put in an application after speaking to the manager and she actually called me back in for an interview.

She enjoyed interviewing me and offered me the job. The position would start in just a few days. I was up for it but in the back of my mind I knew I was getting induced.

"I would love to accept the position, but I didn't know it would be so soon. I applied a few months back and I am scheduled to be induced on the seventeenth and that's just a couple of weeks away. Then six to eight weeks to recover and the holidays will be over."

"You're right. Oh, I'm sorry. Well check back with us and see if we may have a position to fill. It was such a pleasure meeting you. And good luck on your new blessing."

"Thank you so much. I really appreciate you offering me the position."

The next morning I went over Michele's after I dropped off Nadia at school. Her friend Sabrina pulled up at the same time beside me with a friendly smile.

Sabrina was as short as my sister but she was a little on the heavy side, pretty dark skinned, big hips and a big behind with long jet black hair.

"Hey lady, you ready to have that baby?" She asked as we met at the stairs.

Why do people always ask pregnant women that question? They clearly see you big as hell, short of breath, wobbling while you walk but no I just want to walk around like this for let's say another six months...no problem.

"Heck yeah, I'm ready to drop this load, but like my aunt would say it's easier to tote them around in your stomach than on your hip." I laughed.

We settled in on the couch with Michele.

"Have you found a place yet?"

"No."

"When are you due?"

"They are going to induce me in two weeks so I can be at home for Thanksgiving."

"Oh, no girl we got to find you a place to stay!"
Sabrina closed her eyes and started speaking in tongues.

"Thank you, Lord. Thank you! Come on and go with me I'm going to find you an apartment. We'll be back sis."

I followed her out the door and got in her car. She started asking me a lot of questions as to what lead to my current situation.

"I have nothing for the baby, no place to stay and no money."

"Don't worry about anything. God always makes a way out of no way."

We pulled up into an apartment complex called Wild Wood. They looked fairly decent, but who was I to complain in my situation.

As we walked into the apartment it was set up as an office with the Manager sitting at her desk.

"Good Morning sister."

"Good Morning sister, how are you?"

"She was a heavy set white lady with semi curly hair. I couldn't tell if she had Hispanic in her or not. She wore glasses which made her more homely than professional.

"Oh, I'm blessed and you."

"You know highly favored. Who do you have here?"

"This is my other spiritual sister. We need to get her in an apartment before this baby comes."

"Oh, hey darling I'm Ms. Stacy what's your name?"

"Danielle, nice to meet you."

"So when are you due?"

"In two weeks."

"Oh Lord. I don't have anything that soon. Let me look through these stack of work orders. Where are you staying now?"

"With my God family, temporarily until the baby comes."

"Where are you from sweetheart. Do you have family here? Is this your first baby?"

"No. I have a twelve-year-old daughter. I'm from California but we've been in Georgia four years now. My father and my sister live here in Tifton. I was actually living in Atlanta and the guy I am pregnant by asked me to move out of his apartment when I lost my job."

"Are you kidding me?"
She started speaking in tongues in an instant.

"You shall not be deceived by the acts of the devil. We cancel the assignment of the enemy! You are the head and not the tail. You shall be placed above and not beneath. We claim this in the name of the almighty Jesus!"

They both took my hand and started screaming in tongues praying to the Lord. I was looking at them from the corner of my eye as I had my head bowed, but I received that prayer.

"What do you want the Lord to do for you? Here write down whatever it is and we are going to wrap it up and give to God."

"I wrote husband house and family. That is the first

thing that came into my heart."

"Let me have it and we are going to place it in this box. Never open it just leave it as a reminder of God's gift."

"Okay." I replied.

"I'm going to look through these applications. I'll keep your application on top of this stack. I'm sure we have one being worked on that could be move in ready in two weeks. I will call you as soon as I hear from Maintenance."

"Oh, thank you so much."

"Don't worry God is gonna make a way."

"Okay."

I don't know what Marquise had planned he had not mentioned anything or even asked what I needed for the baby. I tried to plan a baby shower but everyone was busy, so that panned out to nothing.

I rode with Michele to Wal-Mart to get the rest of the stuff for Thanksgiving dinner, and I was also going to pick out a car seat. I did not pay my car note this month. I used my check to buy everything I needed for the baby. We had a one week countdown come Monday. I wasn't waiting on Marquise to ask me what I needed. I would just ask him to buy the basinet when he came down. He had planned on taking off a week for the Thanksgiving holiday to spend with me and the baby.

As we pulled in the parking lot I spotted that famous Expedition. No matter how many Expeditions I saw I always knew without a shadow of a doubt that that was his truck. It had been so long since we ran into each other. The last time I saw him I was going into the Winn-Dixie and he was coming out with a bouquet flowers in his hand. I remember someone saying he was getting married soon.

"Oh my God, that is Charles truck!"

"Where?" Michele asked.

"Over there! I know that truck anywhere. I'm staying in the car. I'm not ready to see him yet."

"Get out the car girl!" Michele demanded.

"No!"

I gave her a dirty look. She just wants to gloat at the fact that we didn't end up staying together. She doesn't even care that my heart is still broken behind that man. *I don't care if I am pregnant by someone else.* I got out of the car...While I was in the store, I tried my best not to run into him. To no avail, as soon as I turned the corner into the next isle there he was.

"Hey Dan."

"Hey Charles."

"You pregnant? Oh my God. I don't think I've ever seen you so beautiful."

"Oh my, really? Thank you."

"We should just elope right now and leave everything behind."

"Can't really do that considering you're the one already getting married?"

"Who told you that?"

"Who else?"

"Oh, my sister?"

"I believe so."

"Well I believe I may be making a mistake but hell you only live once."

"If you say so..."

"So you good everything going okay with you I see."

"Yes, everything is fine."

"I'm glad to hear that. Well let me get back to my mom's. You know all my family's over there. It was good seeing you Dan."

"You too."

He turned and walked away and took my heart with him. If he only knew all the hell I was going through. Everything was so different and complicated now. I have nowhere to belong. Never thought of how embarrassed I should really be in my circumstance.

Michele dropped me and Nadia back off at Ms. Marie's. I had all my things still neatly packed up in the closet. I just kept the items in the bag and placed them on top of my bag of clothes.

"The apartments called today. She said you could call her back any time that she would have the phone on until seven this evening."

"Did she say anything about the apartment?"

"No just said to call as soon as you got in..."

"Wild Wood Apartments this is Ms. Stacy."

"Hey Ms. Stacy this is Danielle returning your call."

"Hey Danielle I have good news. I have apartment ready for you to move in. Had you had the baby yet?"

"No, ma'am. I go in Thursday. So when can I move in?"

"As soon as you can get over and sign the lease and get your key."

"I'll be there first thing tomorrow. What time do you open?"

"I open at ten but come after lunch. I have a few appointments and I'll prepare your file and I still need that form from your worker."

"Okay then I'll do that in the morning and make copies of everything else and meet you after lunch. What time?"

"One o'clock. I'll have everything ready for you."

"Okay. Thank you so much Ms. Stacy. I'll see you then."

"You got the place?" Ms. Marie asked.

"Yes, she said I can meet her tomorrow and get my key."

"Praise God! That way you can be all settled in and won't have to take the baby out here and there."

"I know and I can be in my own spot."

"Nothing like having your own, I know exactly how you feel baby."

"I really appreciate you letting us stay here."

"Ah honey, shoot you family. You like my daughter and my sister wrapped all in one."

The next day I dropped Nadia off at school and headed right up to the DFCS office to see my worker. She gave me the information I needed to give to the apartments. I went back home and packed all my stuff in the car. I went to my dad's office to tell him the good news.

"Hey Daddy." As I leaned to kiss him on his forehead.

"Hey baby doll! How you doing today?"

"Just fine. I'm on the way to Wildwood to pick up my keys."

"Your keys? You got an apartment."

"Yes!"

"Thank you, Jesus. How much will your rent be? Nothing, basically I don't have an income."

"Do you have furniture?"

"No. All my stuff is at Marquise's God mother's house. I have all my other stuff though. Like my dishes, pots, microwave, my bathroom stuff and my televisions. I don't have my bed though."

"I'll get you a mattress over there tonight."

"Okay thank you daddy."

"You have any money."

"No sir. I spent it on the car seat for the baby."

"Okay, take some money and go get you some groceries

and whatever else you need."

"Thank you." I replied as he handed me a hundred-dollar bill.

I went over and waited in front of the manager's office. To take in what would be my next residence and journey. I didn't know what the apartment looked like but the way the office was laid out I would make it work. I was wondering, what was the reason for this struggle? I knew in my heart I would raise this baby by myself. I waited so long and had tried to pick the perfect relationship in order to feel confident not to have any fears about bringing a child into this world. It was definitely not planned but they say everything happens for a reason or in this case would it be you have to be held accountable for your actions.

I hadn't shed a tear yet. I stayed strong and standing through my storm. I sat and imagined what this baby would look like. What my next steps would be? I would have to ask Marquise if he wouldn't mind bringing my furniture down. As I looked around the complex was fairly quiet. Everyone should be at work.

The door to the office opened. That was my queue to get my paper work and squeeze myself out of my front seat. I had to keep the seat pulled back so that my stomach fit behind the steering wheel with my arms stretched straight to turn it.
I walked in and greeted Ms. Stacy.

"I have your file waiting and ready to go. Did you get the copies from your worker you needed?"
"Yes, I have them right here."

"Great let me make copies. Okay so let's go over the lease and restrictions of income based housing."

She let me know no one else could be on the lease and anyone who stays overnight more than five days is considered a resident and is in violation of the lease. She asked if the child's father would be coming to stay with me. I assured her he lives in Atlanta and would not be staying here. Since these are income base apartments and I have no income I would be added to a program and would receive a supplement of ten dollars per month for living in the complex. That was crazy. She wrapped up my file and after obtaining all my signatures and walked me to the apartment.

It wasn't too far from the office. Just the next building over and it was upstairs. When I walked in it wasn't bad at all. The carpet was new the counter tops were the same smooth light wood brown. I guess that would be considered the breakfast nook because there really was no place for a dinette set. I could have a few bar stools for seating. The refrigerator was actually new the stove was clean. Of course, I made note of eye pans I would need to buy instead of wrapping them with foil. I hated that look. Of course, there was no dishwasher, what was up with these apartments and no dishwasher. Guess that was the South. There's another item on my list, a cute dish rack, black and silver of course, matching garbage can and a toaster. My microwave was black. My mom had upgraded my last one and had it delivered from Spiegel. *Oh, focus Danielle, you need food first.*

We did our walk through. The bathroom was a nice size, and the bedrooms perfect in size and were side by side in the square shaped hall way. I made a list of what I needed. I couldn't spend all the money on food. We needed a few household items and I had to buy pads of course. I had been consumed with that show, "Bringing Home Baby" all summer. A few of the episodes showed some of the mothers having emergency C-Sections. That was one thing I did not want. It seemed so scary and to have your baby cut out of you oh Lord. That would be the worst.

I only pushed two times with Nadia and she came right out. No stitches at all.

I unpacked the things out of the car and sat in the middle of my bedroom floor. Still no tears, I just sat in silence. I was thankful to be in my own place. I made a mental list of what I needed as I cleaned the kitchen, bathroom and the refrigerator and put everything in its place. I picked Nadia up from school and we went to Walmart.

When we pulled up to the apartments Nadia looked puzzled.

"Who lives here?"

"We do!"

"We have our own apartment?"

"Yes."

"So, we aren't going back to live with Marquise in Atlanta?"

"It doesn't look like it. He hasn't asked me to move back."

"Oh well, that's cool. I wanted my own room anyway." She laughed.

We headed up the stairs with the groceries. She liked it okay. She even did snow angels in the middle of her bedroom floor. I didn't think to even consider what Marquise would think. I had no real desire to go back after he put us out. I wasn't mad I just rolled with the punches and did what I had to do to make us and the baby comfortable.

My father and my brother in law showed up with the mattresses. A twin set we put on the floor for Nadia and Queen size for me with rails. My step mom sent over some sheets and a comforter. They didn't even match. She had a closet full of brand new sheets and towels. These were old and one was ripped, but it was cool. I was thankful until I could go buy my own.

"This is nice Danielle. You already have everything hooked up In its place. You go girl you don't let any grass grow under your feet. I'm happy for you."

"Thank you, bro.,"

"Now we're just waiting on the baby to come." He added.

"Yes, they are going to induce me on Thursday. So, I won't be in the hospital on Thanksgiving. I didn't want to take the chance of going into labor with my due date on the 20th."

I called and had the phone turned on. I waited to call Marquise from my house.

"Whose number is this?"

"Mine. I got an apartment so I could be settled by the time the baby gets here. You'll be here, tomorrow right?"

"Yes, I took time off for Thanksgiving so I could stay up there a few days with you and the baby."

"Did you get the bassinette?"

"No."

"Why not what is the baby going to sleep in?"

"In the bed with you..."

"That's not safe Marquise. You could accidently suffocate the baby. Are you serious? You haven't even asked if I needed anything else for the baby?"

"Relax woman, I'll get it when I get up there."

"Okay..." I replied hesitantly.

I guess I would never understand this man. He was just a different breed. He still had no compassion or showed any extra concern for my wellbeing. He was still paying my car insurance though. My note would soon be behind a few months.

Our first night in our own place was peaceful and quiet. No worrying about mice running around and we could walk on the brand-new carpet bare foot. I bought some plastic storage bens, one for Nadia and one for the baby and new hangers. I wanted all white for Nadia, all black for me, and of course little pink ones for the baby.

Marquise arrived like clockwork at nine. He said he would be on the road by six after work. I heard the bass from the corner slowly approaching the parking lot and then it stopped. I looked out my bedroom window and saw him getting a huge white box out of his back seat of his mustang. I had purchased a cute light blue tube top pajama set with big Hawaiian flowers to wear while he was there.

I went down the stairs to greet him and show him back up to my apartment. The big white box was my basinet. He remembered!

"Hey!"

"Hey, how are you doing?"

"I'm okay, ready for tomorrow to get here."

He followed me inside and dropped the box on the floor and I showed him to my room and he pulled his Calvin Klein travel bag off his shoulders and put it by the door.

"Have you eaten I made dinner?"

"I grabbed a few sandwiches from the store earlier. I'm fine thanks."

"Okay just checking."

I was disappointed he wasn't hungry. I made all his favorites. Fried pork chops with rice and gravy and salad. I baked a cake and had some ice cream in the freezer just in case he wanted dessert.

We sat on the couch in the living room and watched television while I put the basinet together. We still didn't have much conversation. Nadia was over to Michele's. He asked why I didn't let her come to the hospital with us. I never even thought about it. I remember Michele letting my nephew in the room with her. I guess I just thought it would be too much. You can't blame a person for their decisions if new ideas are never brought to their attention. Michele said she would bring her to the hospital as soon as they got out of school.

That night I showered and made sure I had everything packed and the baby bag was ready. I was sort of nervous when it came time to go to bed. I hadn't known what to expect. Would he volunteer to sleep on the couch? I did announce that I was going to bed as he watched television. He grabbed the remote and turned off the television. My stomach dropped at the thought that we would lie in bed together after all these months. I never imagined that I would actually be alone during my pregnancy and not have any sex. Would we talk about all that has happened? Do I face him or turn my back towards him? So many questions raced in my head. I lay down and turned my back to him. Praying he would wrap his arm around me the way he used to. As I lay there propping the pillow under my belly his hand reached over as his warm breath enveloped my neck. I felt butterflies in my stomach. I didn't think he desired to touch me at all. My thoughts raced... *had he been distracted by another woman all this time?*

In silence, he kissed the back of my neck and began to rub my breasts. I felt the back of my knees begin to sweat. I hadn't been close to Marquise in months and I almost forgot how to respond. Do I continue to lay to see where he takes it or do I caress his hands and invite their touch to continue? I couldn't take it! I turned to welcome his kisses on my neck praying his lips would search for mine. As our lips connected I placed my hand behind the back of his head to embrace our kiss. I could feel his hard penis on my butt as his hand guided my pajama bottoms down to my knees, he in turn escaping his black boxer briefs. He kissed the back of my neck while guiding me onto my knees with his other hand pulling me from my chest positioning me to receive him from behind. I moved the pillow to support the weight of my stomach. He kissed my ass rubbing his hands over my back. Searching for me gently, I overflowed with juices anticipating him entering the depths of my soul. I longed for his attention. I was realizing how much I missed him and wanted him in my life.

His touch took my breath away. My heart pounded as my body gloved him remembering his form. He penetrated deeply filling up every inch of me.

"Am I hurting you?"

"No, I'm okay. Don't stop baby. I need you."

Everything was overwhelming, his thrusts said he missed me, my scent, my touch but no words had been exchanged. What was he thinking? Did he realize he had missed me as well?

I could always tell if a guy had been having sex because he wouldn't come as fast, if he hadn't he would come faster. He didn't. I tried not to think about it. We lay together with his arm around my belly just as he did when we started our relationship. Not saying a word.

CHAPTER FIFTY

That morning we headed to the hospital. We registered and got settled ready to be induced. Once I was induced it seemed to be taking forever. The pain crept up and I kept my head under the blanket so Marquise wouldn't see the ugly faces I was making. Michele had arrived, and Heaven called to check on me.

"Hey honey, how you feeling?"

"In pain."

"Who all up there?"

"No one, just Marquise and my sister just walked in."

"Okay, I'll be up there a little later."

"You don't have to come. Ain't nothing going on."

"Okay, then I'll just call back to check on you."

"Okay thank you."

"Okay love you girl."

"Love you too."

I didn't feel like any company. I guess I was acting possessive over Marquise I didn't want to share our time together with anyone else.

"How is she doing?"

"Not too good. The contractions are kicking her butt."

"Hey sis, how you doing." She greeted peeking under the blanket laid over my face.

"I'm in pain!"

She kept rubbing my leg and giving all these different instructions to help me. I really wasn't in the mood to even hear her voice.

"Shut up already!" I yelled.

The medicine was not working. It started the contractions but I was not dilating at all. Those two hours seemed like all day. The pain was just ridiculous. I requested an epidural before it was too late. That seemed to take another two hours.

"Where is he? Did they page him?"

"They said they did."

"Well he is taking forever!"

The anesthesiologist finally arrived. I had remembered watching all those episodes on TLC when they would get the epidural shot. You'd have to be really still and brace yourself sitting up. I wanted Marquise to come hold me instead of me hugging on some random nurse.

"Come on daddy, help mama be very still."

I held on to him and I swear I couldn't even hold my breath. It felt like that needle was going up my whole back. Jesus! It was over and I was able to lie back down hoping for the contractions to make me dilate. That didn't work either. The next step was to burst my water. The doctor put his two fingers to my cervix and when the water burst it was dark brown. The baby had had her first poop. It was called Meconium. If inhaled it could partially or completely block the baby's airways. They ordered a STAT C-section.

Wouldn't you know just my luck! The one thing I feared most after watching TLC all summer. It was show time. They rushed me into the operating room with Marquise right by my side. They talked me through everything.

"Do you think you could give me a tummy tuck while you're down there?" I teased.

"I'm afraid not sweetie."

Marquise laughed. I felt nothing maybe a little tug but not much. It's a girl! She was here, our baby was out safe. They had to make sure there wasn't anything in her airway. Marquise put her on my chest. She looks like... and the first words out of his mouth were...

"I know she better turn black."

"You're so crazy, she will. She looks just like Jordan."

Jordan was Marquise's oldest daughter. I was exhausted. They took the baby away with Marquise to get her cleaned up. I must have dozed off when I woke up I was in a new room and Marquise was not there.

He soon returned with a bag from Red Lobster. How dare he? He didn't bring me back anything. I didn't say a word. The only visitors I had were Ms. Marie and Heaven. My step mom came also in place of my dad because he had caught the flu.

"If you were in Atlanta this room would have been packed with my family." Marquise stated.

"That would have been nice." I replied.

No one else came by at all. I stayed in the hospital five days. Marquise stayed four days sleeping in the chair beside the bed. It wasn't until the day he was leaving the nurse showed us that it let out into a bed. Now why would they have him sleeping like that and never say anything?

When he left, I walked him down to the lobby. Things

still seemed so awkward with us. I went to give him a hug and a kiss and he just patted me on the back and said he would call to me later. I rode the elevator back up to my room feeling so empty and alone once again.

I would be discharged tomorrow. I couldn't find anyone to come pick me and the baby up from the hospital. I called everyone I knew and no one was available and it was raining. Wow. I called my dad again and he said he would ask Michele if she would pick me up. Mind you she lived right across the street. She came alright. She called from her truck to tell me she was downstairs.

I waited for the nurses to assist me and help me gather my things but no one came after I signed my discharge papers. I waited outside my door to get someone's attention to bring me a wheel chair no one was at the desk. I packed up my bag and put the baby in the car seat and walked to the elevator. When I got downstairs Michele and my step mom where waiting in the truck in front of the automatic doors. No one bothered to get out and assist me with the baby. Nor even open the door for me. They just sat right there in their seats looking straight ahead. I had to put the baby and my bags in the seat and climb up into the back seat of the truck. They pulled up around the corner to my apartments and again no help. I climbed out and put the bags on my shoulders and leaned over to get the baby from the middle of the seat. I thanked them for the ride and shut the door. I walked up the stairs with my bags and the baby. Making sure she was covered from the rain. I tried not to cry from anger. Nadia was still at Michele's. She would come home tomorrow after school.

I settled in my room and put the baby in the basinet. I sat on the edge of the bed and watched her sleep. I then began to cry. I had nothing, no food, no money and no one here to help me. I was going to be raising another baby by myself again. I was up for the challenge, it just wasn't going to be today or tomorrow. I called my grandmother the next day to let her know I had had the baby and that I was home. I spent Thanksgiving alone. No one dropped off a plate or even called to check on me. I was told I wasn't supposed to do too much moving around with my C-section but I had no one to help me, and I had to take care of Nadia too. I hadn't eaten and I wasn't producing any milk. My nipples where bleeding and it hurt so bad I thought she was going to suck them off. She wasn't getting any milk and she was crying nonstop because she was hungry. I called my mom to let her know what was going on and that I was home and alone. She told me to check my mailbox because she had sent me some money for the baby. I thanked her and told her I would. When I went to check the mail, it was there. Three hundred dollars, that money came just in time.

That next week I received calls from all my aunts letting me know that they had sent money in the mail for me. My longest conversation was with my aunt Chelly. She was always a good listener and she gave sound advice. She told me she talked to my grandmother and that they all agreed to send money until I got on my feet. I told her the whole situation with Marquise, my job and how I had lost everything. She asked me why didn't I just come home and I told her I didn't want to. That I liked being in Georgia. They told me to spend the money on whatever I needed to. If I needed to catch up my car note then do that, bills, food or even clothes. It was for me to do what I needed. I believe in that one week I received fifteen hundred dollars. I know my two aunts sent three hundred, and my grandmother and my Aunt Jean sent me two hundred and my mom sent me another two hundred.

I was so thankful each time I saw a new envelope in my

mailbox. I didn't have to pay any rent since I didn't have an income, but I still had Georgia Power and gas, cable, and phone. I caught up my car note and stocked up on milk, diapers and food. Then I got a call from Marquise. He was on his way. What a surprise. Did he miss us already?

No, he came to drop off my sofa and love seat. He stayed for the weekend. He held the baby and even fed her, changed her. They had fallen asleep on the couch. She was looking so tiny lying on his chest. We had a good weekend. We talked about our situation. By Sunday he was packed and ready to head back to Atlanta. He stopped me at my bedroom door. I guess he was having a change of heart.

"There's nothing I wouldn't do for you and my baby right now."

"Are you still going to marry me?"

"Except that."

"What do you mean except that?"

"Let's just see how things go. I want you to come back home."

"To Atlanta? To your place?"

"Yes."

"Why you ask now and I just moved in here."

"Well you didn't tell me you were getting a place."

"Well did you think I was going to have the baby and still stay with Ms. Marie?"

"I don't know. Just come back when Nadia starts Christmas break. Then you can be home for Christmas."

"Okay if you say so I will."

"Thank you."

We stood in the doorway of the bedroom and he pulled me close and we began to kiss. I didn't know how to take that since my feelings were still so hurt from the big picture. I walked him downstairs and tried to wrap my mind about what was just said. Christmas break was only a week and a half away. I looked around my apartment. I didn't know what to do. My family had sent me money and now I was going to go right back to the guy that put me out. I had some thinking to do.

Cary stopped by to see the baby. I don't know how he found out where I was staying but in Tifton you can find out just about anything.

"She is so pretty Dan. You know she should have been mine. You just left a nigga for dead."

"No I didn't. You know I was trying to get to Atlanta. That's why I had all them jobs."

"Well where that get you? You right back home where you supposed to be." Little did he know I was on my way back again, without notice.

CHAPTER FIFTY-ONE

I packed up my apartment and the baby and headed to Nadia's school to check her out early. It was her last day before Christmas break. I went into the office to get all the necessary paper work to enroll her in school in Atlanta. As we walked back to the car I was surprised to see Michele had pulled up. Damn! This was all I needed. No one had come over to my apartment to see the baby or called to check on me so I was leaving alright without as much as a good bye. Fuck'em!

"Hey, how you doing?" Michele asked.
"Don't say a word." I whispered to Nadia.
"Oh hey!" I answered without a pause in my step to stop and talk.

I put the baby in the car so fast Michele wouldn't have time to even look at her. I just hope she didn't pay any attention to all the bags in the car. She was trying to talk to me about something that had to do with my nephew but I wasn't paying her no mind. I cut her off abruptly.

"Girl let me get out of here before I'm late."

I jumped in the car and kept it pushing out the parking lot and hopped on I-75 north. I always timed myself to get to Atlanta in two hours going ninety the whole way, but not this time with my babies in the car. I gave myself a big enough window to get there and unpack and have everything in order by the time Marquise made it home from work. He had left the key above the door ledge for me like he used to do before he gave me a key. This time he had moved into a three bedroom at my request so I could turn the third room into a nursery. I was surprised he listened. I found the new condo with no problem. I had to go to the office and add my name to the lease. When I unlocked the door, I was surprised it was a different layout. You walked right into the kitchen from the foyer. The Master was smaller and the bathroom only had one sink. I didn't like it but I appreciated him listening. There was a Bed-in-a-Bag from Macy's on top of the empty mattress, also per my request. I had no hesitation telling him I was not going to sleep on any sheets that may or may not have been occupied by another woman. I didn't even want to think about it. He found it funny but I was so serious. When I opened the shower door it was filthy, I almost jumped out of my skin. That would be my first task to clean while the baby was asleep. I had Nadia claim her room and hang all her clothes in the closet. She took the room next to ours. The third bedroom had French doors at the top of the hall. She said she was too scared to sleep that close to the front door and I for sure wasn't putting my baby that far away from us. The basinet set up shop next to my side of the bed.

I opened the closet and oh my word. What was he thinking throwing all his different clothes on top of one hanger? Everything else seemed to just be thrown in there. Geesh! I made the bed and added my new pillows from my place. His were old and flat. Did he ever buy anything new? I made the baby comfortable on the bed of pillows so she could watch me as I cleaned out and rearranged her daddy's closet. I turned on the CD player to start me on my cleaning mode. I was hoping to be done before he got home to surprise him but that didn't work, halfway in he was standing at the bedroom door admiring my presence as I transformed his closet. Each item placed separately on a hanger from slacks to jeans, short Polo's to long sleeve. Color coordinated from light to dark. I even put his tie hanger to use that he never opened.

"What are you doing home?" I asked.

"I left early. I was too excited to stay at work." He replied as he picked up the baby.

"Awe that's sweet did you miss us?"
The closet was just about complete. He was impressed. I didn't have many clothes.

"You have more clothes than me!'

"They're old, I buy stuff that won't go out of style. You'll just think I shop a lot because I'm always in a shirt and tie at work."

"Yeah that makes sense I'm not a real shopper either. Going to catholic school my mom just shopped in seasons. Back to school clothes, winter clothes and summer clothes."

As I cleaned off the bed Marquise laid the baby back down. She had fallen asleep as he kissed her puckered lips.

"She is so pretty."

"Thank you." I smiled.

"I forgot to show you something. He walked out of the room.

I followed him to the front door and he was already half

way down the stairs coming around the corner with a Christmas tree. A real one.

This was going to be the best Christmas after all. I was back home so far so good. Later that evening we settled in bed. I had given the baby a bath as he watched. Nadia was in her room watching television. We were going to his aunts for dinner tomorrow so they could see the baby.

"There's something I need to talk to you about."

"Sure, what is it?"

"I don't quite know how to say it."

"Does it have to do with you seeing someone else while I was gone?"

"Yes." He replied.

"Oh God, well just say it. So you were seeing someone while I was away." I demanded.

"Yes, but it's not what you think."

"What am I thinking? You either were or you weren't? You asked me to come back so it must be over right? You chose us right?"

"Yes, I did but it's more complicated than that."

"Oh God Marquise is she pregnant?" I blurted out in hopes to being totally wrong.

"Yes." He replied.

My heart sank. *No, this nigga didn't ask me to come back home to be with him but failed to mention the most important piece to the puzzle.*

"Is she going to keep it?"

"Yes."

"Well how far along is she?"

"Five months..."

Look for the third in this series
of the "Lukewarm" trilogy

"Here I Am"

Order and follow Angela M. Holmes at
www.amazon.com/author/angelaholmes.itsmystory